Also by Kathy Morgan

Yvonne Parker Mystery Series
Field Murder
Death on the Village Green

Woodford Mystery Series:
The Limner's Art
The Bronze Lady
Death By Etui
The Mystery of the Silver Salver
Deadly Philately

Also by Kathy Morgan:
Silver Betrayal

Short Stories by Kathy Morgan
Snowflake, the Cat Who Was Afraid of Heights
Plan C
Farm Shop Trauma

This book is a work of fiction. Names, characters, places and incidents are the product of the author's imagination or are used fictitiously. Any resemblance to actual events, locales, or persons living or dead, is coincidental.

Copyright September 2025 Stormybracken Publishing Kathy Morgan.

Printed by KDP.

1st edition September 2025

The author Kathy Morgan asserts their moral right under the Copyright, Designs and Patents Act, 1988, to be identified as the author of this work.

All rights reserved. No part of this publication may be reproduced, copied, stored in a retrieval system, or transmitted, in any form or by any means, without the prior written consent of the copyright holder, nor be otherwise circulated in any form of binding or cover other than that in which it is published and without a similar condition being imposed on the subsequent purchaser.

A CIP catalogue record for this title is available from the British Library.

Death on the Village Green

An Yvonne Parker Mystery

by
Kathy Morgan

For Mum

Character List (in order of appearance)
Tom Archibald a policeman, with dog Stan and horse Ben
Yvonne Parker an antiques dealer; her dog Zebedee and horse Toby
Charlotte Perry Ritchie runs a local bakery with her mum; Arab chestnut mare Sparkle
Charlie Perry Ritchie Charlotte's husband
George Gumbleton Yvonne's boyfriend, works in the Jimmy Mack empire, manages a local restaurant The Abbess Aethelgifu known locally as TAA
Jack Perry Ritchie Charlotte's brother-in-law; antiques dealer; birth name John
Lindy Speake her horse Astrid; part of the family who run Kenyon Hall
Alison Leighton-Jones a local beautician; married to Tabitha
Tabitha Leighton-Jones Alison's wife; sheep farmer
Tim Smith one of Tom's colleagues in the local police force
Detective Sergeant Bridget Smalley
Commander Jemima Tattersall
Sally her horse Poppy
Jim Mack celebrity chef who owns The Abbess Aethelgifu
Colin George's ex-wife's new husband
Maisie Day business partner of Alison
Rob Kemp antiques dealer

Bernie Campling antiques dealer; father to Nigel and Rufus
Nigel Campling one of Bernie's sons
Rufus Campling one of Bernie's sons
Lesley Martin a manager at TAA
Alan an antiques dealer
Alex an antiques dealer
Beau Parker Yvonne's older brother
Nicole Yvonne's younger sister
Katie Moon TV name of Yvonne's youngest sister, TV antiques expert; married name **Catherine Bawtree**
Amelie Yvonne's older sister
Gabriel Yvonne's older brother
Raymond antiques dealer
Christopher Boucher Yvonne's cousin; antiques dealer
Terry Smith friend of Yvonne; antiques dealer
Sylvia Nelson antiques auctioneer
Sue Cooper wife of Jim Cooper
Jim Cooper scrap dealer
Rachael Hall antiques dealer
Darren one of Raymond's apprentices
Antonio and Luca the Ronco brothers, gangsters
Lucy Beau's wife, Yvonne's sister-in-law
Gregory antiques auction house porter

Chapter 1

When Tom Archibald wasn't working as a policeman in Dorset, his recently discovered favourite off-duty activity was to go horse riding, and today he was enjoying riding his new horse, leading a group of friends through Wincombe Woods on the outskirts of Shaftesbury, until a scream nearby made everyone jump.

Three months earlier he had met Yvonne Parker, an antiques dealer, during a difficult time in his life and she had rekindled his enjoyment of being around horses. Tom had not ridden since he was a teenager, over thirty years ago. Circumstances meant that Yvonne and her dog Zebedee, a brindle and white Staffordshire Bull Terrier cross, ended up staying with Tom and his dog Stan, a scruffy dog of indeterminate breed, at his mum's house on Bimport in Shaftesbury. Tom had been badly injured while on duty, and as Yvonne kept her horse on a nearby farm it became a natural thing for Tom's rehabilitation to join her once or twice a week to walk with the dogs while she rode her horse around the fields. Inevitably as his recovery progressed he started riding her horse, Toby, while Yvonne walked alongside, and then he took the opportunity to look after Toby while Yvonne went away on holiday. The other livery owners were on-hand to help, and Tom found he was enjoying the time spent at the farm, and his dog Stan certainly loved being one of the many dogs who either joined their horse-riding owners around the farm's fields or were left at the farmhouse on the occasions when the routes were unsuitable for dogs.

As so often happens in the equestrian world, someone was looking for a home for their beloved horse because they could no longer keep him. Yvonne and Charlotte Perry Ritchie, a fellow livery owner in her mid-twenties who ran a local bakery with her mum, went along with Tom to meet the horse, whose name was Ben. Tom immediately fell in love with Ben, and as Ben's owner was satisfied that he would be going to a good home, both Yvonne and Charlotte approved of the match. Ben moved onto the farm on a week's trial, although no one involved really believed he would be going back, and for the past month Tom and Ben had been developing their relationship. Everyone kept warning Tom it would take at least a couple of years to form a good partnership, but so far Tom had felt his and Ben's bond getting stronger and stronger.

This afternoon Tom, Yvonne and Charlotte were enjoying an evening hack in late September. They appeared to have the woods to themselves because it was too far for the local dog walkers to get back home before dark, and although the light was dim within the trees Tom and Ben could easily see to lead the way along the tracks. It was an adventure to ride here in the relative darkness because their usual night-time routes took them across open fields close to the livery yard, and into an area of woodland easily accessible without having to ride on country lanes or roads running through the town. Ben, a black cob with a wide white stripe down his face and measuring 15.2hh, was enjoying the easy canter along the woodland track, closely followed by Charlotte on her Arab chestnut mare Sparkle who was three inches smaller than Ben, and Yvonne and Toby were bringing up the rear. As always when riding behind Charlotte and Sparkle, Yvonne admired how Charlotte's long red straight hair caught in a low ponytail beneath her riding hat matched her horse's tail. Yvonne didn't think Charlotte had bought Sparkle because they had the same colouring, but it was certainly a striking look. Yvonne's own dark brown hair was short and tucked under her riding hat without the need for hairbands or intricate hair styles.

Toby was huge in comparison to the other two horses, with his Irish Draught heritage mixed with something else big and last time she measured him Yvonne found he was standing 17.2hh. As the track took them along the edge of the woods they were moving through dappled shade, then bright light from the setting sun, and then blinded by the contrast of the darkness as they cantered again through the trees. For the past month the three friends had regularly hacked out together at all hours of the day and often with other livery owners, but this evening was the first time any of them had ridden this route. They had studied the big map on the wall of the kitchen at the yard, and Charlotte had walked the route with her husband, Charlie Perry Ritchie.

When Tom brought them to a walk, he called over his shoulder 'These woods are quite spooky at this time of day aren't they!'

'Sparkle is spooking at the patches of sunlight' laughed Charlotte.

'Watch out, there's a muddy patch here' said Tom, as Ben carefully negotiated the boggy ground.

Yvonne was thinking about what she'd like to eat when they reached the end of their hack, at the Benett Arms in the village of Semley. As if reading her mind, Charlotte said 'I hope they still have the chilli on the menu. I've been thinking about it all day!'

'Is it good?' asked Tom.

'It's delicious!' Yvonne called from the back of the ride.

'We won't need to wait for someone to choose from the menu if we're all having the same' laughed Tom. 'I wonder if George will make it an even four.'

'Probably!' said Yvonne. She checked her watch, 'He said he was going to walk up the road with the dogs to meet us so he's probably just leaving the livery yard in the horse lorry about now. I'll send him a text and ask him to put our order in when he gets there.'

They continued in silence as they enjoyed the peace and quiet of the woods, with just the gentle sounds of the horses' bare hooves on the earth track as they walked.

Then Tom asked 'Shall we have another canter before we reach the road?'

That was when a scream deep in the woods over to their left startled them, and even the horses twitched.

'Why does nature have to be so cruel?' complained Charlotte, as she leaned forward to stroke the chestnut hair on Sparkle's neck to soothe both the frightened mare and herself.

'It's the circle of life' said Tom as Ben started to walk a little faster. Tom asked him to slow the pace again. 'That was probably a rabbit being taken by a fox.'

'It doesn't make it any kinder' muttered Charlotte.

Yvonne, in her late forties and a little small at five foot six inches to be riding such a big horse, was having to duck under more branches than the other two, as Toby was at least eight inches higher than Ben. She had been leaning forwards on his neck when the scream made him start, so she was easily able to grab hold of his thick black mane to steady herself. Even though she was used to night hacks and hearing all sorts of scary noises, she could feel her heart thumping and her senses on high alert after that scream. She decided she probably wouldn't ride through these woods after dark again and was glad they were having a lift home in the horse lorry kindly driven by her boyfriend George Gumbleton, rather than returning along this route after their pub dinner.

The woods were alive with sounds as the sunlight faded and the evening drew in, with deer suddenly dashing away from the group of riders, unseen bodies rustling through the undergrowth as badgers went about their nocturnal business and smaller mammals scuttled out of their way. Soft calls and shrieks announced the presence of numerous owls and the occasional pheasant. The horses were relatively relaxed about all the activity around them, although every now and then one of them would be disturbed by a movement nearby. It was the swooping bats which were making the riders more jumpy than usual. They agreed to stay in walk until they were out of the woods.

Once on the road they again enjoyed a bright and clear Autumnal evening. The three riders each wore a highly visible harness with white lights on the front and red on the back, and even though they could see more easily now they were out of the woods, they switched them on, so they were more visible to other road users. Yvonne's harness was orange, Charlotte's was yellow, and Tom's was blue, and they were also wearing reflective tops. The horses had lights fixed to their tails, as well as reflective leg wraps. Charlotte jumped off Sparkle to switch the horses' taillights on and used a grassy bank to remount easily. The friends quietly chatted as the horses clip-clopped down the narrow country lanes through Donhead St Mary, Donhead St Andrew, and onto the lane into the village of Semley leading to the local village pub, riding alongside each other, with Charlotte and Sparkle between Tom and Yvonne.

Charlotte giggled 'We must look spooky to anyone else travelling on this road!'

They tried to catch sight of their reflections in the windows of a house, but the glare of their lights interfered with the images. Looking over to their right across the valley they could see the shape of Old Wardour Castle among the trees, and further round were the lights in the windows of New Wardour Castle, which had been divided into apartments over thirty years ago. Owls and the horses' noisy bare hooves on the road provided the soundtrack for the next mile. No one else was riding, driving or walking along the lane, the inhabitants of the few houses they passed were safely shut indoors.

'I'm hungry' said Yvonne. 'All that moving furniture and painting walls has worked up an appetite.'

'Are you ready to reopen your antiques shop?' asked Charlotte. 'I know my brother-in-law Jack is excited to be selling in there again soon.'

'Yes, we are nearly ready for the public again. Jack has been a real asset and has got stuck in with the others who are redecorating and cleaning up the rooms. I think he is almost as excited as I am to be reopening. He's roped your husband in to help with moving furniture and other heavy items, did you know?'

Charlotte laughed 'Oh yes, I know! I don't think Jack gave Charlie much chance to refuse. Charlie is always complaining that Jack will never let him forget he is the older brother, and still bosses Charlie around as though they were ten and six years old again. When will you be moving back home?'

'In the next few days. It will be lovely to be in my own bed, much as I enjoyed staying in Tom's spare room and am grateful to him for letting me and Zebedee stay there. It will make life so much easier to be living on site while I organise getting the shop ready. Three new antiques dealers are arriving with their stock tomorrow, so we should be ready to open on Wednesday.'

'Don't forget you were doing me a massive favour when you moved in' said Tom. 'The timing was ideal for me since I was so badly injured and couldn't do much for myself at the time, let alone look after Stan.'

'You have made a great recovery. I bet you didn't think you'd be horse riding less than two months after that incident' said Charlotte. 'You don't seem to be having trouble with your wrist or leg anymore.'

'Thank goodness my body seems to be healing better than expected, because at my age everything takes longer.'

'Hey, you're not much younger than me so don't start complaining about your age' teased Yvonne.

'You're older than Tom?' Charlotte's tone was incredulous.

'Thanks' muttered Tom. 'I don't look that old.'

'Sorry, sorry!' Charlotte tried to placate him. 'I'm sure it's because women moisturise their faces better than men do.'

Yvonne was laughing 'I am only a few years older than Tom but thank you for thinking I am younger than him.'

'Are you fifty yet?' Tom asked, a little nervously. He didn't want to offend her, but he was forty-six and didn't think she looked any older than he did.

'Next year I will be' said Yvonne. 'I am looking forward to it. I don't have a problem with ageing. I loved being forty and think that fifty will be an exciting time for me. Charlotte is right, Tom, you are making an incredible recovery. How are you feeling after all that trotting and cantering under those low branches?'

'Really good, thank you, although I am keeping a light support on my wrist while I ride Ben. Funnily enough my leg feels better than it did before, but I am being diligent about keeping up with the strengthening exercises to make sure it doesn't relapse. I did own up to my physiotherapist that I am riding, but as he is also a horse rider I knew he would understand.'

'It does help if they are sporty' said Charlotte. 'Mine is great to, and she totally understands my need to get back in the saddle as soon as possible whenever I have done something silly to myself.'

'You are right, and of course horse-riding wasn't even on my radar when it happened' laughed Tom. 'I have Yvonne and the rest of you at the farm to thank for that as well. I am sure it has helped with the physical therapy I need to be doing to fully recover, rather than hinder it as so many people have been quick to warn me.'

'You are going to miss Yvonne once she has moved back to her own home' observed Charlotte.

'I am' he sighed, 'although I think Stan is going to miss Zebedee more.'

Yvonne laughed 'The dogs will always be meeting up for playdates at the farm.'

'Even though you are moving back home soon, you are both coming to my house for Sunday lunch this week, and we are still going to be riding together most days' said Tom. 'I don't think the dogs' social diaries are going to be a problem.'

'True! We even have George well-trained, and he's brought them to the pub for us this evening.'

'Thank goodness for George' said Tom. 'I appreciate him coming to collect us this evening, because I'll admit I'm not keen on riding back through those woods in the dark. I am ready for my dinner too. The food is always good at this pub.'

'There it is' said Charlotte, as the lights of The Benett Arms glowed in the distance.

'That looks like George towards us now, with two dogs' said Tom, peering through the gloom at the tall figure of a dark-haired man with a dog either side with lights on their collars.

'Let's ask him to take a photo of us so we can add it to our livery yard Facebook group' said Yvonne.

A scream interrupted their conversation, and stopped everyone in their tracks, including the person with the dogs.

'That was no rabbit' said Tom and asked his horse to trot towards the noise. Charlotte had no choice but to follow him, because Sparkle was not going to be left behind, and Yvonne certainly didn't want to be left on her own in the middle of a dark country lane when someone was screaming. All three horses trotted down the road in a less calm manner than they had been walking seconds earlier. Yvonne saw that George was running with the dogs cantering beside him towards the noise, which had not stopped. The sun was setting fast, and natural light was disappearing. All they could see were shapes on the common in front of them, but it was hard to discern what was happening.

In less than a minute the horse riders and dog walker had arrived at the source of the noise. All three riders dismounted, and by an unspoken agreement Charlotte stayed with the horses, holding their reins, while Tom and Yvonne sprinted as best they could in their riding boots and hats to the edge of the common land. Although Tom had left the army many years ago, Charlotte thought he looked like a soldier as he ran, his dark hair covered by his riding hat and although only a couple of inches taller than Yvonne he had the air of physical authority of someone who had served in the military. By the light of their body-worn lights they could see that George was already on the phone to the emergency services.

After checking he was connected to the operator, Yvonne rushed past George towards the person on the ground, who was no longer screaming. Tom was already on his knees attempting to assess the body for signs of life. Yvonne heard George say to the operator 'We don't know yet, but the man looks to be seriously injured. There is blood everywhere!'

The pub was emptying of people, all running towards them.

'Stay back!' shouted Tom. 'Yvonne, make sure they stay on that side of the road. No one is to come over here. This is a crime scene. I think someone has tried to kill him.'

Yvonne did as she was told, and with several other members of the public created a human cordon. The village pond was a natural barrier, and most people had run along the road towards the Common. It wasn't difficult to keep the onlookers where they were on the road junction because no one wanted to get in the way of the people trying to save the person's life.

A shout from someone in front of the dairy made everyone turn in that direction. Several people moved rapidly backwards, away from the prone figure on the ground. There was another body, and this one was past the point of being saved.

Chapter 2

The pub-goers of Semley were well-behaved, comprising mostly of builders, electricians and an all-female book group, and the crowd moved opposite the pub, standing in groups on the Green behind the pond, being terribly British and not wanting to gawp at the tragedy on the Common, but keen to know what was happening, united in their horror of the commotion in their quiet friendly village. The people nearest the dead body stayed where they were, unsure what else to do. Several followed Yvonne's lead and took up positions along the numerous roads which led into the area and marshalled any traffic by turning them away. Fortunately there were a handful of people who had emergency life-saving skills, and they crossed the road to help. Tom, looking every inch the policeman in his blue hi-viz body harness, was joined in trying to save the man's life by Lindy Speake, one of his fellow livery yard owners, and Alison Leighton-Jones, a local beautician who had been enjoying supper at the pub with her wife Tabitha.

'There's a pulse' said Lindy crouching next to the man with her fingers on his neck. She put her hand in front of his face 'He's breathing, but it's shallow and he is unconscious.'

Tom and Alison were trying to locate the injury. From her shoulder bag Alison produced two pairs of disposable gloves, offering one to Tom. 'They'll keep peroxide off your skin, so I'm sure they'll protect us from his bodily fluids' she said as she pulled on the gloves after quickly tying her long blond hair into a bun and out of the way.

'Thanks' said Tom 'There's so much blood on his clothes I can't work out where it's coming from to stop it.'

'Here it is' Alison said, as she pulled up the man's t-shirt and exposed a wide cut in his side. 'I need something to press onto it.'

Tom produced a First Aid kit from one of the pockets in his riding gillet and unzipped it. 'This will work,' he said, as he unwrapped a dressing. 'It's sterile, and absorbent. I've got more gloves in here if we need them. Let's see the wound?'

'How come you're walking around with a complete First Aid kit in your pocket?' Lindy asked.

Tom shrugged 'I always have it on me when I'm out with the horse, just in case either of us needs it. This is the first time I've used it, although I was thinking more of grazes to my arms if I fell off, or scratches to his legs from brambles if we go off-road, rather than the victim of an attempted murder. Here you are, use this.'

Alison allowed Tom a brief glimpse of the bloody mess on the man's side, before pressing the dressing firmly into place. Tom said over his shoulder to George, who was still on the phone to the emergency services 'Tell them it's a suspected knife wound, and that there is a second victim. Tell them the attacker will still be on the scene, because this has happened in the last few minutes.'

While George relayed the information he scanned the dark figures nearby in case he could see who had done these terrible things, Lindy checked the man's breathing, and looked worried. 'He's getting weaker.'

There was a small cheer from the onlookers at the sound of sirens in the distance. Yvonne decided she was no longer needed to keep the crowds at bay or as a traffic marshal and collected the dogs from George on the way to join Charlotte with the horses, keeping her eyes averted from the body being worked on. Charlotte had managed to untie everyone's lead ropes from their saddles and had already attached them to the halters each horse wore underneath their bridles, and tied their reins safely out of the way, making it easier to hold onto all three horses. She handed Toby's orange lead rope to Yvonne, kept hold of Sparkle's yellow rope in one hand and Ben's blue rope in the other, and they moved the horses further along the Common, as an ambulance on full blue lights and sirens swept around the corner and past the pub from one direction, and two police cars zoomed down the road past the village shop, and stopped effectively blocking the road to prevent any other vehicles driving into the area. The other marshals melted away from their posts, including those surrounding the dead body, to re-join their friends on the Green or walk back to stand outside their homes, and the scene changed from vague figures in the gloom to blinding blue flashing lights and tinny voices blaring from police radios.

Yvonne and Charlotte remained with the horses and dogs well away from the action, watching as figures ran to the injured live body, and George, Lindy, Tom and Alison passed on what they knew of the incident to the emergency team.

The plan had been to have a leisurely pub supper sitting at the picnic tables on the Green, a grassy area opposite the pub, as the sun faded and darkness fell, with the horses securely tied by their halters and lead ropes to the lorry George had driven down to meet them. While they and inevitably the dogs, tucked into plates of chilli and jacket potatoes, the horses would have been munching on hay nets. This was something Toby and Sparkle had done a few times together at the local airfield or at a couple of pubs Yvonne, Charlotte and other livery owners had visited, but this would have been Ben's first time. Tom had chosen to make his and Ben's first pub trip with Yvonne and Charlotte because he knew they and their horses would be confident and help Ben if he became worried by anything. None of them had anticipated the scene surrounding them. There was no way they could reach the lorry parked opposite the pub where George had already hung the hay nets to the outside of the lorry, but the horses were happy to tuck into the grass on the Common, apparently unconcerned by the noise and bright flashing blue lights and activity going on in front of them. Yvonne and Charlotte were sure their horses had never been in an environment like this before, but other than occasionally raising their heads when another vehicle arrived, the horses' focus was on the grass.

Over the next few minutes more police cars appeared and were parked at strategic points to prevent road access to the area, and an air ambulance landed at the other end of the Common. By this time George and Tom had joined Yvonne and Charlotte, George took the dogs back from Yvonne, and Charlotte handed Ben back to Tom. Between them they moved the horses and dogs into the graveyard on the other side of the road just before the helicopter landed, and even the noise and down-draught didn't interfere with the horses' concentration on helping the groundsmen maintain the grass around St Leonard's Church.

'I'm surprised they haven't panicked' observed Tom.

'Me too, especially Sparkle. You're a good girl' said Charlotte as she stroked her horse's neck. 'It must be the influence of your two horses. Are we safe here? We don't know who the attacker was, or how many of them there were.'

'I should think whoever it was is lying low, with so many police on the scene' said Tom. 'We need to keep alert in case someone flushes them out, but if they are local they are probably long gone now.'

'That must be a good sign' said Yvonne, as they watched the air ambulance crew walk back to their helicopter carrying the patient on a stretcher surrounded by medical equipment.

All the chatter which had been going on in the crowd on the other side of the road stopped. An eerie silence covered the area. The blue flashing lights of the police cars continued to light up the scene, and a couple of police officers made their way towards them in the graveyard. Behind them five white unmarked vans had been allowed through the police cordons, and the number of official people in the area appeared to have quadrupled. Floodlights were being set-up, more tape was being fixed across the roads and around the Common, and the sound of police radios filled the air.

'Good news?' Tom asked the police officers as they arrived.

'As good as can be expected for one of them' said Tim Smith, one of Tom's colleagues in the local force. At over six foot two he towered over Tom. 'The one you were working on is alive, at least for the time being. The medics think they have a good chance of getting him to hospital in reasonable shape, and then the specialist team can take over.'

'Where are they taking him to?'

The second officer, Detective Sergeant Bridget Smalley, a woman in her fifties slightly taller than Yvonne with her curly grey hair tied in a loose bun below her uniform cap, spoke 'They are flying to Bristol, Southmead Hospital. We're treating him as the victim of attempted murder. The second man, sadly, is a murder victim.'

'Let's hope there aren't any more bodies, dead or alive' said Tom, nervously glancing around.

'You and Alison did a good job of trying to save that man's life, and the medics were saying it's thanks to you they could take him away from here alive. Any idea who he is? Or who the dead man was?' DS Smalley asked.

Tom and George shook their heads.

Yvonne kept quiet but shook her head too. Like Tom and George she had not walked over to view the deceased, but she did know who the man was whose life was saved. He shouldn't have been anywhere near her, but she wasn't ready to start sharing. His identity would be revealed soon enough. She thought it likely she would know who the murder victim was too and was relieved she had not seen that face. She had more than enough images of the dead etched in her brain, without adding any more.

'You didn't see any weapons? I'm sure you would have said, but I have to ask' said DS Smalley.

'No, I didn't see anything in the immediate area' said Tom.

'I had a brief look around the live victim on the Common but it certainly couldn't have been described as a thorough search' George said apologetically.

'Don't worry, that's what the forensic team are here for' Tim reassured him. 'We're ready to clear the area of everyone who doesn't need to be here, and that includes you. This graveyard must be thoroughly searched. Is the horse lorry anything to do with you?'

'It's deductions like that which will make you eligible for promotion' teased Tom. 'Yes, we were going to take the horses back home in it.'

'Be prepared for another astounding deduction' Tim warned. 'Was it you who drove it here, George?'

'Yes, I came down with the dogs and parked up at about half-past six. I didn't see anything unusual, just the regulars sitting out at the tables eating and drinking. We walked up the road in the direction I knew these three would be coming from.' To Yvonne he said 'I was planning to walk the last section of your ride with you all.'

Tim asked Yvonne 'Did you see George?'

'Yes, we spotted him and the dogs walking ahead of us when the screaming started.'

Tim nodded 'And where had the three of you come from?'

Tom answered 'The road through the Donheads from Wincombe Woods. We were together the whole time, and as Yvonne said we saw George on the road up ahead just before the screaming began.'

'Did you see any vehicles or people on your way here?' DS Smalley asked.

The three riders looked at each other and shook their heads. Tom said 'No, we had the roads to ourselves from the Donheads to Semley.'

Apparently satisfied that none of the four were involved in stabbing the man, Tim said 'We'll get you out of here as soon as possible, but I don't think that will be for at least an hour. As we are in Wiltshire the team from Warminster have arrived, and they will need to speak to you. Are the horses going to be alright here?'

Yvonne nodded as she said 'We were just commenting how chilled they all seem. There's enough grass in here to keep them occupied for hours, although hopefully we won't be here that long!'

'Is this your new one?' DS Smalley asked Tom. 'He's gorgeous.'

'Yes, this is Ben. We're still getting to know each other, but if he can cope with this chaos then there's not going to be much more we need to find out about each other' Tom stroked his horse's black neck. 'He's not keen on the blood on my top and has checked it out thoroughly by sniffing all around, but other than that he is being amazing. I am so proud of him.'

'My kids want to start riding, but my wife isn't keen' said Tim. 'My sister and I loved it when we were young. You never know, I might follow your lead and end up with a horse of my own.'

'Ha it's a slippery slope! First you have one, then your kids will want one' said Charlotte.

'Each' laughed Yvonne.

'True. My wife might have a point after all. I'm glad you're all OK at the moment, and we'll get you out of here as soon as we can' said Tim. 'So long as you feel safe we'll leave you to it for the time being.'

The police officers re-joined their colleagues, and the group were left alone in the graveyard, watching the professionals as they worked. The sound of the horses munching the grass came to the fore, and the dogs began to strain on their leads and pull George to various delicious smelling spots amongst the graves. George tried to ensure they respected their surroundings, and no one walked over a grave or wee'd on a gravestone. He was also keeping his eyes peeled for any signs of a fight, weapon, or worst-case scenario, a body.

Charlotte switched on the torch on her phone so she could read the epitaph on a memorial stone topped by a horse and rider. 'In loving memory of Lieutenant George Dewrance Irvine Armstrong The Sherwood Foresters, Aged 36 years, Died August 3rd 1915' she read aloud.

'Oh that's sad' said Yvonne. 'He must have been killed fighting during World War 1. Isn't there something about the number of hooves a horse has on the ground that denotes how the rider died?'

George came over and peered at the statue 'Yes, I think you're right. I can't remember what it is, but let's look it up when we get out of here and have some internet signal.'

'And look, underneath it says "Also of his mother Elizabeth Jane Armstrong Died August 5th, 1937". So he had no wife or children?' said Charlotte.

'Or father, and possibly no siblings' observed George. 'I wonder what the story is here?'

Tom said 'I don't know what his story is, but inside the church there is a stained-glass window in memorial to PC Yvonne Fletcher, who was killed while policing a protest outside the Libyan Embassy in London, forty years' ago.'

'That's right' said Yvonne. 'It was designed and created by an artist called Henry Haig, who knew Yvonne Fletcher. She used to baby-sit his children when she was a teenager. Even though I didn't live around here then, and was young, I have always remembered that brave policewoman because of her name.'

A voice behind them said 'The window is also worth viewing.' Tim Smith reappeared behind them. 'She was only twenty-five years old when she died.'

Charlotte looked shocked 'That's my age. I can't imagine how her family and friends must have felt.'

'And her colleagues' said Tim. 'Under this tree here is a plaque in her memory, look'.

Everyone turned to where he was pointing his torch light, and read the inscription. For a few moments the tragedy they were currently experiencing was forgotten.

Tim broke the silence 'There's also a memorial to her on the Commons in Shaftesbury. But onto the latest violent crime, George please can you collect the lorry and bring it over here. You three can load your horses on the road outside the graveyard, and then the four of you can go. The Commander doesn't want loose horses to add to her challenges, but you will need to be available for interview in the morning. I have your names, addresses and contact details, and of course she knows Tom, so she has said that you are to clear the area now.'

'Oh is the Commander Jemima Tattersall?' asked Tom.

'Yes, thank goodness. I was worried we were going to get one of the others.'

Tom nodded 'She is definitely the best.'

'In what way?' asked Yvonne.

Tim explained 'It's not just that she is the most efficient and practical, but the other two we could have been landed with are more interested in press conferences and how the optics look, than actually solving crime. Jemima Tattersall will make sure there are proper searches conducted, and the investigations behind the scenes will take place.'

Yvonne frowned. 'Don't you think a heightened police presence will be needed in the next few weeks? People want to be reassured after a violent attack like this. At least one person dead and another seriously injured? This is Semley, not London.'

Tim noticed she looked frightened. It wasn't easy to see in the dark, and she was wearing her riding helmet but he knew Yvonne well enough to recognise her expression was not as relaxed as Charlotte's. He knew it was understandable, given recent events concerning her business colleagues. 'I'm sure there will be plenty of us out and about Yvonne, don't worry. You can always contact me or Tom if you're worried about anything, you know that.' He put his hand on her arm to reassure her, and she nodded although the look of fear did not leave her face. 'This is a Wiltshire Police investigation, but they will be including us in Dorset Police because of the location so close to the border. Please talk to either of us if you need to, any time. Old Sicknote here will be back at work any day now.'

Yvonne's face relaxed into a smile as Tom responded to Tim's comment with 'Oi! I have been proper poorly! And for your information I am back to work tomorrow.'

'I'll go and get the lorry now' said George, and he headed off in the direction of the pub with the two dogs.

'I could really do with having a wee' said Charlotte, looking around the graveyard for somewhere suitable. 'I don't want to be visible with all those lights over there, but I don't want to have a wild wee on someone's resting place. I also don't want to fall over a dead body or be attacked while I'm crouching with my knickers down.'

'If you can wait until we've got the lorry, you can use the toilet in there' said Yvonne.

'Oh I forgot about that! I'm used to having my little potty in my trailer' laughed Charlotte.

'Here's our toilet facilities arriving' Tim pointed to the latest vehicle to arrive on the common.

They watched as a mini village grew in front of their eyes. The forensic tent over the body had already been erected, and a large white lorry with FORENSIC UNIT in black on the side was backed up to it, enabling private access between the two. A second huge lorry, this time black and without any markings was parked across the front of the forensics' lorry, and a low loader began to unload a small block of showers and portaloos nearby.

Seeing Charlotte's questioning look, Tim explained 'That black lorry has accommodation so the officers and scientists can work around the clock. There are a few small bunks and a kitchen area, as well as office space in there.'

'It's lucky the weather has been dry for the last few weeks' commented Yvonne. 'None of those vehicles would have been able to drive onto there in August, it was so wet.'

'Good point' said Tim. 'Let's see if they can all get off when this investigation is over.'

'I wonder how long that will be?' asked Charlotte.

Tim shrugged. 'It should be a couple of days if we can find out what has happened soon enough. The trouble is that now it is dark we are hampered in our investigations in a little village like this, with no pavements or streetlamps, or even many inhabitants. The main thing we need to find is the weapon and the attacker, or attackers.'

'That would be good' Yvonne commented wryly. 'I don't suppose you even know if there was more than one person involved?'

Tim shook his head. 'I can't tell you anything yet. There must have been a few witnesses to the attacks, and hopefully we are already talking to them.' He looked over to where small groups of people could be seen gathered around three or four police officers. 'I can't believe no one saw anything, even in this quiet village. George is taking his time isn't he?'

Yvonne peered at her watch 'He is taking a while isn't he. Hopefully he hasn't lost the ignition key or something daft like that.'

'I'll go and see what's taking him so long' said Tim. 'Jemima wanted you lot out of here as soon as possible. I think she is nervous about the horses being amongst all this noise and traffic movement.'

After he had walked out of earshot, Charlotte said 'I really can't wait any longer. Tom, please can you hold onto Sparkle while I disappear around the other side of the church?'

'Of course. I think I'll need to go after you if George doesn't hurry up.'

'And me' said Yvonne, who was more relaxed, although the strain of the last hour was still telling around her eyes. 'And I'm starving and could do with a drink. Isn't it annoying when you need a wee and you're thirsty at the same time?'

Charlotte came back looking a little flustered 'There is literally nowhere to go without some police person popping up with a torch. They are searching the land all around the church, which is probably why they want us out of here. I am no longer worried about being attacked, but I am worried I am going to wet myself!'

Tom said 'I am sure we are in danger of contaminating the crime scene, particularly as the weapon or weapons haven't been found yet. We only know where the man died, but we don't know where the attacks started.'

Seeing how desperate Charlotte looked, Yvonne said 'Just go over there in the corner behind us. Me and Tom won't look, and if anyone comes past they'll think it's one of the horses having a wee.'

While Charlotte hurried away behind the memorial of Lieutenant Armstrong, Tom and Yvonne began a relatively loud conversation about where they were going to eat, as it was obvious the pub had been closed for the evening. Suddenly they were blinded by the headlights of Yvonne's horse lorry. Shielding their eyes, they checked the horses weren't startled by the light, but none of them raised their heads from the long grass. There was a yelp behind them, and instinctively both turned to look just as Charlotte hurriedly pulled her riding breeches up.

'Nothing like being in the spotlight' she laughed. 'Luckily I had finished!'

George called out of the window 'Chilli on board! Sorry I was so long, but although the police have closed the pub for the evening they let the kitchen finish what they had started. They have packed the rice up in a covered dish, and the chilli is in a saucepan so we can reheat everything if we need to. I'll take their cookware back tomorrow.'

Even though the horses loaded easily the process took about twenty minutes by the time the horses had been untacked, and their saddles and bridles stored in the tack lockers, the ramp at the back of the lorry lowered, and the horses walked up into the lorry one by one into their travel sections. The ramp was secured back in place, the humans and dogs installed in the cab and the living area, and at last George drove them away.

'Thank you George!' said Charlotte as she collapsed onto one of seats in the living area of the lorry and snapped on her seatbelt.

'No problem' said George, 'although someone is going to have to direct me out of here because I can't go the way I came. The road has been blocked off by the police.'

It was a slow journey back to the livery yard at Hannam, as George negotiated the winding narrow lanes of Semley, Donhead St Andrew, and out onto the A30 known locally as the Salisbury road. Yvonne had offered to drive, but George, who was more used to driving food delivery lorries on the odd occasion there was a shortage of drivers, was enjoying the challenge of taking care of three horses on board.

'I'm having to take more care about braking and accelerating, and cornering' he explained. 'Fruit and vegetables don't mind if you swing around a corner, but I don't want the horses to fall over.'

'How come you have an HGV licence? I thought you were a senior manager in the Jimmy Mack restaurant empire?' asked Tom. 'More used to driving your flash sports car than donning the hi-vis and being in charge of a 7.5 tonne lorry?'

'It's not flash!' protested George, as he manoeuvred the vehicle carefully across the small bridge over the river Nadder, outside one of the former mills in the village.

'Oh I think it is' teased Tom. 'A silver Aston Martin is the very definition of a flashy sports car! At least your old Jaguar didn't stand out at first glance.'

Yvonne and Charlotte were nodding agreement, so George had to acquiesce 'OK, OK, it is a little bit flashy. But I'm worth it' he grinned. 'I still have my Jaguar. It's what I use for driving around the country, for the exact reason you have pointed out. The Aston draws too much attention, and I wouldn't want to leave it in some of the car parks I have to use. It's bad enough leaving the Jag. To answer your question, we had a real problem a few years ago with recruiting and retaining lorry drivers to deliver food to our restaurants, and as Jim has always taken the view that his managers need to be able to do any job within the company, he paid for some of us to train for HGV licences. It came in useful for a few months, but the labour market has settled down now and I wasn't planning to renew it. Although if you lot are going to have adventures like this I might need to.'

'I'd rather not have any more adventures like this' said Yvonne. 'But yes, we're planning on riding the horses to places further afield or start some distance from the yard and hack back. If you're willing to be our chauffeur we'd appreciate it.'

'Especially if you're going to organise the catering too!' laughed Charlotte. 'That chilli smells delicious. Lindy was saying earlier today she would have joined us with her horse Astrid this evening, but she didn't have anyone to drive her lorry and didn't want to ride back to the yard on her own, and I am sure other livery owners like Sally would be up for a ride like this one. The more of us riding through Shaftesbury would make it safer and a more pleasant experience.'

'That's a good idea' said Yvonne. 'Safety in numbers.'

'I wonder if I can persuade my husband to help. Although Charlie doesn't have an HGV licence. He doesn't need one to drive his company's vehicles for work.'

'He wouldn't need an HGV licence to drive Lindy's horse lorry because it is a three-point-five-ton box and can be driven on a normal driving licence' said Yvonne.

'You don't have any plans to encourage him to get into horses too?' Tom asked. Yvonne thought there was a hint of hope in his voice. 'Or you George, you don't fancy learning to ride?'

'I can ride' George said.

'What!' said Yvonne. 'I didn't know that!'

George grinned 'My mum had horses, so it was expected in our family.'

'You are an international man of mystery' laughed Charlotte. 'An HGV licence, can ride horses, what else are we going to discover about you today?'

'I haven't ridden for years' confessed George. 'I don't have time to go regularly, so there doesn't seem much point in starting. I'm happy to drive your lorry while you enjoy yourselves with your horses, and I can go for a walk or a run with the dogs. And if Charlie wants to come too, Charlotte, that would be even better, so long as Lindy doesn't mind someone else driving her vehicle.'

'I'll ask him when I get home. Lindy has already said she'd like to join us on these trips, so unless she has someone else in mind he could be ideal' said Charlotte.

George drove into the parking area of the livery yard, and turned off the lorry's engine, relieved to have made it safely with his precious cargo. Yvonne's horse lorry lived at the yard, alongside several other lorries, horse vans and trailers, and he, Tom and Yvonne had travelled down in Yvonne's car with the dogs. After they unloaded their horses and turned them out into the fields with their respective herds, and emptied the lorry of their saddles and bridles, Tom made an attempt to clean the victim's blood from his clothes. There wasn't much because he had been kneeling on the opposite side of the body to the wound, but he knew Alison would have been covered, and he wondered how she was getting on. Whereas his clothes were salvageable hers probably needed to be binned. He pulled on a spare hoodie Yvonne had found for him in her lorry and put his soiled clothes in a dustbin bag and popped them into a corner of Ben's empty stable to deal with another time. He decided he probably would throw them away.

George took the hot food out of the lorry and into the liveries' kitchen area where he laid the table with random plates and cutlery donated over the years by hungry riders. For some reason there was a matching set of glass tumblers, and a big white china jug painted with sunflowers which he filled with cold water. The chilli and rice had survived the journey and were still hot, and within minutes the dishes were empty.

'That was delicious' said Tom as he leant back in his chair and patted his stomach, looking surprisingly masculine in the pale pink top bearing the words BOOBS Breast Cancer Awareness across the front. 'I didn't think

I'd be eating much after tonight's events, I don't usually after dealing with something like that. How much do we owe you George?'

'I haven't paid for it yet' said George, as he stood up and began to collect the dirty plates. 'It was all a bit chaotic as the police were trying to ascertain if the pub was part of the crime scene, so I said I'd pay when I take the dishes back.'

'I suppose they'll be closed tomorrow, will they?' asked Charlotte. 'They have a regular order with us at the bakery, but I imagine they won't be needing it in the morning.'

Tom shrugged 'If it is part of the crime scene it could be closed for several days, but even if it has nothing to do with it I can't see that area being open to the public tomorrow.'

'They still have to feed all the bed and breakfast guests' said George. 'When I left they were being told they had to stay in their rooms until they had been questioned, and everyone had to vacate the premises by seven o'clock tomorrow morning.'

'That won't be a problem' said Yvonne. 'They're all working in the building trade and will have left for work well before then. Come on let's go home. It's been a traumatic night, especially for you Tom.'

'I think I'll walk home' said Tom. 'I feel as though I need some peace and quiet, and a half hour walk in the dark along the lanes will be just right.'

'Are you sure?' asked Yvonne. 'We're all going back to your place anyway.'

'I'm sure, thanks. See you all soon' said Tom, and he clipped Stan's lead to his collar and headed out of the door.

'I hope he's going to be OK' said Charlotte. 'I know he's in the police and must come across traumatic scenes in the line of duty, but that was a horrific event, particularly as that other person had already died. I'm feeling shaky and I didn't really see anything.'

Yvonne gave her a hug 'I know what you mean. Shall we give you a lift home? I can run you back tomorrow to collect your car?'

Charlotte hugged her back. 'Thank you, but I'll be OK. I feel I need to be doing something and driving a few minutes up the road will be a start. I'll follow you two back to town.'

Chapter 3

Yvonne had planned to drop George at his flat, where he lived above the restaurant he managed, The Abbess Aethelgifu, known locally as TAA, before going back to her temporary home in Tom's house on Bimport, but she was feeling quite jittery after the evening's events, and although it wouldn't be long before Tom and Stan walked home it was George she wanted to be with. They had to drive past Tom's lovely old, detached house on the way to the high street where George's home and business were located a couple of minutes away, and as they drove up St John's Hill towards Bimport, Yvonne said 'Would you like to come in for a nightcap or shall I drive you straight home?'

'I'd love to have a nightcap, and then I can walk home afterwards' George said, pleased that she had asked him. 'It's been quite a night.'

He had wanted to say something earlier, but theirs was a new relationship, and George often felt he was being prevented from getting to know her properly while she was a guest in Tom's house. Yvonne had to move out of her own home when it became the focus of a police investigation, but it had been too soon to suggest she and Zebedee move in with him. Tom had been severely injured at the time and it made sense for Yvonne to stay with him, so the option of staying at TAA was never discussed.

Yvonne zapped open the electronic gates and parked her car on the driveway next to Tom's black Volkswagen Golf and walked around to the back of the house to unlock the kitchen door while George unclipped Zebedee's harness from her seatbelt on the back seat, and lifted Toby's saddle and bridle out of the boot. It was a routine the pair had fallen into in recent weeks when George would join Yvonne and Zebedee with Toby around the fields and lanes. He was a tall man in his fifties, a keen road and trail runner and appreciated being able to run with a dog and jog alongside his girlfriend and her horse, occasionally pulling ahead when horse and rider walked a section, and then being overtaken when they picked up the pace and cantered up a hill or along a grassy verge. It was a long time since he had been in a relationship where he could enjoy a shared activity other than eating, drinking and sex, not necessarily in that order, and although they had only known each other a few months he couldn't imagine life without Yvonne and her animal family.

Since his marriage break-up, which had been acrimonious and filled with bad feeling on both sides, he had thrown himself into a series of short-lived relationships with gorgeous thirty-something career-women who were attracted to his good-looks and close proximity to his boss, the celebrity chef Jim Mack who owned The Abbess Aethelgifu and many other restaurants around the country. George in turn was attracted to their toned and manicured bodies and their drive for and success in business. George was of the view that women in their thirties have lived long enough to be interesting but not so long they are cynical, and after the turmoil of his marriage breakup he found their company exciting.

The relationships consisted of wining and dining and incredible sex for a few weeks, with party invitations and plenty of plus one engagements keeping his social life full and boosting his self-esteem. Inevitably they either petered out or came to an abrupt end when their work diaries clashed with personal or social dates, because he wasn't willing to compromise his business life which he loved but involved long hours and days away elsewhere in the world, and neither were they. He had no wish to marry or have more children, because he already had four grown-up sons and daughters of whom he was very proud, and in his early fifties he wasn't looking for a second family or a housewife. He was perfectly capable of cooking and cleaning for himself and doing his own laundry. He did love the thrill of a new relationship, the anticipation of the first few dates, the tantalising exploration of each other's bodies, enjoying having someone interested in him and his thoughts and opinions with no demands other than his company.

If someone had told him three months ago he would meet and fall in love with a woman approaching fifty who was more likely to be dressed in casual t-shirts and jeans and smell of horses than smartly cut designer outfits and smell of Gucci, he would have laughed. Yvonne was very different from the women he had been dating in recent years. She was comfortable in her world which was a healthy balance of animals, friends and work. She wasn't impressed by his status as close confidant of a celebrity chef, and not interested in networking or being seen in the right places. When they went out for dinner or a drink in the local pubs she wasn't on the lookout for who was there and concerned about her appearance, or constantly pointing out flaws on her face or body. From the first time he saw her standing in a field next to her horse he had felt that immediate tug of attraction, and during their first night together he had fallen in love. Unlike the women he had been dating who had all, without exception, made the first moves and been confident about their sexual demands, George had been enjoying the easy progression of his relationship with Yvonne. Their courtship had been gentle and taken much longer than he had become used to. He soon realised Yvonne was not looking for a relationship, but he found her fascinating and thought about her all the time when they were not together. He knew he was more invested in their relationship than she was, but he didn't care. Or at least that's what he told himself.

They had had the 'how many people have you slept with' conversation, and while she shared there had been a few short-lived relationships in her late teens and early twenties before settling down with her husband, but no one since that marriage ended, he had decided it was wise to stick to the old chestnut of heart-breaking first love followed by a one-night stand before he met his wife-to-be, and had glossed over the sexual partners he'd had in the years since his marriage broke up. He didn't think

Yvonne was the type of woman who would accept his post-marriage relationships, nor did he wish to own up to them to her. The women he had been dating in recent years were slim and wouldn't have been seen dead in anything which wasn't form-fitting and revealing a substantial amount of toned and tanned flesh, were fussy about what they ate but seemed to drink anything available in vast quantities, and never went anywhere that wasn't fashionable in their circle of acquaintances. Of course he had been excited by all those firm bodies under his fingers and lips, the pleasure of being desired by a younger woman was intoxicating, and being the envy of other men in the room at parties was often all the aphrodisiac he needed. But it took a lot of energy to maintain that level of interest. When he was with Yvonne he could relax and have fun. They could meet up in local pubs and cafes, or have kitchen suppers and takeaways in their respective homes, go for walks with Zebedee, or spend time apart but together in the fantastic countryside around them while she was horse riding and he was running. He loved how much she enjoyed sex with him, and whenever they were together he wanted to hold her hand as they walked or put his arm around her when they sat down together. He had forgotten how pleasurable kissing was, and although it inevitably led to other things in the privacy of their own homes, or in Yvonne's case Tom's home, he loved having a quick snog in a quiet country lane or when no one else was around on Castle Hill. He was aware that he missed her so much it hurt when they were apart, and he wasn't sure he had ever felt like this about anyone before, not even his wife.

George met his wife when they were at school, studying for their A levels. They had both been in school sports teams, and were happy to be on the side-lines and cheer the other on. He was proud to have such a gorgeous girl on his arm and was the envy of his team-mates most of whom were awkwardly trying to attract the attention of a member of the opposite or the same sex without being cruelly rejected. When they left school she trained as a hairdresser and was working her way up to open her own salon, but over the years while he had been immersed in his career within the Jimmy Mack company, she had been well-supported by her family as she gave birth to one baby after another, picking up a few hours of hairdressing work here and there when her mum and grandma could baby sit. As their family grew they moved from a small two-bedroom flat to a three-bedroom flat, and then a large new-build eight-bedroom detached house with an acre of garden on an exclusive development. The children no longer needed their granny or great grandma to baby-sit them, and her family were now too far away to easily pop in for a coffee or supper. Her clients were ageing and either in care homes or had died, and she wanted to open her own salon with a friend. George was happy for his wife to do whatever she wanted, so long as he didn't need to be involved, and so he put up the money for her to rent the high street premises with her business partner. The hairdressing business was an immediate success, and soon she was working long hours, with rarely a day off. The children were always out when he came home, and so was his wife. As a consequence he stayed away for longer, not bothering to come home for a night here and there when he had consecutive trips. Birthdays and Christmas became wonderful family gatherings when everyone would make an effort to be in one place at the same time, and for several years he and his wife enjoyed hosting many members of the wider family over the Christmas period, working well as a team decorating the house and garden, preparing the spare rooms for the guests, and shopping for food and drink which they prepared and cooked between them. She and her business partner opened a second salon without needing financial input from George, and his career was everything and more he could have dreamed of.

For her fiftieth birthday she asked him for a divorce.

For George this came out of the blue. He was completely devastated. He had no idea there was anything wrong between them, and after the initial shock when he felt a physical pain and temporarily lost the ability to breathe he came back fighting. Who was he? How long had it been going on? Had they done it in his bed? On and on the shouting and accusations were flung between them as she denied there was anyone else involved and let rip about all the times she had been left to fend for herself, picking up sick children from school, attending school concerts and parent evenings alone, rarely being able to have a glass of wine because she had to be their children's taxi service, dealing with the upsets and tantrums which are inevitable when one or more teenagers live in your home. The break-up didn't take long, because she didn't want to save their marriage and George had to go away for three weeks thus illustrating the main reason for the split. While he was away she had a fantastic birthday party with friends and family at a local safari park, put the family home up for sale, and with the children began to view potential new homes in town. George could see all the birthday posts on his children's social media and scoured every picture and video for signs of another man, but either he had been careful to avoid being in front of a camera or he really didn't exist as his wife was still claiming. When he returned to the house he looked for signs of his rival but found none. One of his sons assured him he didn't mind his parents splitting up, another said he was looking forward to moving back into town where all his mates lived, and both of his daughters told him they loved him and would come and visit him in his new home. None of them expressed regret. None of them assumed they would be living with him. Miserable and outnumbered George gave in, signed the divorce papers and accepted Jim Mack's offer of an apartment next to his in London, only an hour away from his former family home and within visiting distance for his children. George's career in the Jimmy Mack company had been more than that of a manager in the restaurant business; he was also involved in the security branch which worked with national and international security services, usually for the UK government, and because of the nature of the work was not able to talk to his wife about it. But he had come close to telling her in an attempt to save his marriage. He knew she was owed an explanation for all his absences from their family, but in the end he had to accept the work was more important to him than family life.

Nevertheless that first Christmas was dreadful. His wife went away for three weeks to visit friends in Australia so there was no big celebration with family and friends, although he was partly relieved because he knew he wouldn't have been invited but he had also hoped it may be an opportunity for a reconciliation. One of his sons came to see him before Christmas, his daughters and his other son came to see him after Christmas, and no one was available for New Year's Eve which had always been a big family event and one he had thought everyone valued as much as he did.

Fortunately Jim Mack had plenty of work for George, and every hotel he stayed in was well equipped with a gym. During his married years George had no time for playing sports, and limited time for basic fitness other than a couple of boot camps every year with the security teams and a couple of short runs every week, and he had been putting on weight without noticing. After that lonely New Year's Eve he resolved to get fit, not easy in your late forties after over twenty years of taking the lift at every opportunity and endless business lunches and dinners. At six foot two he was carrying excess weight and topped the scales at twenty stone. Now at fifty-two he was slimmer and fitter than he had been for thirty years, running several miles three times a week, lifting weights, and taking the stairs whenever he could. He had a good relationship with his children, but he and his ex-wife no longer communicated. She had remarried and was apparently happily living in the house she moved into when they broke-up, with her new husband, Colin. According to his children Colin was a lovely man, with adult children of his own, and now Christmases and birthdays were spent with their extended family. George had to work hard not to feel resentful, and most of the time he was successful, but he was lonely. His working life had left no time for keeping in touch with school and college friends, or joining groups or clubs outside of work, and the nature of his work meant there was little opportunity for making friends. Meeting Yvonne and her friends had felt like a big step in the right direction because they all had their own families, social lives and businesses, while still having time for each other. This evening had been a good example of that, when three people had been horse riding together, he had been able to join them without having to ride too, and when a shocking event happened a couple more friends were nearby and joined as a team.

Tom had given Yvonne the use of the boot room next to the kitchen to store all of Toby's tack and grooming kit, and while George hung up the bridle and placed the saddle on its stand he reflected that driving the lorry full of horses and riders back to the livery yard, and with its cargo of chilli and rice, had been one of the most fulfilling experiences of his recent years, and he hoped they would be doing it again soon without the terrible events on Semley Common of course. When he moved to Shaftesbury he had believed he was treading water while he focused on a serious work commitment and avoided all news of his ex-wife and her new family, but now he was wondering if this could be a more permanent and positive move.

Yvonne looked around Tom's kitchen trying to decide what she wanted to drink. It had been a long evening, and she was exhausted, but her mind was too busy to settle. She discarded the idea of a hot drink and noticed a small bottle with a Quillfeldt stopper which had been part of a hamper Alison and Tabitha had given her the previous Christmas. The pretty handwritten label 'DRINK ME' convinced her to pour a couple of small glasses, and when George came in he joined her at the kitchen table with a glass of homemade sloe gin, while Zebedee curled up in one of the two dog beds in front of the Aga.

'So how was the hack?' George asked. 'We didn't get a chance to talk about it. I know you were excited to be exploring a new route in the dark.'

'That seems a lifetime ago' said Yvonne with a shiver. 'We were trying to work out if it was you walking towards us before everything kicked off. It's amazing how quickly it gets dark.'

'The three of you were clear to see, with the reflective leg bands and little lights on your stirrups. That reminds me, I took a few photos of you all. I have no idea how they came out. How dark was it in the woods?'

'Not too dark, although I think Tom got a bit spooked when a fox started calling to her young. He was in front, leading the way. He and Ben have formed a great partnership already, I'm glad Tom decided to buy him.'

'Here you are' George passed his phone over to her with the photo app opened.

'These make us look great! You can clearly see us all lit up like that. Can you ping them to me please, and I'll share them with Tom and Charlotte?' Yvonne drained her glass and got up from the table. She checked there was enough water in it before moving the kettle onto the hot plate of the Aga to bring it back to the boil. 'Would you like another glass, or a cup of tea?'

'Thanks, that sloe gin hit the spot, but a cup of tea would go down nicely now.'

George stood, and carried the two empty glasses to the sink where he washed and dried them, before returning them to the cupboard. In unspoken agreement Yvonne and George took their mugs up the stairs to Yvonne's temporary sitting room, which had been one of Tom's sisters' bedrooms, and sat together on a sofa which was fashioned from a single bed with big cushions lining the long side along the wall. It was impossible to sit on it in an upright posture, and so as was their custom, George sat next to the small coffee table at one end with his legs outstretched across the width of the bed, and Yvonne sat with her right leg tucked under her body next to him. Zebedee padded into the room and flung herself down on the floor at their feet only to spring back up and charge down the stairs when they heard the back door open.

'Tom and Stan are back' said Yvonne. 'I hope Tom is alright after his efforts to save that man.' Despite the heat from the mug in her hands she began to shiver, and hurriedly took another sip. They could hear Tom moving around his kitchen before the sound of his bedroom door closing. His bedroom and bathroom were off the kitchen, and until Yvonne moved in the whole upstairs of his house had been unused since his mother emigrated to Spain earlier in the year, leaving Tom with her scruffy dog Stan and her house.

'The way he and Alison set to work like that was impressive' said George. 'They both got stuck in without any hesitation, and I am sure if he can be saved they will have done so. When you think how damaged Tom's body was a few weeks ago I think he is amazing to be back in shape to perform CPR. His police training kicked in, and he was there. Alison was a surprise though; I had no idea she was so proficient in life-saving techniques.'

Yvonne shook her head 'No I didn't know that either. She was brilliant the way she joined Tom. They made a great team. I am in awe of Tom for taking his rehabilitation so seriously, when you think he was able to ride his horse for a couple of hours and still run over to an injured body and try to save the person's life.'

Yvonne finished her tea and reached across George to place it on the coffee table, before shifting on the sofa and snuggling into George's chest. Automatically he put his arm around her and pulled her close. George kissed her forehead and said 'It's all thanks to living with you for a few weeks that he got his love of horses back. He's made a great recovery from those injuries, and I'm sure it's because you gave him a reason other than getting back to work to keep up with his rehab exercises.'

'I don't know about that' said Yvonne. 'I think Tom is the type of person who has boundless self-discipline and would have got back to fitness regardless of any influence I might have had. But I do agree that having to be one hundred per cent recovered for Ben's sake helped with his enthusiasm for the gruelling effort. That and having the Shaftesbury Lido so easily accessible every morning. He never missed a session, whatever the weather.'

Now it was George's turn to shiver. 'Just thinking about early morning outdoor swimming makes me cold. So would you do that route again?'

'I don't know. It wasn't nice to ride along the busy roads of Shaftesbury, and other than first thing on a Sunday morning I don't know when it would be different.'

'So potentially you could do a breakfast ride to The Benett Arms?'

'Yes, yes we could, but it's a lot of roadwork when we can just ride across the fields up to the airfield. Riding in Wincombe Woods was good, but perhaps we could just drive the horses in the lorry to the Donheads or Semley, ride in the woods, and then drive them home again missing out all the encounters with heavy traffic in Shaftesbury. I don't know, I'll see what the others think. With everything that went on we haven't had a chance to discuss it.'

'If I'm around I can always drive you. There is a route I run which takes in both Wardour Woods and Wincombe Woods, although there is quite a bit of roadwork on those lanes in the Donheads and Semley. I could drop you all off at Wincombe Woods and meet you at the Benett.'

'That's a good idea, thanks, I'll have a look at a map. That reminds me, you never said you could ride!'

'Didn't I? There's probably a lot we don't know about each other. Can you believe we only met three months ago?'

'A lot has happened in those three months.' Yvonne yawned and sat up. 'I'm going to have a quick shower and then go to bed. You are welcome to stay tonight if you want to? I know you wanted to sleep in your own bed before your early start, but to be honest I'd rather not be alone tonight if you don't mind staying with me?'

George could hear the slight tremor in her voice. 'Of course I'll stay. I must admit I'm not keen on spending the night alone either. That was a shocking experience. I keep thinking about Tom and Alison; I hope they are alright. Those two had far more to do with the man than I did.'

'At least Alison has Tabitha, but Tom is on his own' said Yvonne.

While Yvonne had her shower, George, followed by Zebedee, took their cups downstairs to the empty kitchen, gave them a quick wash and set them dry on the draining board. Stan appeared from Tom's end of the house, and both he and Zebedee asked to go out into the garden. Inevitably in the course of his security work he had seen and been involved in far more serious scenes than the one they came upon that evening, but George had not lost his humanity and had still been affected by the incident and knew he needed to take a few moments to assimilate what he had seen and heard. He stood outside the back door listening to the noisy quiet of the town as many of its inhabitants slept. There was the background noise of a few cars, murmurings of people as they walked along the lane outside, and owls talking with each other. The snuffling of the two dogs was relaxing, and he wondered what animals they could smell in Stan's garden. When the pair of them decided they had spent enough time outside they pushed past him, and went their separate ways, Stan towards the end of the kitchen and through the door to Tom's rooms, and Zebedee straight up the stairs to Yvonne's bedroom. George closed and locked the door and followed Zebedee up the stairs.

Yvonne had already finished her shower and was quickly drying her hair with a hairdryer. She often styled her short dark brown hair straight which George though made her look glamorous if a little more serious than she was naturally, but tonight she was fluffing the strands between her fingers as she ran the hair dryer over her head resulting in a soft curly style which George preferred but had not yet told her. There was still a lot they needed to discover about each other.

'I let the dogs out' he said on his way to clean his teeth. Their relationship wasn't so new that he didn't have his own toothbrush in her bathroom, and vice-versa.

'Thank you!' she called out over the noise of the dryer.

Hair dried, teeth cleaned, it wasn't long before they were snuggled together under the duvet in Yvonne's temporary bed. George hadn't realised how exhausted he was. His body felt heavy, and he knew it wouldn't be long before he was fast asleep. Yvonne was tired, and comforted by his warm presence in her bed, but she couldn't relax. She couldn't banish the image of the body on the ground from her mind. She kept going over the events of the evening, and the shock of seeing the injured man, the brutality of the attack at odds with the excitement of their ride through the woods.

'You're shaking' whispered George, as he drew Yvonne closer to him. She snuggled into his chest, fitting comfortably alongside his body with his arm holding her to him.

'Why are you whispering?' she whispered back and started to giggle.

'I don't know!' said George, and he began to laugh.

Within a couple of minutes both were fast asleep.

Chapter 4

The next morning Yvonne met her friends Alison and Tabitha Leighton-Jones and Maisie Day for breakfast in a local café. King Alfred's Kitchen was in a typical thirteenth century building with the entrance door opening into low ceilings and thick beams, which was why 'Duck!' was worn on the staff uniforms. Although the ground floor was full of atmosphere and cosy, the four women preferred to sit at a big table on the first floor where there were high ceilings, looking out of a large window revealing a view of Shaftesbury High Street and great people-watching opportunities. Ollie was behind the counter and took their orders for tea, coffee and cake (Tabitha) and toasted teacakes (everyone else), and then the friends walked up the stairs to their chosen table.

'How are you Alison?' Maisie gave her friend and business partner a hug, their long blond hair almost indistinguishable from each other's as their heads touched. People often mistook them for sisters, since both were tall and slim and were rarely if ever seen in public without make-up, but they were not related and had only met ten years earlier. 'I heard all about your efforts to save that man's life yesterday.'

'She's a bit shocked, aren't you love' Tabitha rubbed her wife's arm. 'You didn't sleep much last night. We stayed up until almost three in the morning talking about it.'

'That First Aid training course we did last year came in handy, and don't worry about me, thank you Maisie. I'm in better shape than that poor man' Alison said. Yvonne thought she looked amazing, her hair was as usual smooth and straight hanging down her back, and her make-up was perfect, as you would expect from someone who was in the beauty industry. If Yvonne hadn't seen for herself the traumatic events she would never have guessed. When she looked closely she could see the tiredness around Alison's eyes and a tightness around her mouth, but otherwise she looked like her normal sunny self.

'You were amazing the way you ran towards him and got stuck in trying to save his life' said Yvonne.

'It wasn't only me; Tom and Lindy were also trying. That poor man. We were so relieved when the paramedics arrived. I have never had to deal with a real body before, only those Annie dolls in the resuscitation trainings I have done. Thank goodness Lindy was there too. It took the three of us to stem the blood and keep checking his vital signs. I imagine she has First Aid training from working at her family's country hotel, because she was very good.'

'Do you have any idea who the victim was?' Maisie asked.

Alison shook her head 'no, no idea. He didn't look like anyone I know, and Tom didn't know who he was either. I don't suppose I'll be told when his identity is revealed.'

'I think the scariest thing was that one man was already dead and a second was violently attacked in Semley!' said Tabitha, who rarely wore make-up and whose long dark hair was stuffed as usual into her farmer's baseball cap, with long tendrils escaping. Yvonne knew that Tabitha would have been up and out checking her sheep not long after she said that Alison had finally fallen asleep, and probably had less sleep than Alison. 'Lindy, Alison and Tom were probably quite safe by the time they reached him because there were so many of us around, but it's a sobering thought to think that two people could be stabbed and no one sees who did it.'

'Is that what happened?' asked Maisie. 'They were stabbed?'

Alison nodded. At that moment Renate appeared with their drinks and toasted teacakes, and the next few minutes were spent distributing cups and saucers, milk and tea, plates and teacakes and Tabitha's slice of cake.

'Who stabbed him?' Maisie asked.

They looked at each other shaking their heads. Tabitha answered 'No idea. I suppose it is possible the two victims could have stabbed each other and there wasn't a third person involved? All we saw was the victim lying on the ground. I didn't see anyone running away.'

'Nor me' said Yvonne. 'No one passed us.'

'You were on horseback weren't you!' exclaimed Maisie. 'How did the horses cope with all the noise and people?'

'Surprisingly well' said Yvonne. 'Especially Charlotte's Arab, Sparkle, because she can be a bit skittish in the calmest of environments, but I think she was so pleased to be allowed to eat the long grass on the Common and in the graveyard she didn't seem concerned.'

'How about Tom's new horse?' Tabitha asked. 'From what I could see he looked chilled out about it all.'

'Ben, yes he was busy stuffing his face too. You can't really train for an experience like that, so we were lucky.'

Alison shivered 'I have never been in a situation like that before. I just went into automatic, and I don't know how I did it. Tom was amazing. He was calm and methodical, really easy to work with, and it's thanks to Tom that man was still alive when the paramedics arrived. I am so glad he was there. He is definitely someone you want by your side in a crisis.'

'The way the police swung into action was incredible' said Tabitha. 'Honestly Maisie, you wouldn't know there were that many policing resources available to us in Shaftesbury! Police officers appeared from all directions, and in a variety of vehicles.'

'They did didn't they!' exclaimed Alison. 'I couldn't believe it. The paramedics turned up really quickly and took over from us without any delay. The air ambulance wasn't long in arriving. The police weren't far behind, and then they just kept on coming. Cars, vans, trucks, there was an almost endless stream of them.'

'They set up a small village on the common within an hour' said Yvonne. 'I have no idea where they all came from.'

'But we still don't know the identity of either men?' Alison asked. 'I would like to know what their story is. Semley is not the sort of place where people get stabbed. You wouldn't get the milk station or the lovely village shop if it was.'

'I think that is why it was so shocking for us all' said Tabitha. 'As soon as we heard the man screaming everyone left their pints and plates of food and ran out of the pub without a second thought. We all wanted to go to the aid of whoever was injured. It certainly didn't cross my mind we were heading out to help the victim of a stabbing.'

'I thought someone had been run over, or someone else was having a heart attack or something like that. Like you, Tabitha, it didn't occur to me there was an attempted murder going on outside. It's just not what happens around here!'

'No it isn't. That is though' laughed Maisie, pointing out of the window. 'Typical Shaftesbury High Street blocked by two lorries and a bus!'

The friends watched as the drivers tried to extricate their vehicles from the traffic jam, exacerbated by more and more cars joining the queues at either end in the narrow road. Eventually one of the lorry drivers had to reverse down the road with goodness knows how many vehicles behind him doing the same to allow room for the oncoming lorry and bus to pass, and the drama was over.

'How's the plans for opening your shop going Yvonne?' Tabitha asked.

'Really well, thank you! It took me a while to fall back in love with the place after the police handed it back to me, because it felt horrible to think people I worked with had been using it as a base for their criminal activities. The holiday to Ireland helped me to gain some perspective, and with your support, and from the antiques dealers, once we started to rejig the layout and decide who was staying and who was joining us it all came together quickly. The antiques dealers are already painting and decorating it. I am so lucky to have their support, and they are more enthusiastic than I am to be honest.'

'Oh, you will be again' Tabitha said, encouragingly. 'You know how much you love your shop and being surrounded by all those antiquey people.'

'You do!' exclaimed Alison. 'It's because of your enthusiasm that we have started watching antiques-related programmes on the telly.'

'I always watched them' said Maisie 'but since meeting you I feel I have a little bit of knowledge, which makes watching them even more enjoyable. I can't wait for you to reopen Angel Lane Antiques, because my husband's birthday is coming up. It's a big one; he's going to be fifty!'

'It's our generation isn't it' said Yvonne. 'We're all rapidly heading to fifty.'

'We're not!' chorused Tabitha and Alison, laughing.

'I'm sticking with forty for a while' said Alison.

'Me too' said Tabitha, 'although I don't mind ageing.'

'I remember being forty' laughed Yvonne. 'It feels like another lifetime!'

'It's your birthday soon isn't it Yvonne. Are we having a party?' Maisie asked, looking hopeful. 'I want another chance to wear the shoes I bought for Tabitha and Alison's wedding.'

'Now that is a good idea' said Alison. 'You could wear your Matron of Honour dress if you wanted to, Yvonne.'

'I hadn't even thought about a party!' said Yvonne. 'I have been so focused on getting my home and shop back, moving out of Tom's and gathering my antiques dealers together, my birthday was going to be just a date in my diary.'

'After all you did to get our wedding reception back on track, and we believe even better than it would have been as originally planned, sit back and let us organise your birthday party.'

Yvonne looked worried 'Goodness, you're not going to plan something as big as your wedding reception are you? I really don't have any family who would come, and my only friends are you three! It's not a big birthday, only my forty-ninth.'

'And George' Maisie said.

'Oh, of course, and George. And Tom for that matter, and Rob Kemp and Charlotte Perry Ritchie, oh you know what I mean' laughed Yvonne.

'I am sure we could have a big party for you if you want' said Tabitha, warming up to the idea. 'There are all your antiques dealers in the shop, all the other livery owners at the farm.'

Yvonne paled 'No please don't, I wouldn't enjoy it!'

Taking pity on her friend, Tabitha said 'I can see that! Don't worry, we won't have a huge surprise party for you. Although if anyone wants to do that for my fiftieth I'll be up for it. Fair warning for nine years' time!'

Alison laughed and kissed her cheek 'Noted.'

Maisie said 'I'm with Yvonne, don't do that for me either. I'd much rather have a nice meal with my friends and another nice meal with my family.'

Yvonne nodded 'That sounds more like my kind of celebration.'

'Look, we'll just organise a fantastic party for a select group of people' said Alison. 'How does that sound?'

Yvonne relaxed and a huge smile spread across her face 'That sounds perfect. Thank you!'

Chapter 5

Yvonne Parker, Rob Kemp and John Perry Ritchie stood together near the back of the chapel in Salisbury crematorium, watching in silence as the curtains were drawn by some unseen automatic function and the coffin disappeared from view. Yvonne was surprised to find her eyes welling with tears, and surreptitiously dabbed away the evidence with a tissue from her jacket pocket. She rarely wore her navy-blue suit except for events such as this and was pleased she had remembered to put some tissues in there. Also in the pocket were a few Fox's glacier mints which she passed to her friends without making eye contact, and they spent the next minute trying to unwrap them quietly. They failed. Yvonne made a mental note to replenish her supply, because the boiled sweets always proved useful if the service was particularly long and boring to stop her yawning, or if she got one of those embarrassing tickles in the back of the throat during a quiet solemn part. Funny how those tickles never appear when you're on your own, she mused. This funeral had been delayed while a post-mortem and inquest took place, and although the cause of death had still not been made public the body had been released to the family for burial. The delay had allowed speculation and rumour to run rampant through the antiques dealer's hometown of Shaftesbury, and the news of his death to spread to the far corners of the antiques world where the rumours were magnified. Antiques dealers do love to gossip. The crematorium was packed with mourners, because the deceased had been popular with the trade and had many friends in the local community.

Yvonne, Rob and Jack, as John preferred to be called, had arrived early enough to be able to sit together, and peering along the row she could see that Rob too was succumbing to the emotion of the event, but Jack remained composed. Yvonne took a moment to study Rob and Jack, who were also antiques dealers renting space in her shop Angel Lane Antiques, and had come along to the funeral of a fellow dealer who had been a regular trader in the shop. There had been several months between Bernie Campling's death and his funeral, and a lot had happened involving the dealers in Angel Lane Antiques during that time, but Yvonne was looking forward to the following week when the disruption and stress would come to an end.

Both men had big blue eyes and dark curly hair, although Rob's was more white than black these days. They were taller than her five foot-six height, but there were a few inches difference between the older and younger man, and both looked smart in sombre suits rather than their usual uniform of jeans and shirt. She could see they were wearing black trainers. She doubted either of them owned a pair of polished black lace-ups. Rob, the older and shorter of the two, was a self-declared petrol-head, whose natural habitat was buried in the former garage at the back of her antiques shop surrounded by bits of classic cars and motorbikes, engines and tools. Jack was forty years' younger, he had recently celebrated his thirtieth birthday, aware of his good looks, and a successful antiques dealer specialising in jewellery, silver and watches.

Yvonne had put effort into smoothing her natural curls for the occasion and was comfortable in her navy-blue shift dress with matching jacket, and because the late September weather was taking a chilly Autumnal turn today she was able to wear her favourite navy-blue suede knee-high boots. Gone were the days when she regularly wore suits and shoes, but when she swapped her riding breeches or jeans for smarter clothing she enjoyed the experience. She appreciated the two men for accompanying her to Bernie's funeral. She had known him since she started working in the Parker family firm more than thirty years' before. Bernie was from an era when dealers travelled from one antiques fair to another, often spending a couple of weeks on the road, dealing out of the back of his van in the queue before the fair opened, stalling out during the day, packing up and driving on to the next one. He had been one of the original dealers to rent space in her antiques shop when she opened nine years ago, and she would always be grateful to him for giving her new venture his seal of approval.

As the mourners filed out, Bernie's two sons and his brother and sister were shaking hands and accepting condolences. The sons were the image of their father, with floppy longish brown straight hair, ruddy complexions, carrying a couple of stone overweight for their five-foot eight height, and with friendly grey eyes topped with bushy brown eyebrows.

'Hello Yvonne, thank you for coming' said Nigel, the elder of the two. Neither son had followed their father into the antiques business, choosing instead to join his sister's family firm of electricians, but both had been dragged around the antiques fairs with their parents as children and had fond memories of Yvonne from those days.

'Of course I came, your Dad has been a good friend to me in the business over the years. I am glad you have finally been able to say "Goodbye". It must have been a difficult few months for you.'

'Yes, it has not been easy that's for sure' said Nigel. 'Our aunt has taken the coroner's delay in releasing his body very hard, and we're relieved for her sake more than ours. Still no final report on the cause of his death, so the waiting isn't over yet. I don't know why they are taking so long because it seems to have been a straightforward heart attack, but they must have their reasons.'

'Dad regained some of his old joy for life when he started working in your antiques shop. I hope you know how thankful we are to you for encouraging him to join you. You will come to the wake at The Abbess Aethelgifu won't you?' asked Rufus hopefully. He developed a crush on Yvonne when he was thirteen and she was eighteen, almost thirty-five-years ago. He had never grown out of it.

Yvonne's heart sank. Bernie had been a lovely man to know, and she liked his sons to pass the time of day with in the pub or the shop, but she rarely attended funerals, let alone wakes, and had lots of things she would rather be doing that afternoon. The fruit and vegetable plants in the little greenhouse on the decking outside her flat above the antiques shop needed to be either pulled out or tidied up for the winter, and she wanted to spend some time tending to them. Hoping for moral support she glanced at Rob, who didn't help by nodding and saying 'We wouldn't miss it. It starts at two o'clock this afternoon, doesn't it?'

Yvonne drove them back to Shaftesbury in her blue VW estate. She had spent a lot of time the previous day cleaning the horse and dog hair off the seats and scrubbing the spilled sugar beet from the car's boot. She hoped no horse food or animal hair was adhering itself to Rob or Jack's smart clothes.

'I didn't realise there still hadn't been a cause of death announced' said Jack. 'What's that all about?'

'I don't know' said Rob. 'I'm not sure how these things work. But as they have released his body to the family I don't suppose there are any ongoing investigations.'

'Was it a suspicious death then?' asked Jack.

Rob shrugged 'Not that I heard. We all thought dropping dead off a bench on the green opposite the Benett Arms in Semley was a good way to go. I don't think anyone else was involved, so unless Bernie committed suicide and that's why they are not saying much I don't know why there hasn't been an official conclusion.'

'Unless there has been and the family just aren't saying what it is' said Jack. 'I'll shoot off after one drink, if you don't mind.'

'I'm not staying long. I wasn't going to go at all' Yvonne said.

'There will be some stories about the old boy' said Rob. 'I'm looking forward to it. Bernie had been in the business for years, and I know there will be lots of people wanting to reminisce about the good old days.'

Yvonne groaned just as Rob knew she would, and the three friends burst out laughing.

'I only knew him in recent years when he used to come into the shop on his day to work in there. He spent the day drinking tea and eating cake while he talked about what had sold in which auction or antiques shop, although he never seemed to buy anything. Everything he put out on his stand came from his shed in the garden, and he would always joke that he was downsizing. His knowledge was phenomenal' said Jack. 'But you two must have known him in the days when he was a force to be reckoned with in the antiques trade. Wasn't he one of the biggest dealers in the country?'

'He was, yes. Bernie Campling was a giant of an antiques dealer' said Rob. 'He worked all day, every day, and made a fortune. He bought that big house on Bimport when he was only in his early twenties, and sent his sons to Port Regis and then onto Bryanston School. His wife was the one who kept his bookkeeping together, making sure enough money was going through the accountant to show for their spending, but we all knew he hid a lot from the tax man. Everybody did in those days.'

'Not everybody' Yvonne remarked. 'Some of us worked within the law.'

'You're too young to remember' said Rob. 'By the time you were working in the business the money was disappearing. The big American buyers stopped coming, and along with them the opportunity to fill shipping containers with stock.'

Bernie's wake was being held in the courtyard at the back of the TAA restaurant in Shaftesbury high street. Yvonne parked her car behind her home and shop in Angel Lane a couple of minutes away, and they walked through the public car park to Bell Street which runs parallel to the high street, and in the open black iron gates of the private space, secluded from the noisy, busy shop-filled road beyond. The manager, Lesley Martin, and her team had worked with the Campling family to transform the area into a celebration of Bernie's life. The mammoth task of clearing Bernie's home of fifty years was just beginning, and his sons had thoughtfully chosen a handful of his prized possessions to decorate the courtyard. An oak coffer, a garden statue, a Captain's chair stood alongside photographs which had been printed and displayed on the stone walls. There were pictures from his childhood showing Bernie with his older brother and younger sister on a sandy beach, with his parents and grandparents at a wedding, and beaming from ear-to-ear astride a bicycle. More photographs showed Bernie on his wedding day with his young bride, to whom he had been married for over forty years before she pre-deceased him twenty years ago. Bernie laughing with fellow antiques dealers at a showground somewhere in the north of England, Bernie wearing a Christmas cracker paper hat, Bernie eating an ice-cream. Jack bought the first round of drinks and then disappeared to talk to another group of dealers, while Yvonne and Rob joined fellow local dealers as they shared memories of Bernie.

Bernie's sister had been overcome with emotion at the crematorium and decided not to come to the wake, but his older brother was there with various members of his immediate family and was holding court in the large room next to the courtyard where the folding doors were fully open. Everyone else was out in the open-air courtyard and either standing around in small groups or settled in big red sofas and comfortable wooden chairs with padded dark green cushions. Although the temperature wasn't too cold for the time of year, several fire baskets and a couple of fire pits were providing colour as well as warmth.

'I'm going to miss my old friend' said one man, a tear in his eye. 'I only met him in recent years, but he could always be relied upon to be in The Ship Inn a few evenings a week, and we'd meet for a pint or two and a chat. He never mentioned he was ill the last time we had a drink together, so I hope it was quick in the end. It was a heart attack wasn't it?'

Rob shook his head 'He didn't say anything to me either, but yes I heard it was a heart attack. He appeared to be in reasonable health last time I saw him, and that must have only been three days before his death.'

'For the past eight years Bernie was one of the marshals for the cycle race' said another man. 'I could leave him in charge of two or three others because he knew what to do, and where to go. Every year, rain or shine, he'd be there calling out encouragement to the cyclists as they came up St John's Hill, and he was great at keeping the traffic in check.'

'Who's clearing his house?' asked someone else. 'Of course, it won't be the treasure trove it was before he was burgled that time, but I bet there is still a lot of valuable and collectable stuff in there.'

'Not as valuable as whatever he kept in his shed' said Alan, an antiques dealer in his seventies with a shock of white hair. 'I've been in his house loads of times, and never saw anything particularly valuable. But I have never been in his shed, and don't know of anyone who has, do you?'

A general murmur of agreement rippled through the gathering crowd, and the conversation turned to stories of what had been stolen, and who had lost money as a result. The memories were interrupted by Lesley and her team appearing with trays of hot sausage rolls and tiny cold quiches, before the details of the burglary at Bernie's house were resurrected again.

'Want another?' asked Rob, indicating Yvonne's glass.

'Yes please' she said and gave up all ideas of gardening that afternoon.

Rufus and Nigel joined in the conversation.

'Poor Dad,' said Nigel. 'The bastards who stole those antiques so soon after Mum's death really put the boot in.'

'I'll never forget how devastated Dad was' said Rufus. 'He never felt safe in his own home again, and he felt terrible that all those dealers had entrusted their livelihoods with him, and he'd lost so many people's income. He loved being in your shop, Yvonne. He would talk about the people who he'd seen that day, and the items that were brought in to be sold, but he missed life on the road and the camaraderie that went with that. I don't think he was ever truly relaxed after that burglary.'

A gloomy silence fell over the courtyard.

The brothers remembered it as a dreadful time, watching helplessly as their father virtually became a recluse. They had been concerned about his mental well-being as he grieved for the loss of his soulmate of forty years. Their mother had been ill for about five years before the cancer finally killed her, and in that time Bernie had adapted to being her carer after many years of having all his laundry and housework done and his meals cooked for him. As his wife's health declined he began to do the weekly food shop, learned how to prepare her favourite meals, and discovered where the washing machine and tumble dryer were in the old house's scullery. When their mother died Nigel and Rufus were not concerned about how their father would cope with cleaning and feeding himself, but he had lost the sparkling personality he was famed for. The gentle teasing and amusing stories were gone, and he looked as though he had aged several years. His lack of enthusiasm for the business he had lived and loved since he was a young lad of fourteen was perhaps the most worrying aspect of his grief. A handful of friends, including Alan, popped in at least once a week for a cuppa, some of them bringing cake, or fresh bread, or produce from their gardens. Nigel and Rufus took it in turns to cook a roast dinner in the family kitchen every Sunday, sometimes with their friends and family, sometimes just the two of them with their father. Bernie's brother lived an hour away but had relinquished his driving licence after an unfortunate incident with a neighbour's garden wall, and once a month Rufus drove to the other side of Salisbury to collect him and bring him back for the Sunday roast. Rufus would be taking him home after the wake and was pleased he had brought him because the old man seemed to be thoroughly enjoying meeting friends of Bernie's and swapping stories about him on what could have been a desperately sad occasion. Burying any sibling was awful, but somehow it must be worse to outlive a younger sibling. Bernie's sister was still driving competently and lived near Devizes. She regularly came down to see him during the week and bought the pair of them a takeaway of Bernie's choice at least once a fortnight.

For a man who had been used to bantering with hundreds of people every week at auctions and fairs, having his social circle reduced had been an enormous change for Bernie, and one he seemed to have been resigned to. But things went from bad to worse when, after one of the takeaway evenings with his sister enjoying a meal from the nearby Aroma Indian restaurant, while he lay fast asleep in his bed, thieves broke into the house and stole hundreds of thousands of pounds worth of stock, the majority of which belonged to other people. The first Bernie knew about it was when one of his friends turned up with a couple of sausage baps from Reeves the Bakers for breakfast and found the smashed lock on the back door. His friend pushed the door open, trying not to leave his fingerprints or smudge any the burglars may have left and called up the stairs to Bernie, who had just stepped out of the shower and was oblivious to anything that had happened that night. The police were called, Bernie tried to give them a list of stolen items but struggled to remember everything that had been in the house, and the sausage baps went cold.

'Poor old Alan probably lost the most' said one man. 'He'd given Bernie an eighteen-thousand-pound marble statue to sell to one of Bernie's clients.'

'Eighteen thousand?' echoed Jack, whose group of friends had migrated over to the older dealers and was now standing behind the sofa where Yvonne was sitting. Yvonne noticed that Jack had ditched his one drink pledge and was sipping at a fresh pint of Butcombe.

'I lost six thousand' muttered another dealer. 'He picked up a portrait miniature for me the day before, and it was stolen along with everything else. I had a customer lined up, and I had to let her down. She never bought anything from me again.'

'You lost a lot more than six thousand' observed one of the dealers. There was a general murmur of agreement.

'I suppose I did, but these things happen' he shrugged. 'There were a lot of us in the same boat. Bernie reckoned the bastards had got away with over three hundred thousand pounds worth of stock, and of course none of it was insured. The whole trade was affected in one way or another, and Bernie was never the same again. That burglary was devastating for him. He was terrified to leave the house, and terrified to stay in it. I remember he didn't come back and start trading for at least six months after it, and even then he stopped travelling to markets he couldn't drive back home after that night. He never stayed away from home after that.'

'That's true, and the fairs for the next few weeks were subdued as people who had been promised money or goods by those who had lost antiques in that raid came to understand they were never going to receive them.'

Yvonne was nodding. She had been responsible for seven antiques fairs and forty-two shops at the time and had witnessed the trade almost grind to a halt for a while after she experienced a shocking event which led her to dramatically alter the direction her life was going. Yvonne made the gruesome discovery of her cousin, Christopher Boucher's murdered body, and although the murderer had been tried and convicted the reason behind the crime had never been made public. But Yvonne knew the reason, and she knew it was connected with the crime at Bernie's house. She wished she didn't.

The conversation turned to an anecdote about Bernie's transit van, and the mood lifted as they discussed the modifications he had made to ensure he always had access to hot coffee or cold vodka. Yvonne was glad she had come and was enjoying listening to the men and women as they reminisced about a much-loved member of their trade. The atmosphere was generally happy, with lots of laughter as fond memories were shared. Bernie's sons were making their way around the mourners, listening to stories and sharing tales of his antics. People took themselves away from the groups and stood alone, drink in hand, looking at the pictures on the greenstone walls surrounding the courtyard, before re-joining their friends and acquaintances gathered around the warming firepits dotted around the space.

Yvonne became aware of a change of tone in a discussion going on in one corner of the courtyard. A rotund grey-haired man was becoming animated about something and had drawn a crowd around him. Peering through the bodies, Yvonne could see that he was bending down and gesticulating at one of the items of Bernie's which was decorating the courtyard in his honour. Several other men were taking a closer look, a variety of spectacles being removed from pockets and worn for a better view of whatever it was the man was getting upset about. As if drawn by a magnetic force, people began to drift over to the kerfuffle, and Rob and Yvonne joined the flow of bodies.

'It's Alan' whispered Rob. 'The one whose marble statue was stolen.'

'So I see' Yvonne whispered back.

'That's my bloody statue, I'm telling you' Alan had begun to shout. 'Look, look, right here, this is the stain on her back where she'd been leant against the fence. Look!'

'What's going on?' said Jack.

Rob turned to explain 'I think Alan believes he has found the statue Bernie reported stolen.'

'I think Alan could be right' observed Yvonne quietly so no one else could hear.

Chapter 6

The mood at the wake changed from relaxed to angry. Alan marched over to Lesley, who was supervising the changing of one of the beer barrels, and demanded 'Where did that statue come from?'

Bewildered, Lesley looked over to where he was pointing. Turning to Nigel who was standing with an empty pint glass, waiting for the beer supplies to be restored, she asked 'Isn't it from your dad's house?'

'Um, er' stammered Nigel, as he took a few steps to get a better view of the statue, before nodding his head in confirmation 'Yes, yes that was in Dad's office.'

'No it certainly wasn't' shouted Alan, whose white hair was contrasting strongly with his red face. 'Your father and I spent many hours in his office, and there is no way that statue was in there. I would have seen it. Where did you get it from?'

Nigel looked a little frightened in the face of this angry man and opened his arms wide in a gesture of confusion 'Honestly, it was in Dad's office. That is where we carried it up from, along with the rest of this stuff.'

Alan took a step towards Nigel, and Lesley calmly moved sideways to place herself between the two men. 'What are you talking about' Alan roared 'None of this stuff was in his office. There wasn't space for it in that room, there was only just about room for his desk in front of the window, and a couple of armchairs by the fireplace. Why are you lying?'

Rufus came to his brother's rescue 'Nigel is telling the truth. We found all of this in his office downstairs, in the cellar.'

In the silence that followed, Yvonne could see several people mouthing 'what cellar?' to each other.

In a grim voice, Alan enunciated the words 'What cellar?'

'The one at the back of the larder. The one he always kept locked' explained Rufus.

Nigel found his voice 'We only found it when we were clearing out the kitchen and the larder yesterday. We didn't know it existed, because the door was behind a curtain, and Mum and Dad stored apples from the orchard in wooden crates in front of it. You're talking about the room at the back of the house he also used as an office, overlooking the garden. We called it the snug. The office we're talking about is the size of the footprint of the house, with no external windows or doors, and the only access is through the door in the larder and down stone steps.'

'We were so excited when we found it yesterday' said Rufus. 'I wish we'd known about it when we were growing up. It would have been a perfect place to play.'

Nigel nodded 'I could have kept my drum kit down there and played any time of the day or night.'

'We could have put the table tennis table down there, and there would have been plenty of room to play football whatever the weather' said Rufus.

Everyone stared at the two brothers. Previously unheard noise of the vehicles on the roads outside became loud. A couple of motorbikes were roaring through the High Street, and a bus was idling at the bus stop opposite St Peter's church.

Yvonne stepped forward 'Alan, show me the mark you are so sure proves the statue was the one you gave to Bernie to sell.'

The mourners were transfixed by the drama unfolding before them, and they turned and moved closer to the corner where the marble statue was on display, parting so Alan could lead the others over for inspection.

'Look, here, this stain on her back is from a nail that was sticking out of the fence in the garden I bought her from' said Alan, as he carefully tipped the statue forwards so Yvonne could see. Rob and Jack took the weight of it from Alan, so he and Yvonne could study the rust mark on the marble.

'Yes, I see it' said Yvonne, and took a couple of photographs with her phone. 'Do you mind if I contact a friend who is in the police?'

Alan suddenly looked as if someone had pulled the stopper out of his body and he had deflated. He sank into one of the cosy red sofas. He flapped a hand in Yvonne's direction 'No I don't mind. Please do. I'm not sure what is going on here.'

As Yvonne made the call, the crowd became animated and people began to look more carefully at the rest of

Bernie's possessions his sons had displayed within the courtyard. Yvonne could hear 'You know, that could be Alex's Captain's chair, do you remember? He had half a dozen and had given one of them to Bernie as a sample for a buyer he said he had.'

'Hi Yvonne' Tom Archibald answered his mobile.

'Tom I think we may have a bit of a situation here at Bernie's wake. We're in the courtyard at TAA. Are you nearby?'

'I'm at home and can be with you in a couple of minutes. What do you mean "situation"? Can't George and his staff manage anyone getting out-of-hand?'

'It's not that kind of situation' explained Yvonne, trying to keep her voice low. 'It's to do with the burglary twenty years ago at Bernie's house and may have something to do with his death.'

'Do we need blues and twos, because that might take a little longer' asked Tom, sounding as though he was talking while running.

'No, but a little sensitivity will be needed.'

It took Tom nearer fifteen minutes to appear through the black gates, and he had brought a couple of colleagues with him, one in police uniform and the other, like Tom, plain clothes. Tom was in his forties and although had left the army many years ago, still had the walk of a soldier as he led the way, his dark hair covered by a black baseball cap. He exuded confidence as he strode in.

Lesley and her team had moved the wake indoors to the large room adjacent to the courtyard, leaving a handful of people including Yvonne and Rob with Alan outside. Lesley called her manager George to join them, and he was observing in the background in case his input was required.

Having established there wasn't a public order situation, the uniformed officer soon disappeared, leaving Tom and his colleague, who introduced herself as Detective Sergeant Bridget Smalley to the antiques dealers. Yvonne had met her for the first time when she was waiting in the graveyard of St Leonard's Church in Semley to be given the clearance to leave the site of the knife attack. She had grey curly hair which today she wore high on her head in a ponytail, smiley blue eyes which Yvonne hadn't noticed in the dark of the churchyard, and was a couple of inches shorter than Tom.

Tom sat next to Alan on the sofa and patted the old man on the shoulder. 'You look as though you've had a shock. Do you want to tell me about it?'

'I'm just trying to take it all in' Alan said, shaking his head and with tears in his eyes. His previously florid complexion was now grey, and his body was swamped by the cushions of the sofa. 'For all these years I have believed my old friend was traumatised by having his house broken into and now it looks as though he was pulling the wool over my eyes. Why? Why would he do it?'

Yvonne's eyes filled with tears for the second time that day as Alan began to quietly weep into a handkerchief he pulled from his trouser pocket. Tom looked up at Yvonne for an explanation.

'You know that Bernie Campling's house was burgled a number of years ago?'

Tom nodded 'Yes, I remember. I was away with the Army at the time, but I know my parents and all our neighbours on Bimport were on high alert for months afterwards. It was shocking because so much was taken, much of it big and heavy items so a van or even a lorry must have been used, and it would have taken time to load it all into the vehicle but nobody heard or saw a thing.'

'Mmmh we may have the answer to that lack of evidence of the raid' Yvonne spread her arm out to indicate the items from Bernie's house which were decorating the courtyard. 'Nigel and Rufus have just been telling us about the cellar in Bernie's house where they found all this stuff. Alan believes the statue is one he gave to Bernie to sell, and several people think that Captain's chair is probably the one another dealer called Alex gave him as an example of half-a-dozen he had for sale. It seems from what Nigel and Rufus are saying, that many of the items he reported as stolen can be found in that cellar.'

'We need to look at this cellar' said DS Smalley. 'I'll process these items and take them to the police station for secure storage.'

'You'll need a sack truck to move the statue' said Rob. 'I'll get one from the shop, if that's alright Yvonne?'

Yvonne nodded, and Bridget said 'Thank you Rob, that will be very helpful.'

Tom asked Yvonne and Alan 'Would either of you be able to identify any other items Bernie reported stolen if we take you to his house?'

Alan shook his head 'I am sorry, I would like to help but I am too upset to do that today. I can't believe he would betray me like that. You remember the damage it did to the trade at the time, don't you love?' he asked looking up at Yvonne.

She knelt next to him and patted his arm 'I do, Alan, I do. It was a dark time, and many of us were affected, although not as much as those of you who had given him stock to sell on. I do understand how you must be feeling. He was your friend, and he lied to you. He stole from you.'

Alan nodded, and fresh tears ran down his grey cheeks. 'It's not just the money, although that was devastating at the time. To think of all those years I sat with him in his office as we discussed the state of the antiques trade while drinking tea or a beer, and all the time, underneath our feet …'

Tom put his arm around the old man and said 'You take your time. It is a lot to take in. Here's George with a cup of tea for you.'

George laid a tray with four mugs, a teapot, milk and sugar on the table in front of Alan, and gave Yvonne a hand standing up. 'Thank you' she said quietly. 'I'm not even going to pretend there was a time I could easily stand up from a kneeling position.'

'Better you than me' said Alan, the ghost of a smile appearing on his face. 'Wait until I try to get up off this sofa!'

Tom poured the tea, and Lesley brought some cake over for them to eat. Within minutes Alan's colour was restored from grey to a healthy pink, and Tom could see the old man's fighting spirit was returning. By the time

Rob and DS Smalley returned Alan was ready to join them in inspecting Bernie's cellar.

'Come on you two,' Tom said to Nigel and Rufus. 'Show us this cellar.'

Together they walked along Bell Street to Bimport, and through the large wooden door on the side of the house, into Bernie's home. Nigel and Rufus appeared as shocked as Alan by the day's revelations; their father's funeral had not turned out as expected. All the effort they had put into planning the service at the crematorium felt wasted, and the pleasure in decorating the courtyard with happy memories felt foolish. Neither had been living at the family home when the burglary took place, but they both lived nearby and had clear memories of how traumatised their father had been at the time. Their pace slowed as they approached their former home.

'It's just through here' said Nigel, indicating an open door at the end of the kitchen.

'After you' said Tom, and the two brothers led the way through the recently cleared larder to a solid oak door, which opened onto wide stone steps leading down into a cavernous room lit by a variety of standard lamps, with several rugs covering the stone floor.

'Oh my god' said Rob, his eyes wide with amazement at the sight of the antique items laid out as though they were in a well-curated museum. 'The old devil.'

Yvonne said nothing at first as she moved through the different areas between the stone pillars. She could remember the list of stolen items because it had been big news in the trade, and everyone had been on the lookout for the thieves attempting to off-load bronze figures, gold sovereigns, and much more. She had circulated the list to the local managers of their shops, and the marshals at their antiques fairs had been given the responsibility for checking every stall in case they had found their way into general circulation. But nothing had been found, or at least nothing which could be clearly identified as originating from Bernie's house. The marble statue Alan spotted in the courtyard was easily claimed due to the rust mark on her back, but it was much harder to claim an oak coffer or an Imari plate. Even so, the antiques dealers were as keen to trace those items as the police, probably even more so because they were integral to the flow of trade.

Tom and DS Smalley positioned themselves at the bottom of the steps with Nigel and Rufus in front of them. The brothers stood looking desolate and watched as Alan, Yvonne and Rob walked around the hoard pointing at this piece and commenting about that one to each other. Rob had produced a notebook and pencil from the back pocket of his suit trousers and was listing items and owners as Yvonne and Alan searched their memories for the items Bernie had reported stolen. Yvonne wondered why he had a notebook in the trousers of a suit he claimed to rarely wear from one year to the next.

'That could be Ivan's Japanese jar and cover.'

'Look at this gorgeous example of a silver tea set. I'm pretty sure that belongs to Jason.'

'Didn't Barry have one too?'

'He did, but he didn't leave it with Bernie. His was sold at auction.'

'I can't believe this' Rufus murmured to his brother. 'I can't believe Dad would do this.'

'I'm struggling with the idea. How on earth did he get all this down here? And look,' Nigel pointed at a control panel on the wall 'he's somehow managed to install a temperature-controlled environment and automatic humidifiers. There is no way all of that was here when Dad bought the house; it is too modern.'

'I agree, it looks about twenty years' old' said Rufus drily.

'It's not just the moral behaviour which seems so out of character, but all this electrical work. I didn't think Dad could do something like this. One of us always sorts out anything electrical which needs to be done for him.'

'You're right. We were the ones who did all the work when he renovated that shed at the end of the garden' said Rufus. 'If he could do all this he wouldn't have needed us to put the lights and heating in down there. He never showed any interest in our work.'

Nigel shook his head slowly. 'Either he has hidden his skills, or he would have had to employ someone who was not local, who we didn't know, and not connected to the antiques trade. It would have to be someone who would not link the reports of the burglary with the work they had done here. A risky thing to do.'

'But a risk which obviously paid off' Rufus gestured to the antiques displayed around them. 'When did he do all of this? Before Mum died? After Mum died?'

'It must have been after Mum died' Nigel said. 'I simply do not believe she would have condoned any of this, and he couldn't have got away with it while she was alive.'

Alan joined in the conversation 'I agree with you Nigel. There is no way your mother would have allowed him to hoard all these things belonging to other people and lie about it. Mind you, I wouldn't have believed it of your father if I hadn't seen it for myself.'

'But if that is what happened it means he did all of this in the months while we thought he was grieving after she died. Surely not' said Rufus as he looked at his brother for reassurance. 'That would mean he planned the burglary and put all this into place in the time between Mum dying and faking a break-down. I don't believe it. He wasn't even capable of coming over to your house for your thirtieth birthday party, or going to any of the antiques auctions, events he would never have missed before. He was destroyed by that burglary, don't you remember?'

'He certainly appeared to be' Nigel agreed. 'I was very worried about him, and thought we were going to lose him within a year of losing Mum.'

Alan sat down in a seventeenth century mahogany Chippendale chair, tears welling in his eyes, and began to speak. 'That burglary shook our local antiques trade. We were all terrified the thieves would come and empty our shops, lockups and warehouses. It was a real shock because nothing like that had ever happened.'

'I remember it well' said Rob. 'It happened before I retired, and I was still working as an engineer. The members of my local auto club had an emergency meeting where we discussed ways we could improve our personal security, as well as that of our collections. I was looking over my shoulder for weeks afterwards, worried that I was being followed back to the garage I rented at the time.'

Alan nodded agreement. 'I remember changing my routes on every journey and going around roundabouts two or three times before taking one of the exits, just to try to spot anyone following me. It was a stressful time. If anyone had been caught, or even suspected of being involved in the theft it would probably have been easier, but we didn't have any idea who had done it.'

'I am sorry' Nigel said in a quiet voice.

'Oh, you have nothing to be sorry about lad' Alan looked up at him and patted his arm. 'It was your old man who did it, not you, and you obviously didn't know anything about it.'

'I didn't' said Nigel.

'Nor me' said Rufus.

Alan sighed 'But he can't have done all this on his own. Someone helped him to carry all this stuff down here. There is no way he could have moved some of these pieces of furniture on his own. Someone knew something, and it's your job to find out who.' He directed the last comment to Tom and DS Smalley.

Tom nodded 'We will do our best.'

Chapter 7

'I think that's the last box' said Tom, as he carried a cardboard box full of dog toys, food and coats into the kitchen. He set it down by the sofa and watched as his dog Stan and Yvonne's dog Zebedee set about removing each toy and placing them on the floor. 'Look at those two working as a team' he laughed.

'They're going to miss living together. Thank you Tom,' said Yvonne, who had begun unwrapping individual pie dishes. Although she had planned to only take a few essential items when she temporarily moved into Tom's house while her shop and flat were closed as a police crime scene, as the week or two dragged out into three months she had made frequent requests to return to pick up more of her belongings. She realised within a fortnight that she couldn't live without these pie dishes, even though when she was only cooking for herself she rarely used them. 'I can't believe how much stuff I had moved into your place.'

The buzzer on the gates outside sounded, and Yvonne crossed the kitchen to check the small monitor and saw her friends Tabitha and Alison waiting for her to let them in. She pressed the button to unlock the gates and opened the back door for them.

'We wanted to check you really are moving back home!' Alison, looking glamorous as always, her six-foot-tall willowy figure dressed in a fitted long green dress, and her long straight blond hair and perfect make-up a good advertisement for the beautician she was, walked into the kitchen with a huge smile on her face when she saw the boxes.

Close behind her, Tabitha said 'Oh good, it's really happening. You must be so happy!' In contrast to her wife, Tabitha's hair was a messy mass of curls shoved into a baseball cap, and she was dressed in her usual farmer's outfit of jeans and a shirt. Tabitha was five foot six, the same height as Yvonne, but stockier and more straight up and down than Yvonne's slim-with-curves figure.

'Oh Tom, are you happy you are getting your house back or is it going to be lonely for you?' Alison asked.

Tom said ruefully 'I think I am going to be lonely for a while. After so many years of living on my own I thought I would hate to have someone else in my home, but Yvonne and Zebedee have fitted into our lives really well, haven't they Stan?'

Stan looked up at the sound of his name from his busy task of emptying the toy box with Zebedee, wagged his tail a few times, and then stuck his head back in the box and pulled out a knotted rope.

'I bet it will be a bit odd for a few days, but tomorrow we're all coming to invade your kitchen for Sunday lunch, and on Monday you'll be too busy working to even notice they are not there' Tabitha assured him.

'He's not getting a chance to miss us' said Yvonne. 'He'll be seeing us almost every day at the farm with the horses. I am really pleased to be moving back into my own home, but I am most looking forward to finally getting my shop reopened.'

'You have taken quite a hit with your income this year, having to stay closed all summer' said Tom. 'Let's hope it's a profitable last quarter of the year.'

'Are you still set for opening next Saturday?' Tabitha asked.

'Yes! There is a lot to do before then, in terms of finishing the redecorating and getting the dealers' stock in there. I won't be around much next week but I hope you will all come to help us celebrate on Saturday.'

'Of course we will!' said Tabitha. 'You know us, we do love an excuse to celebrate something. Plans for your party are going well, by the way. George is letting us use the courtyard at TAA, did he tell you?'

'Oh that's kind of him, no he hasn't said anything.' Yvonne looked worried. 'Isn't that going to be a bit big for us?'

'Don't worry, we're not inviting the town, just the ten on your list. Maybe a few more. If the weather holds we'll sit around on the sofas outside with the firepits going, and if it's too cold we'll sit in the big room inside.'

Yvonne suddenly felt tearful. She had never had friends like these, she had always been so busy working that people she could call her friends were fellow antiques dealers who relied on her for the antiques markets and centres she owned, and she had done her best to remove herself from them in recent years. These three people standing in her kitchen wanted nothing from her except her company, and it was a warm feeling. Realising she was in danger of being ungracious, she said 'I love you guys, thank you.'

'Is there anything we can do to help you here?' Alison asked as she looked around Yvonne's kitchen.

Yvonne shook her head 'No, I don't think so, thank you. We have moved all the cases and boxes and bags, and it's just a matter of unpacking everything which I had better do on my own. But thank you for the offer.'

'Do you have everything? Milk, bread, butter? We can pop out for a shopping bag of essentials if you need them?' offered Alison.

'You're so kind, but no, I really do have everything here. Look!' Yvonne opened the fridge to show the well-stocked shelves and gestured to the work top where a loaf of bread and a box of fruit and vegetables sat waiting to be put away. 'But I am glad you two popped in. I had to have the locks changed, and here are the new set of spare keys for you.' She took a set of keys from the hook by the door and said 'the code to the gate has been changed too. I'll text it to you later. Tom also has a set of keys and the code, just in case anyone tries to break into the shop.'

'OK, that was a good idea' said Tabitha.

'She had to do it' explained Tom. 'It is standard practice after something like that.'

'Of course, it makes sense. Right, we'll leave you in peace, and see you tomorrow. What time do you want us, Tom?' Tabitha asked.

'I told Maisie any time after eleven o'clock, and lunch is served at midday. I think she is planning on arriving on the dot of eleven' he laughed.

'We'll see you at eleven tomorrow! Bye!'

The two women waved as they left the kitchen, and Yvonne said 'I love those two. Now then, it must be time for a cuppa.'

While Yvonne filled the kettle, Tom chose a couple of mugs from a cupboard and popped teabags into each one.

'I've been thinking about Bernie and his hidden treasure, and your reaction to it' Tom said as he busied himself with retrieving milk from the fridge. He waited while Yvonne poured boiling water into the mugs before continuing 'You weren't surprised.'

'I was surprised' Yvonne protested. 'I couldn't believe my eyes when we walked down those stone steps. Bernie always had an eye for display, and his market stall was easy to spot in a row when often one dealer's stock appeared to blend into the next, but since his wife died he'd lost the passion that went into presenting his stock. His stand in Angel Lane Antiques was often in need of a tidy-up between his days working in the shop, and even when he was in there all day he didn't make much of an effort with it. Seeing the way all that stock was displayed in that downstairs room was a reminder of how he used to be. The use of lighting, the way he layered one item above or alongside another, the arrangements of the collections and the wow factor of the single items was all reminiscent of the old Bernie.'

Tom squeezed the teabags and threw them into Yvonne's kitchen waste bucket, before adding milk to their mugs. Yvonne carried the mugs to her kitchen table, and they pulled out a chair each and sat down. 'That's not what I meant,' Tom said quietly, his blue eyes which could be so full of laughter looking serious.

The silence grew between them, until eventually Yvonne said 'Alright. It was curious that none of the items surfaced anywhere after the burglary. Even if the gold and silver antiques had been sacrificed to the melt, there were plenty of wooden items, paintings, sculptures made from bronze or stone, which would not have been destroyed for cash. Nothing ever turned up in auction, or on market stalls, or even in private houses when the owner died and the family didn't know what to do with all the stuff accumulated over a lifetime. I wasn't surprised that he still had some of those items after reporting them stolen. I was surprised by the quantity he had down there.'

Tom waited for Yvonne to continue, but when she didn't say any more he prompted 'Go on.'

Yvonne sighed and sipped her tea. 'Bernie was one of the stalwarts of the antiques trade while I was growing up. There were certain people you would see at every fair, at every market, who would stop for a chat, share some great buy they'd made or sale they were celebrating, and Bernie was one of them. When I was managing the business I could always rely on him to pay up on time for his stand and get on with stalling out without any additional input from us. No quibbles or arguments like some, he just paid up.'

'He sounds like the perfect stallholder' commented Tom.

'He was. He was friendly and helpful, and we never had any complaints about him, unlike so many other dealers.'

'What sort of complaints would you get about other dealers?'

'Oh the usual ones. Some we could dismiss where one dealer had a gripe with another about some deal which had not gone their way but was nothing to do with us as fair organisers, or complaints by members of the public about someone's attitude but we'd usually discover the member of the public had started that dispute. He also wasn't one of the men who made me feel uncomfortable around him, and there were plenty of those, nor did I hear any other women expressing their concerns about him. Some of the dealers had a real drink and or drugs problem, and over time it showed in the way they ran their businesses and in their personal relationships, but I think you get that in all walks of life. It made them difficult to be around, and we ended up banning a few which was a part of the job I hated, but it wasn't worth allowing them into the fair because they always ended up causing trouble and sometimes we'd have to involve you lot. No fair organiser wants to get a reputation for calling the police on a regular basis. But we could rely on Bernie to get on with his neighbours at a fair, and the same went for most of the other antiques dealers, and we didn't get negative feedback from customers about him.'

'But?'

With another sigh Yvonne said 'But. There were no mutterings or rumours about his integrity until that burglary at his home, and even then anyone who began to cast doubt on his honesty was shot down. But. There were people beginning to voice their suspicions about the whereabouts of the reportedly stolen goods, which I think is probably a normal response when something like that happens. Like I said, none of it was seen again which you must know is extremely unusual.'

Tom shrugged in a non-committal manner and motioned for Yvonne to continue.

'I don't think any of us wanted to believe the rumours, because as I said Bernie was someone we could trust. The rumours didn't last because it wasn't long before the next scandal hit the antiques trade.'

'What was that?' Tom asked.

Yvonne shook her head. 'It was so long ago I can't remember what that was. There is always something going on, whether it is someone having an affair with someone else, or someone being taken seriously ill, or an item selling for way above the estimate in auction. Who knows, I can't remember but I don't think it was related to the thefts. It was a while after my cousin was murdered, so it wasn't that. Ever since then I have only heard good things about Bernie. Although thinking about it now, he had been keeping a relatively low profile since his wife's cancer diagnosis five years earlier, and almost disappeared from the scene after his wife's death, so his name rarely came up in conversation. Before that he was an extrovert character, and busy. He would be stalling out at every antiques market, bidding in every auction, selling in a couple of local ones and the London specialist sales, turning up everywhere. After she died he was practically a recluse, and rarely ventured away from our local area. I don't think he was putting anything in any of the auctions, and I didn't hear stories of him being successful in buying from them either.'

Seeing that she was concentrating on trying to remember Bernie's activities after the burglary, rather than on what he wanted to hear about, Tom prompted 'What was the thing which made you suspect Bernie was not the open and honest antiques dealer you had believed him to be, Yvonne?'

With a sigh she said 'Before the burglary we discovered that when my cousin died Bernie had over fifty thousand pounds worth of his stock which he denied when we asked him about it.'

'That sounds like a lot of antiques for someone else to be holding for another antiques dealer. How do you know all this?'

'Because my cousin kept meticulous records in a diary, and Bernie's name and details of numerous items were listed going back fifteen years with no mark to show they had been paid for or returned. I have always known, sorry suspected, that Bernie was involved in some way in my cousin's murder.' Seeing the frown on Tom's face, Yvonne said hastily 'I know, I know, I don't have any evidence of his involvement, and the killer's conviction is solid.'

'But' said Tom slowly 'you have linked Bernie to the circumstances around the murder in your mind.'

'I have' Yvonne nodded. 'Bernie was also murdered, wasn't he?'

Tom grimaced 'You know I can't confirm or deny that, and because I can't I suppose you have your answer. The official verdict is Unexpected Death - Under

Investigation, and that way his family could have the funeral.'

Yvonne narrowed her eyes as a horrible thought struck her. After a few moments she said quietly 'Tom? Was there a body in that coffin at the crematorium?'

Tom gave her the kind of blank look which told her there was not.

'Do Nigel and Rufus know?'

Again she was on the receiving end of the blank look, which she took to mean that they did know but she wasn't sure and decided not to bring the subject up when she next saw them.

Tom said 'So do you think his sons are involved?'

'Absolutely not!' Yvonne was adamant. 'Neither Nigel nor Rufus have ever given me reason to doubt their innocence. They have never been involved in their father's antiques business. They both chose to join their aunt's family's electrician's business.'

Tom's blue eyes were gentle but his voice was firm. 'As they themselves pointed out, that was a specialised degree of skill which went into setting up the electrics in the cellar.'

'I know, but do you really think they would have highlighted it if they had been involved? And why would they have put any of the items on display at his wake if they knew they had been stolen from half the people attending?'

Tom nodded 'You make a good defence. But it isn't a strong one. I think they are the most obvious suspects for the murder and attempted murder on Semley Common, but I am not in charge of the investigation. We'll have to see what the Commander thinks.'

Yvonne protested 'There is a big difference between helping your dad to conceal a load of antiques belonging to other antiques dealers and stabbing them. I don't believe they were involved in Bernie's deception, and I cannot believe they have an aggressive bone in their bodies.'

Suddenly there was a low growling sound from one corner of the kitchen. Stan had retrieved a red rubber bone-shaped toy from the box, and Zebedee wanted it. She snarled at him showing her impressive teeth, and he slowly dropped the toy to the floor and backed away. Zebedee moved in and collected it, before settling down on the floor and concentrated on chewing it, her white and brindle body radiating happiness. Stan nipped around behind her and picked up the green fluffy bird-shaped toy she had been guarding and trotted over to Tom, his scruffy black and white face a picture of glee.

'I swear he planned that' laughed Yvonne. 'Clever boy! I think you'd better take that one back with you. It was probably his to start with, but I have forgotten whose toys were whose.'

'Well, it has been almost three months since you two moved in with us' said Tom. 'Things are bound to have got mixed up. Thanks for your thoughts about the Campling brothers. If you do think of anything else, you know where I am. I'd better be going and leave you to your unpacking. See you tomorrow for Sunday lunch?'

'Yes, thank you Tom.' Yvonne crossed the kitchen to give Tom a hug, something they had got into the habit of doing in recent weeks.

'Hi, I've just popped round to see if you need a hand with anything.' George Gumbleton appeared in the doorway, dressed casually in jeans and a pale pink shirt which looked fantastic against his tanned skin and dark hair. Yvonne thought he looked as though he had stepped out of a magazine photo shoot for luxury yachts with his dark glasses pushed up on his head.

'Thank you George, I think we've moved everything of mine from Tom's house, so it's just a matter of putting everything away in its rightful place.'

'I'll see you both tomorrow, come on Stan' said Tom as he sketched a wave with the hand carrying the fluffy dog toy and left through the doorway George had just entered.

'Yes, see you tomorrow!' called Yvonne.

'Can I help you get this stuff sorted, or will I be in the way?' asked George.

Yvonne ran her hand through her short curly hair as she looked around the room, trying to decide whether she wanted to be alone in her home for the first time in months. Making up her mind she walked over and took his hand and gazed into his soft brown eyes, marvelling as she always did at his long eyelashes. 'Do you know what, I believe there is something you can help me with. Upstairs.'

'I like the sound of that!' said George.

Chapter 8

'Knock knock!' Yvonne and George walked through the open back door to Tom's house, into his kitchen where Tabitha, Maisie and Alison were already seated at the big old pine table with glasses of wine in front of them. They had been discussing Yvonne's upcoming birthday party and immediately shut up when they heard her footsteps outside.

'Hi!' Tom, wearing his usual black top and black jeans but with the addition of a blue and white striped apron, his forearms impressively decorated with tattoos making him look like a naval chef, turned from the Aga to greet them, before turning back to attend to one of the four saucepans in front of him. 'Help yourselves to a drink. I'll be with you in a minute.'

While George poured wine into a glass for Yvonne and helped himself to a zero-alcohol bottle of Guinness, Yvonne opened a cupboard and found a jug. 'These are for you' she said as she filled the jug with water before adding a bunch of white roses to it. She put the jug on the windowsill behind the butler sink and went round to give Tom a kiss on the cheek. 'Is there anything I can do?'

'Thank you, they're beautiful' he said. 'You remembered?'

She nodded, 'Can I stir something, drain something, carve something?'

Tom laughed 'No, I have it all under control thank you.'

He was as good as his word, and within minutes the table was filled with dishes of vegetables, roast potatoes, Yorkshire puddings, and slices of roast beef perfectly browned on the outside and pink in the middle. The dogs, who had been thunderously charging up and down the stairs, suddenly appeared in the doorway looking hopeful. Stan executed his best Sit, while Zebedee fixed George who was usually an easy target with her best begging stare. Everyone ignored them.

'Cheers to the chef!' announced Tabitha, raising her glass. A chorus of 'Cheers' went around the table, and Tom placed a couple of gravy boats on the table with a flourish.

'Don't laugh, but wearing a white top wasn't the best idea I've ever had' groaned Maisie, as she tucked one corner of her napkin in the V of her cashmere jumper. 'My kids always tease me when I do this, but if I don't I'll drip gravy down my front.'

'She's right' said Alison. 'We chose the colour and pattern of our uniforms for work because Maisie seems to attract everything from nail varnish to peroxide, even when she isn't the one applying it. I can be waxing a client's legs in one room, and somehow Maisie gets hot wax onto herself.'

'It's true!' laughed Maisie.

'So long as you don't accidently get it on the client, I don't suppose it matters' said George.

'Well that's the strange thing' said Alison. 'Out of the two of us Maisie is much better at applying make-up or colour to someone's hair. When we have a bridal booking it is Maisie who looks after the bride, because she is so accurate with her brushwork!'

'That's probably because I have ten years' more experience than you. I'm in my mid-forties now, so it's all downhill from here' she said cheerily.

'You don't look it' observed Tabitha. 'You two are great advertisements for your beauty business, with your perfectly straight long blond hair and great-looking skin.'

'Thank you!' said Maisie, raising her glass of wine to Tabitha. 'I am definitely noticing the ageing process these days, but also seem to care less about how I look, so I suppose that is a good thing.'

'We do make a good team' said Alison, as she and Maisie chinked glasses. 'Cheers Partner.'

'Mmmh this is delicious, thank you' said Tabitha as she tucked into the beef, her dark curly hair tumbling down her back for once, instead of stuffed under a baseball cap. 'We don't usually eat meat when we're away from home, but as it's you and you bought this from our neighbours we're making an exception.'

Alison nodded 'Careful Tom, we might be turning up at your door every Sunday!'

'And you will be very welcome, so long as I can turn up at yours for the occasional roast chicken or lamb' Tom laughed.

'Changing the subject' Maisie said, 'do you have a cellar under here like the one in Bernie's house?'

'Good point' said George. 'Bernie's house is only four doors down from here. I know they all look different from the outside, but presumably if one has a cellar they all do?'

Tom gave them a knowing look. 'Yes, we do have a cellar, but I am sorry to say it is not filled with priceless antiques, although my dad did build up a good wine cellar down there over the years. In fact both of these bottles are from his collection.'

'Cheers to your dad' said Yvonne, raising her glass of red.

'Cheers to your dad' said Maisie, raising her glass of white.

'It would have been his birthday today' said Tom.

'That explains the roses. Nice touch Yvonne' Tabitha too raised her glass in a toast.

'Can we see the cellar after lunch?' asked Maisie.

'Of course you can. But as I said, it really isn't very impressive.'

'What is happening with the contents of Bernie's cellar?' asked Tabitha. 'Did he keep a record of who all the items belonged to?'

'Fortunately for us he did keep meticulous records, which has made our lives easier, but nothing will be returned to the original owners for a long time yet because there is an ongoing investigation. Until then everything is being stored in the silver vaults off Chancery Lane in London.'

'Oh right, when's it all going to be taken up there? From what Alan was saying in The Ship there is a lot of stuff to cart up those stairs, and it will take a few van loads and several people to move it all.'

'It took seven van loads, and as many men to move it all on Wednesday' said Tom with a smile.

'What!' Tabitha looked impressed. 'You've moved it all already? That was quick.'

'That was quick' said Yvonne. 'We only found it all on Tuesday afternoon.'

'We couldn't guarantee the security of it with our policing team in North Dorset so the powers that be took it out of our hands. They can work quickly when they want to' he said with a wink.

'How come no one saw anything?' Yvonne asked. 'I haven't heard a word about it, and I am sure I would have done. It's not every day Bimport gets blocked by seven vans being filled with high value items.'

'We all heard about it when that lorry driver ignored the no access for seven-point-five ton HGV's signs and grounded his lorry on St John's Hill' laughed Tabitha. 'To make matters worse the back doors hadn't been securely shut and all that meat from the abattoir at Manston spilled over the road to add to his misery!'

Yvonne noticed Tom was keeping his head down and concentrating on his food. 'Do you know something about that?'

'Ooh was it a distraction?' exclaimed Tabitha.

'No!' said Maisie.

'He is keeping very quiet about it' observed Alison.

'The vans weren't all lined up in a row, with the antiques being carried out one at a time' explained Tom, making it clear he wasn't going to talk about the meat lorry. 'I doubt there is ever a time when you could park three vans on Bimport, let alone seven. The vans were variously disguised as trade vans, and the drivers parked them along Bell Street and the High Street while one was being filled, and then swapped the full one for an empty one and so on. Bernie had electronic gates like mine, and so no one would be able to see all the antiques being loaded into the back of each van.'

'Do you mean to say we have had hundreds of thousands of pounds worth of antiques parked up with hundreds of people walking by and no one knew a thing about it!' exclaimed Maisie.

George and Tom exchanged a look, before Tom nodded and said 'Not for the first time.'

'What do you mean by that?' Tabitha demanded.

'The town has a lot of valuable assets and they may or may not be stored in the relevant buildings' he explained. 'Think about it. We have several churches, a town hall, a couple of museums, numerous clubs, all of whom have ceremonial items and bits and pieces which have been handed down through the centuries. Some of them are stored in local vaults, but over time businesses close and buildings change hands, so it is not unusual for objects worth hundreds of thousands if not millions of pounds to be transported through our town and local villages without any fuss or fanfare.'

'I keep all of mine out in the open in my fields' laughed Tabitha.

'If you put it like that I suppose my little shop probably has hundreds of thousands of pounds worth of stock, and when the dealers drive in to buy or replenish their stands we could easily have tens of thousands of pounds worth of antiques hanging around in the car park. I am interested in how long it took to empty Bernie's cellar?' asked Yvonne.

Tom grinned 'How long do you think? You saw what was down there. What do you reckon?'

Yvonne thought for a moment. 'I think if you had people packing everything up in the cellar before the removal started, it probably took about four hours to fill the vans. The packing will have taken about the same length of time, so start to finish I am going to guess nine hours minimum, twelve hours maximum.'

'Any other guesses?' Tom opened the debate up to the rest of the table. 'Would anyone like to narrow down Yvonne's time frame because she's in the right area.'

'Well that's not fair because none of the rest of us saw what was down there' said Tabitha, 'but based on what Alan was saying, and knowing that Yvonne tends to get things done in a tidy fashion I would guess nearer the twelve hour mark, so I am going to guess eleven hours forty-five minutes.'

'Tabitha is right, Yvonne does tend to get things done quickly, so I am going to guess eleven hours thirty minutes' said Alison.

'I think you are underestimating how fast seven men can carry things up those stairs' said Maisie. 'Remember not everything will have needed to be carried singly, because it sounds as though there were a lot of small items which could be packed away into a large box meaning less journeys to and from the cellar, so I am going to guess ten hours.'

George had been studying Tom's face as the three women gave their answers. 'I think even twelve hours sounds exceptionally fast for such a big job when you think stone statues and Captains' chairs were involved, but I think Tom is being a touch misleading with his information because I reckon you can fit up to four vans in the driveway of that house. Also Maisie is right and from the sound of it most things were small enough to fit into pockets, so I am going to guess nine hours fifteen minutes.'

Tom looked around the table 'Anyone want to change their answer?'

'I don't think I'm right, but go on, tell us who won' Tabitha said, 'and what did we win?'

'Ha ha, this is No Prize Sunday' laughed Tom. 'Yvonne, of course, has won. It took just under twelve hours to pack all the items for transporting them, and to load them into the vans. You made a good point, George, about how many could fit into the driveway, but the team were not going to draw attention to themselves by parking in there, and Maisie you were right about the small items but of course they took forever to wrap and fit securely into the packing cases. The team came down on Tuesday evening and stayed at The Benett Arms in Semley and were up and packing everything in the cellar by seven o'clock in the morning. I am glad that no rumours of their work got out into the local area, because I am sure at least one of you five would have heard about it if they had.'

Yvonne shook her head. 'This town is amazing. Someone fails to pick up after their dog and everyone knows about it, but seven men can work all day removing an expensive load of goods from a house and no one bats an eyelid.'

'I do wish more people were caught not picking up after their dog' commented Maisie. 'I don't know that I have trodden in it with my artificial foot until I slip on the next step forwards.'

There was a general murmur of agreement around the table.

'The Benett has been allowed to reopen now has it?' asked Tabitha.

'Yes, they were cleared for reopening the next day' said Tom. 'Everyone was questioned, and it appears the altercation between the victims and their attacker or attackers must have happened away from the pub. No one inside saw or heard a thing until that scream.'

George said 'That must have been a relief for the landlords.'

'So what happens now to the antiques?' Alison asked. 'How easy is it going to be to identify the original owners and return their items to them?'

'That will be quite tricky' said Tom. 'Although I am sure the dealers will be able to recognise their stock, and as I said Bernie did keep a list for his own records, none of it is detailed enough and the lack of proof of purchase is going to be a sticking point, isn't that right Yvonne?'

She nodded 'We rarely have detailed receipts for things we buy because it isn't practical. If Alan has a receipt for his stone statue it probably states something like "£3000 received for miscellaneous goods" because he bought it along with several other items from a woman who was moving house and needed to clear the buildings and garden.'

'Exactly' said Tom. 'And the chap who gave Bernie the Captain's chair to show to a prospective buyer is unlikely to have proof that the chair he gave to Bernie is the one we found because any receipt he has won't have identifying features listed. He could show a receipt for a chair and it could be any chair, or even if it was described as a Captain's chair that doesn't mean the one we have is his.'

Tabitha laid down her knife and fork and sat back in her chair. 'That is awful! Those poor people. I can imagine how difficult it would be to reclaim sheep if someone ripped out their ear tags, but I am sure I would get them back if they were found alive.'

'So how does it work?' asked Maisie. 'How come he had all these antiques belonging to other dealers?'

Yvonne explained 'It's a common thing in the antiques world. If we know and trust someone we let them take an item away for valuing or speculative selling. Privately we may make a note of it, for example I write it down in my diary but that's so I don't forget because my memory's not great, rather than an official thing to do. Most dealers don't because they have phenomenal memories and can remember buying an antique badge twenty-five years ago, who they bought it from, how much for, where they then sold it and how much for. If I had given let's say a five stone diamond ring made from eighteen carat gold to Bernie to take away to show to a client of his, my little note would have said "Ring to Bernie" and that's it.

Nothing about that would identify the ring to the police or a court.'

'Oh I see' said Maisie. 'That system does require a lot of trust. How often does it go wrong?'

'Very rarely, thank goodness' said Yvonne, 'and I have never heard of anything on this scale before. Usually the warning signs are there, so word soon gets around if someone owes money, or in the old days wants to write post-dated cheques. I should think that is how Bernie got away with it for so long, because he always paid his debts, and continued valuing and selling things for the dealers while hanging on to one of their antiques. It wouldn't have been unusual for him to have something for a year before selling it for a decent profit for the dealer it originally belonged to, so you can see how he could accumulate a large amount of stock in the months preceding the so-called burglary.'

'I wondered how come he had so much, thank you. In that case what was his motivation, because he couldn't sell it, and he couldn't show it off?'

George said 'It doesn't make sense, does it? From what everyone says about him he was a dealer through-and-through, and in my experience although they are usually hoarders and have mountains of stock, they don't normally have it displayed in the way he did.'

'No, it's usually packed in shipping containers or stored in warehouses' agreed Yvonne. 'There are dealers who have a private collection of antiques, for example top hats, or I know of one dealer who had a fantastic antique horse-drawn coach. They won't necessarily have their collections on display to the public but given half-a-chance they will usually want to show them off to fellow dealers. Perhaps it is still too soon since their discovery, but I haven't heard of anyone else who knew anything about the items Bernie was storing in his cellar. The whole thing is out of character because he doesn't appear to have collected anything new since the burglary, and from what I could see almost everything he had down there was given to him in the year before. Perhaps he was more deeply affected by his wife's illness and death than we realised.'

Maisie said 'It could have been that. Grief can affect us in different ways, although it doesn't explain why he carried on with the deception for the next twenty years. I didn't know him very well, other than someone to say "Hello" to when I came into your shop.'

George got up from the table and began to clear the plates. For the next few minutes everyone was busy cleaning and tidying the kitchen, all the time telling Tom to stay sitting down. They were familiar with the room and where the cutlery, plates and glasses lived. The dogs were finally rewarded for their patience with a bowl each of left over vegetables which they practically inhaled. George filled the kettle and put it on the Aga, while Yvonne began to take tea and coffee orders.

'Before we do that, would you like to have a quick peek in the cellar?' Tom asked.

'Yes, please!' everyone chorused.

Tom led the way to the back door but instead of turning right and walking through it, he turned left and opened a second door.

'Where did that come from?' exclaimed Tabitha. 'I have never noticed that door before.'

Tom laughed 'It has always been here! Come on, follow me. Careful on the steps Maisie, they are not even heights.'

'OK, I will be' said Maisie, who always had to be mindful of walking with her prosthetic leg on uneven surfaces.

He switched a light on and walked down the stone staircase, followed by four humans and two dogs.

'Wow!' breathed Maisie. 'This is exactly how I imagined it would be.'

There was a single bare bulb hanging in front of the stairs, throwing a bright light onto the stone floor. Racks of bottles covered the walls, and brick dust and cobwebs covered the bottles. Vacant floor was limited, and they all almost filled the empty space. The dogs were madly sniffing along the racks and trying to stick their heads as far underneath the bottom layers as possible. While Tom stayed near the stairs, the other four friends browsed along the rows, brushing dust off the labels and exclaiming about their finds.

'I must confess that I do not have a clue about what I am looking at' admitted Alison, 'but it does seem as though it is a fine collection of wine.'

'I can't believe I have been coming here for months and yet I never noticed that door and didn't know all this existed' Tabitha was looking a little shocked.

'Nor can I' said Tom. 'You must have passed it several times on the way in. Where did you think the old bottles of wine were coming from?'

Tabitha shrugged 'I am ashamed to say I wasn't paying attention. I was enjoying drinking them.'

'I never noticed that door either' Maisie defended her friend, 'nor the quality of the wine, and I must have been here at least a dozen times in the last few months since Yvonne moved in with you. Do all the houses along here have cellars like this?'

'I don't know, but I would guess the ones built around the same time probably do.'

George said 'If Bernie's cellar started out like this one then it must have taken several weeks to work on it so the antiques he was planning to store down there would be kept in optimal conditions.'

Tom said 'I don't think it would have taken too long. These cellars don't flood because we don't have any streams or rivers in our hilltop town, so it won't have needed to be tanked or lined or anything like that. The stone flooring, walls and ceiling wouldn't have needed to be modified in any way. Ventilation, temperature control and maintaining the level of humidity were the main work, and someone with excellent electrical skills did that.'

'Mmmh' George was looking around the space, assessing what would have been involved. 'What do you think, three days' work for someone who knew what they were doing?'

Tom nodded 'I don't know because it's not my area of expertise, but Nigel and Rufus Campling were saying they could have done it between them in a maximum of two days if everything went to plan, so I suppose a minimum of three days for one person.'

'Oh, look what I can see!' Alison was pointing to a section of wall behind one of the racks. 'Is that an entrance to a tunnel?'

'It was once upon a time' said Tom 'but it has always been blocked up since my parents have lived here. I can't think of a reason why people would need to use a tunnel to go to their neighbours' houses.'

'Perhaps the houses were built upon the tunnels' suggested George.

'Which came first? The tunnels or the houses?' laughed Tabitha. 'It's a Shaston-specific quiz question.'

'But who knows the answer?' asked Alison.

'Only smarties have the answer!' the women chorused, before laughing at their own joke. The two men looked at each other and rolled their eyes.

'Shall we go back upstairs for coffee?' Tom asked.

They trooped back up the stairs, and again Tom was told to sit down while everyone else made themselves at home in his kitchen, making a pot of tea and filling a cafetiere of coffee. George had brought a box of chocolates, and Maisie had brought a plate of homemade biscuits. It wasn't long before everyone was sitting down at the old pine kitchen table with mugs of tea or coffee in front of them and passing the box and the plate up and down the table while the dogs lay in front of the Aga. Tom looked around his kitchen at his friends and decided he would try to make this a monthly event. He loved living on his own and enjoyed his own company, and of course his job in the police force meant he was rarely on his own while he was working. Until Yvonne moved in he had enjoyed having the house to himself since his mum had moved to

Spain the year before, after years of living in army barracks and then in a claustrophobic relationship where every moment he wasn't at work was accounted for by his wife. He had moved back to the family home as much to escape her as to keep his mum company when his father died, and in the intervening years had enjoyed the freedom. His mum had her own active social life, and his work rota was one where he kept irregular hours, and so they had never fallen into a routine of dinner on the table at six o'clock in the evening and expecting to know where the other one was in the evenings or on his days off. When Yvonne had moved in they had fallen into a similar arrangement, where if they both happened to be home at breakfast time they would enjoy the company, or one of them would make a cottage pie or lamb tagine for a shared evening meal. Cooking for one meant it wasn't usually worth making that kind of effort, but when you had two or more plates to fill it was an enjoyable thing to do. Yvonne's friends had got into the habit of meeting in Tom's kitchen once a week or so for a takeaway Indian meal or fish and chips. This was the first time he had cooked a roast for so many people in a long time, and he was sure it wasn't going to be the last.

Chapter 9

Eventually the Sunday lunch party broke up, with everyone going off to do their own jobs before retiring to their respective homes for the evening. Yvonne and George went to the livery yard with Zebedee, and while Yvonne and Toby enjoyed a gentle walk around the fields with Lindy and her palomino mare, Astrid, and Charlotte and her horse Sparkle, George and Zebedee went for a slightly more exciting walk up to Melbury Beacon.

'I'm a bit nervous about riding out' said Charlotte, as the three horses walked alongside at an easy pace despite their differences in height. 'That was such a horrible way to end our last ride. Have you heard any more about who the victims were and what condition the one who was still alive is in?'

Yvonne shook her head 'No, sorry, I haven't heard anything.'

Lindy shook her head 'Me neither. I don't suppose I will be told anything although it would be nice to know. I hope he survived.'

Charlotte said 'I hope he did too, but no I haven't either. It feels as though it never happened, because the town has already moved on and is talking about that massive pothole on the A30, and the temporary traffic lights on the road to Gillingham.' She shivered. 'How are Alison and Tom?'

'I have just had lunch with them at Tom's house, and they both seemed fine' Yvonne wanted to reassure her young friend. 'Really, Tom cooked Sunday lunch for us, and Alison was tucking in with the rest of us. He is a great cook, and was in good form, but I don't know how you get over something like that.'

'Nor me' said Charlotte. 'But then neither of us have been in the military.'

'Neither has Alison, as far as I know' said Yvonne.

'She must have some experience of dealing with stabbing victims because she was so cool under pressure. Maybe she has been a nurse and changed career?' mused Lindy.

'I'll have to ask her, because you are right, she was focused on saving that man's life and didn't hesitate to do what needed to be done. I have only ever known her and Maisie as owners of their beauty salon. I wonder what they both did before that?' said Yvonne.

'Have you always been an antiques dealer?' Charlotte asked.

Yvonne hesitated. She disliked talking about herself and her past, but sometimes it had to be done, so she tried to make her history as bland as possible. 'Yes, always, I have never known anything else and I can't imagine doing anything else. How about you? How did you get into owning and running a bakery?'

'By accident I suppose' said Charlotte. 'When I was at school I wanted to be an equine vet but didn't enjoy the first year of the degree course or being away from home.

Mum and Dad were great, because it was a big commitment from them to send me to university, but they said because they could see I had tried to make it work, and how unhappy it was making me, so long as I found work and didn't drift I could leave. I got a job working in the shop for Reeves the Bakers in town, and from there I went to work where they actually do the preparation and baking. I learned so much that Mum decided to do a short baking course, and we began to make cakes and bread for friends in our spare time. When the shop building on Coppice Street came up for sale Mum and Dad suggested we buy it and turn it into a bakery, and I said Yes Please! It was never my plan to have a bakery, and yet here I am aged twenty-five with my own shop. It is funny how life turns out. I get the best of both worlds, having gorgeous evenings like this riding my horse with a friend like you, doing what I love for a living with my family.'

'Don't forget your lovely husband!' said Lindy. 'It would be great if he is willing to drive my little horse lorry for me and Sally so we can join you on future pub rides.'

'Oh isn't he the best! Charlie and I met at school and we have been together ever since. I am so lucky to have married my best friend.'

'I don't know Charlie, but his brother Jack is a lovely young man. God that makes me sound old' exclaimed Yvonne, laughing.

'Jack is more extrovert than Charlie' said Charlotte. 'He definitely plays up to his good looks. Charlie is better looking in my opinion, and kinder and more fun than Jack. We can't imagine Jack ever settling down with anyone, but Charlie has always wanted to be married and have children.'

Yvonne gave her a sideways look, which made Charlotte laugh 'No, I'm not pregnant, yet, but it is definitely on the cards. We do want children, maybe in a couple of years if we are lucky enough to get pregnant, but I do want to get the bakery established first. It is only fair to Mum and Dad after all the investment of time and money they have put into it.'

'That all sounds very practical' said Yvonne, not sure if her life had ever been so planned.

'What about you? Do either of you have children?'

Lindy shook her head 'No, I have never been particularly interested in being a mother. I was always career-orientated and didn't really want to make time for pregnancy and babies.'

Yvonne said 'I am not sure I ever decided not to have children, but it never seemed to be the right time and now it is too late I don't regret it. When I was married my husband's job took him away from home for periods of time and so we never really made any plans for a family. Since we split up I haven't felt that maternal need so many women talk about, nor have I met anyone who I wanted to have children with since.'

Lindy agreed 'Same here. I come from a large family and love having lots of nephews and nieces, and of course now I am of an age where I now have grand-nephews and grand-nieces. But they don't make me wish I had my own.'

The light was fading and a scream made them and their horses jump. 'What was that!' Charlotte was clearly terrified.

Yvonne said quickly 'It's OK Charlotte, that was just a vixen calling to her cubs. Don't worry, we are not going to find anything more sinister than that tonight.'

'Sorry, sorry, I didn't realise how much it had upset me. Of course, I am being silly' Charlotte said in a weak voice.

Sternly, Yvonne said 'You are not being silly, Charlotte. What we witnessed was terrifying and is bound to have its effect on us. Don't brush it off. Why don't you message Tom and ask him for details of someone you can talk to about it. Obviously you can talk with me, and Tom and George, but we are not counsellors, and you may benefit from talking to someone who is. Believe me, it may be the best thing to do.'

Lindy said 'Experiences like that affect everyone in different ways. Don't compare yourself to us.'

'Maybe you are right' agreed Charlotte. 'I feel so stupid because I didn't come into contact with him, like you and Tom and Alison did.'

Yvonne said 'Like Lindy said, don't compare yourself to them!'

'I know! I'll ask Tom for someone to talk to about it. Thank you ladies, riding out here with you two has already made me feel better. It is a really lovely evening.'

'You are welcome, and thank you too! Shall we have a trot?' said Lindy.

The three women asked their horses to trot on, and for a while Astrid, Sparkle and Toby trotted alongside each other. Sparkle broke into a canter just to keep up with Toby's longer stride and Toby decided he would join her. Lindy didn't stop Astrid from joining in, and Yvonne and Charlotte were grinning at each other as their horses cantered together along the grassy edge of the field and urged them to go faster. Sparkle was always up for a gallop and initially she took the lead, but Toby wasn't going to be left behind and he soon caught up with her. Astrid was happy to stay just behind the other two. The wind in her face was making Yvonne's eyes stream, and looking across to Charlotte she could see hers were too. By now they were laughing and urging their horses even faster. As they approached the brow of the hill they both asked their horses to slow down, and Lindy and Astrid shot past.

'Sorry, I couldn't resist!' laughed Lindy, as blowing hard through their nostrils Astrid, Toby and Sparkle easily came back to a walk, lengthening their necks out and lowering their heads as they walked in long loose strides, their backs swinging easily.

'Wow that was brilliant!' Charlotte's cheeks were red and she was out of breath, grinning from ear-to-ear. 'Good girl Sparkle! It's good to be able to let her stretch out like that and know we can stop when I want to, because that wasn't the case a few months ago. I would never have trusted her then, but that was so much fun!'

With matching rosy cheeks Yvonne laughed 'It was, wasn't it! Well done' she stroked Toby's neck.

'Look, there is an owl!'

Yvonne and Lindy peered over to where Charlotte was pointing and saw an owl flying low along the hedge line. Lindy saw it first 'Wow, that is a beautiful sight.'

Charlotte said 'It's your birthday soon, isn't it Yvonne? Tom Archibald invited me and Charlie to your party.'

'Yes, Tabitha, Alison and Maisie are kindly organising the party for me, although 'party' may not be the right description. More of a gathering, because it's only going to be small and low-key. If it was left to me I wouldn't be having one, but their excitement is contagious, and now I am looking forward to it too. I don't think anyone has had a party for me since I was eighteen!'

Lindy said 'We'll have to have a Birthday Ride for you too, with everyone who can make it from the yard.'

'That's a great idea! We should always do that for everyone at the yard, although with over twenty of us we'll be having a Birthday Ride every other week' Yvonne laughed.

'No harm in that! What do you think, shall we have a breakfast ride up to the airfield on the nearest Sunday to your birthday?'

'We could do it yes, that way everyone can come whether they ride, walk or drive up there, if they want to of course. We haven't had a yard ride for a while, everyone has been so busy recently. It's a good excuse. I'll put a message up on our board in the kitchen when we get back. Although weren't we going to have a Halloween themed ride this month?'

Charlotte said 'Oh yes I had forgotten about that, we were, weren't we. I don't suppose there is any reason why we can't do both, have your Birthday Breakfast ride one

Sunday morning, and a Halloween-themed ride up to The Old Two Brewer's pub one evening? It would be great fun to get everyone dressed up in costumes and walk along the lanes through St James.'

Lindy said, warming to the theme 'We could do a sponsored pub ride through Shaftesbury, starting at The Half Moon pub while there is still some daylight, riding up the grass verges of the A350 to the fire station and along to Bell Street and arriving at the King's Arms, then down the High Street to The Mitre, and on down Gold Hill to the Two Brewer's, back to the yard by ten o'clock at night.'

Yvonne's phone pinged and she pulled it out of the thigh pocket of her black and orange riding tights. 'Talking of my birthday party, Tabitha has messaged to say she wants me to go and choose the menu. What does party food for a middle-aged woman's non-big birthday party look like?'

Charlotte's phone pinged, and after checking it she said 'Tom has messaged to ask me to make your cake! What type of cake, and what flavour would you like?'

They spent the rest of the ride back across the fields in a steady walk chatting about party food, cakes, partywear, and music, not really noticing the light dropping, the sun disappearing, and the moon taking its place. When they rode into the yard Charlotte was as relaxed as the horses, and Yvonne was full of enthusiasm for her party.

'You look happy!' commented George, who was sitting on the low wall of the grain ramp outside the stables with Zebedee lying by his side.

'We've been talking about Yvonne's birthday party' explained Charlotte, as she swung off her horse and landed gently on the ground.

Yvonne and Toby sidled up to the wall, and Yvonne carefully dismounted onto it, something she had discovered was kinder to her body than jumping down to the floor. 'I haven't had a birthday party since I was a teenager. Did you have a good run? Zebedee looks tired!'

Zebedee half-heartedly wagged her tail and lifted her head slightly, before resuming her prone position. George patted her 'I think I may have found her limit' he laughed. 'She set off running three times as much as I did, shooting here and there following scents on the ground. I thought I was going to have to put her on the lead, but after about five minutes she settled into trotting alongside me and stayed like that for the rest of the run. Good girl' he said to her as he rubbed her ears.

George helped Yvonne to untack Toby and turn him out. Zebedee stayed where she was.

After saying goodbye to her friends, Yvonne drove them up the hill to Shaftesbury, and invited George to her home for a light supper, which he prepared while she had a quick shower and she cooked while he showered. They spent a relaxed evening chatting and inevitably ended up making love in her bed. Yvonne felt far more relaxed in her own four-poster bed than she had sleeping as a guest in Tom's house, and less inhibited which was just as well because George's run had taken some of his energy, but he rallied and was soon matching her with enthusiasm.

When Yvonne awoke the next morning George was placing a cup of coffee on the bedside table next to her.

She smiled at him lazily 'Thank you, that's kind of you. Did you sleep well?'

'Like a log' he grinned. 'So did you, I think? You didn't stir when my alarm went off.'

'Best night's sleep I've had in ages. Do you have to leave now?'

'I do' he said regretfully, and briefly kissed her on the lips. 'I'll see you when I get back from Ireland.'

After he had gone, and Zebedee had taken his place next to her on the bed, Yvonne noticed a text on her phone from Tom which simply read 'We need to talk'. No greetings, pleasantries, or indication of what it was about. That could only mean one thing. She felt sick.

Grimacing, Yvonne ignored the coffee and headed for the bathroom. She loved her bathroom, which was tiled floor to ceiling in white with turquoise and silver detail, had a huge jacuzzi bath and large walk-in shower. Standing under the powerful shower she rehearsed what she was going to say, because even though he hadn't said what he wanted to talk about, she knew what it would be. Ever since they had come across the injured man on Semley Common she knew she would have to have this conversation with someone, and she was dreading it. If she said too little he would keep asking; if she said too much she would lose the hard-won battle to cope with the events surrounding the discovery of the dead body of her cousin.

It had been a traumatic time and was the catalyst for a complete change of life for Yvonne. She ended her connections with the successful family business and walked away from everything and everyone she was familiar with. After almost twenty years she had reached the stage where several days would go by without that dreadful vision of her cousin's body popping into the forefront of her mind, but inevitably something would happen and she would see it again, as clearly as the day she found him. She realised she was crying. She couldn't remember the last time she had cried about it. Giving in to the outpouring of grief she turned her face up into the stream of hot water and sobbed, letting the shower wash the tears away.

After what felt like several minutes, Yvonne turned off the shower and stepped out onto the soft silver-coloured bathmat and wrapped herself in a large turquoise towel before vigorously rubbing her hair dry with a matching smaller towel. She chose a delicious-smelling mango moisturiser by TROPIC and rubbed it into her skin. Feeling refreshed and ready to face Tom, she texted her reply 'Bring croissants. See you in 20 mins'.

'Well' she said to Zebedee, whose white and brindle body was curled up in a tight ball at the end of the bed but her brown eyes were watching every move Yvonne made. 'I think it's a casual jeans and long t-shirt kind of meeting.'

Dressed in a bright blue top and faded blue jeans, with her short dark brown hair drying naturally and therefore curly, Yvonne jogged down the spiral stairs to her kitchen with her dog close behind. Once Zebedee's breakfast was in her bowl, Yvonne filled the kettle and then moved over to the back of the kitchen to unlock the door and leave it open so Zebedee could go out to the small garden after she'd eaten her food. Yvonne was enjoying being back in her own kitchen and decided to make their tea in her blue china teapot instead of the usual dunking tea bags directly into mugs. The buzzer on the gates which led into the Angel Lane carpark outside announced Tom's arrival, and seconds later Stan and Zebedee raced into the kitchen together, playing chase in and out of the chairs around the large old pine table.

'It's as though they haven't seen each other for months' commented Tom drily as he walked in, holding the paper bag containing two almond croissants. 'I see you're settling into your home. Teapot, matching milk jug, and matching side plates. We're eating posh this morning! Do you have a matching vase?'

'Oh Tom that's kind' said Yvonne, as Tom held up a bunch of sunflowers.

'They're from my garden'

'Not the ones along the back wall of the house?'

'Yes, don't worry, there are still plenty there. It's been a good year for them, and I thought you'd appreciate their sunny faces for a few days while they last.'

Yvonne had enjoyed staying at Tom's house, although she was very happy to be back in her home, and one of the best bits had been to enjoy the large garden which extended from the back of the house on Bimport with fantastic views across the fields to Melbury Hill and as far as Shillingstone. She had never had a garden of her own, although was doing her best on the decking area outside her flat above the shop. Tom's garden had been his mother's pride and joy until she moved to Spain the previous year and left him to take care of the family home. The sunflowers which grew against the brick wall of the house always brought a smile to Yvonne's face, and she was touched that Tom had thought to cut some for her.

'Here's some eggs as well, fresh from the chickens' bottoms,' he laughed. It had been a running joke between them about who was going to the end of the garden to collect the freshly laid eggs in the chicken heaven he had created down there.

'Thank you! I must admit I haven't bought any since I moved back home, so I appreciate these, thank you.'

They busied themselves with pouring milk and tea, and tucking into the delicious, sweet pastries while the dogs lay on the sofa together. Eventually Yvonne said 'What do we need to talk about?'

Tom drained his mug, and poured himself a second after first checking if Yvonne needed a top-up. He sat back in his chair looking steadily at Yvonne and said 'Tell me what you know about why those men were attacked on Semley Common.'

Yvonne stalled 'What? Why do you think I know anything?' she asked attempting and failing to sound calm.

'If I didn't before I do now!' Tom exclaimed, his dark eyes more serious than she had ever seen them. 'Your face is giving you away. Come on, tell me.'

Grudgingly Yvonne conceded. 'Alright, although I don't know why he was attacked, I do know the name of the man whose life you saved.'

She paused, trying to collate her thoughts into a cohesive form.

'Go on' Tom prompted gently.

'His name is Beau Parker, but you know that already.'

Tom nodded and motioned for her to carry on, his eyes now calmer and holding her gaze, encouraging without pressuring.

Yvonne sighed. 'He is my brother Beau. Beau Parker. My older brother.'

Chapter 10

Yvonne was surprised and annoyed to find tears pouring down her face for the second time that morning. She thought any feelings for her brother had long since disappeared. She stood and went to the counter, tearing off a piece of kitchen roll and wiping her eyes, relieved that she hadn't chosen to apply make-up when she was getting dressed. Tom allowed her time to compose herself. When she sat down she looked at him accusingly. 'But you knew that before you messaged me this morning, didn't you.'

Tom nodded. 'I did. I thought you might like to know he is alive, although it is still too early to tell what his recovery will be like. Please, tell me about him.'

'Are you here officially?'

'I can be if that's what you would prefer. We can head over the road to the police station and make this a formal interview. Or we can stay here in your kitchen, and you can tell me what you know.'

'What do you want to know?'

'Just talk about Beau, your brother. What was he like when you were growing up?'

Yvonne smiled, staring unseeingly into her mug. 'He was the funny one. Always making jokes, playing pranks, smiling all the time. He made your heart lift when he came into a room. He wasn't particularly good at sport, but good enough to be in the school football and cricket teams. He had the same auburn colour hair as me' she glanced up at Tom and touched her hair 'this is dyed dark brown, and the red tints are added.'

Tom nodded, unsure whether she was expecting a response. He hadn't given a lot of thought to the colour of her hair and didn't know if what she was telling him was relevant or just her way of putting off what he needed to know.

Yvonne continued 'Curly too, and we were closer in age than any of our other siblings.' She stopped and showed no sign of starting again.

Tom prompted her 'He is only a year or so older than you?'

Yvonne nodded. 'Yes, we went through our teenage years with the same group of friends. We had two younger sisters and an older brother and sister, but we didn't socialise with them in the same way. We were nicknamed 'The Twins' because we were nearly always together and looked very similar. Up until we were about fourteen Beau was always taller than me, but when we were fourteen and fifteen I caught up with him, and as I chose to have short hair too we played up on that nickname. We lived in jeans and t-shirts in those days, and even our parents and siblings sometimes had trouble to tell us apart, particularly if we were not together and they didn't have the other one to compare with the one in front of them. When I was fifteen I grew these' she gestured to her chest 'discovered my sister's make-up, and as she loved to dress me up too in her clothes we stopped trying to look like each other. Beau grew taller than me and I grew my hair longer, but we still hung out with each other whenever possible. It was reassuring to have my brother nearby when we started going to parties and pubs. There was always someone to walk home with or catch a late bus. He was also the first of us to achieve 'A' levels, and I was the second. I followed him into the family business, and together we expanded the number of the company's antiques centres and antiques markets.'

'How did your older brother and sister feel about the fact their younger siblings were taking on more senior roles than them?' Tom was curious about the family dynamics. Sometimes the most innocuous information could be the vital clue.

'Neither of them were interested in the administration and management of the business. Our older sister is an amazing seamstress and she branched out into her own vintage clothing company, separate from our family, and our older brother was more interested in working for other people in their auction houses. He didn't want the responsibility which comes with management positions. Our younger sister, Nicole, didn't really know what she wanted to do and sort of drifted into the business after she left school, but she married young and has moved around the world with her husband's job so she didn't work with us for long, whereas our youngest sister knew from the age of five years old she wanted to be on television and she's always popping up as an antiques expert. You've probably seen her, Katie Moon?'

'Oh really?' Tom shifted in his seat and a sparkle appeared in his eyes. 'She's the one with the long curly black hair and is always smiling? I like her!'

Yvonne rolled her eyes 'The one who is always hanging out of her tops and wears ridiculously tight leggings so everyone can see how toned her bum is you mean. I'm amazed you didn't know that she was my sister, since you knew about Beau.'

Tom shook his head. 'I didn't know. She must keep her professional life separate, because all we knew was that your youngest sister's name is Catherine Bawtree and she lives with her artist husband in a former rectory in Sussex. I only started to watch antiques programmes with you, and I don't remember you pointing her out.'

'I won't have done. I don't shout about our connection because she doesn't want to be associated with the rest of us. I don't blame her. She changed her name for television, which was a sensible move because otherwise our cousin's murder and the scandal surrounding it would probably be the first thing to show up on any search of her name. Her real name is Catherine Parker. She would not like her relationship to either me or Beau to be made public, and I think she is right to make that decision to try to distance herself from us.'

Again Yvonne paused, and this time Tom let the silence grow until she eventually spoke. 'It was a horrible decision you know. To inform on him, on my brother Beau. I didn't make it easily. But I don't regret it. I don't think I could have lived with myself if I allowed him to escape justice. I certainly couldn't have gone back to the way our relationship was before. But it was awful, and I still hate it as much as I did then. I don't think I will ever find peace with it.'

Tom nodded. His heart went out to Yvonne, but he kept his expression impassive as he said 'I have read the reports from that time, but I would like to hear your recollections please, if you can?'

Yvonne stood up abruptly, and Tom thought she was going to leave the room but he made no attempt to stop her. Instead of walking out she began to open cupboards searching for something. 'I knew I had some somewhere in here' she muttered as she opened a large bag of salt and vinegar flavoured crisps and poured them into a blue and white pasta bowl. She put the bowl on the table and opened a bottle of red wine. 'If I'm going to talk about this, I need alcohol. Do you want some?' without waiting for his answer she poured the wine into two glasses. Surreptitiously Tom checked his watch. Half-past nine in the morning was a little early to be hitting the red stuff, and not permitted during working hours, but he decided not to object for fear of putting a stopper in the flow of information. He took a sip of wine to show solidarity with Yvonne, who was not holding back and had already taken three large gulps from her glass. Tom took a handful of the crisps and put them on his plate. Slowly he began to eat them, the crunching noise breaking the silence and making him feel self-conscious. It did the trick and stirred Yvonne into talking again.

'Alright, let's go for it' she said, and put her glass down. Staring at the table because she couldn't meet his eyes, she began to speak. 'Beau and I made a good team. Mum and Dad were still very much involved with the business when we started, but they had worked extremely hard since they were teenagers and had brought the six of us up while doing it. Mum's family were antiques dealers and pawn brokers, with many shops throughout London, Surrey and Sussex. Dad's dad, our grandfather, worked for them, but my dad worked as a porter for a big London auction house. He and mum opened their own antiques shop, and then a second and a third. Then they started a monthly antiques fair at one of the racecourses, then a second antiques fair, then a third. Beau and I took their business model and opened larger antiques centres in the Midlands and the Cotswolds and started some more antiques markets near those locations. By the time we were in our late twenties we had a multi-million-pound company, and Mum and Dad were taking six-week cruises in the Caribbean. We were working all the hours seven days a week, at least three hundred and sixty days a year. We took Christmas Day and Boxing Day off, New Year's Eve and New Year's Day. We both took a fortnight off when we married our respective partners, and even timed our weddings so we didn't interrupt the flow of the antiques markets. Neither of us took any other time off for holidays or sick days. We worked non-stop and loved it.

'We learned on the job and made mistakes along the way usually by trusting people who didn't deserve our faith, but we built a good team around us. As time went by we could delegate to managers for the day-to-day organisation of the antiques centres, although we travelled around the country so one of us could be on site at least once a week to check the books and the presentation of the shops. It is important for the rest of the shop that the dealers regularly check and update their stock on the individual stands and give them a dusting now and then. We rarely had any issues once they were set up, and we managed to keep our good members of staff while assisting those who were not such a good fit to find alternative work. We tried not to upset the ex-members of staff, because if there is going to be trouble it usually comes from disgruntled ex-employees.' She sighed and took a sip of wine, grimacing as she realised she'd rather be drinking tea. Tom saw her expression and guessed what was wrong, so he stood up to make a fresh pot, gesturing for her to carry on talking, not wanting to interrupt her.

'The antiques markets were a different matter. We found we needed to be on site before they opened, stay throughout the day or days they were running, and remain after they closed. We tried delegating but there were too many staff, too many dealers, too many variables such as the weather and number of customers. We both enjoyed being in among everyone, and thrived on the atmosphere, but it was exhausting. It took a few years, but by the time I sold the business we had built up a good crew who moved from one market to the next, knowing who did what and what needed to be done without being directed to do it. We had some amazing dealers who stalled out at every market, wherever in the country we were, and we had regular buyers who could be relied on to turn up whatever the weather.'

Again Yvonne stopped talking, and this time Tom said 'You sound as though you miss it?'

Yvonne sighed 'I don't miss it. I did enjoy it, but once I stopped I realised how much life I was missing out on. Yes, I miss the people, the buzz of the fairs, the adrenalin rush when the gates opened and the first buyers came in, but I don't miss the long hours of driving on motorways, the aggressive men and women we encountered probably once a day, the stress of dealing with disagreements between dealers in the antiques centres or at our fairs. If it hadn't been for the murder of my cousin I probably would have carried on working like that until I burned out. I miss working with my brother because we had a fantastic partnership, real teamwork you know? I will never have that again, with anyone else. We always agreed with each other, supported each other, neither of us felt the other was slacking off or leaving the heavy lifting for someone else to do. He was great at diffusing a situation whereas I was better with the admin, but together we made everything work well and it certainly wasn't always my job to balance the books or his to resolve a disagreement. I was lucky to have that time with him, but I now realise it wasn't healthy for me. I am fitter now I am approaching fifty than I was in my twenties. I love my little antiques shop, being able to go for a walk with my dog or ride my horse every day. If it hadn't been for my brother being responsible for killing my cousin I wouldn't be here now. Although the recent murders have taken the shine off it all a bit, and now my brother has turned up here too it feels as though those two worlds are overlapping.'

Tom put a fresh mug of tea in front of her, which she took and held in both hands after pushing the wine glass away. Tom removed it, and his, and placed them both on the draining board. He asked 'You mentioned to me you suspect Bernie Campling of being involved with your cousin's death. Can you tell me why you think that?'

'Because he was driving away from the shop as I was driving towards it' Yvonne said. 'Nothing more than that. I don't know if he was there when the actual attack was taking place. Bernie wouldn't have had any reason to be in the area, other than to visit my cousin. It was also odd when he denied knowing anything about all that stock my cousin had recorded as giving to him. Of course now I realise he was hoarding lots of antiques dealers' stock, but at the time it was something which jarred. Not much to go on, and certainly no proof, but it all means something.'

Tom nodded 'I think you are probably right to be suspicious. When did you last hear from your brother, Beau?'

Yvonne shrugged and shook her head. 'We haven't spoken since the trial. My sister in Norway, Amelie, kept in touch and visited him in prison when she came over to England, but she hadn't told me he had been released. In fact' she sat up straighter in her chair and looked at Tom 'I should have been told officially he was being released, but no one has said anything. Did you know?'

'Your victim liaison officer should have kept you informed when Beau came up for parole and again when he was released' said Tom carefully.

'I don't even know who that is now. I expect the original person has long since retired. He was ancient when I last heard from him.'

'Do you think Amelie would be willing to talk to me about Beau?'

'I don't see why not. I'll message her now.' Yvonne went to pick up her phone, but then stopped and said 'Will someone have told her he has been attacked?'

Tom shook his head 'No one through official channels will have informed her. His wife is listed as his next of kin, so whether or not she will have had time to tell Amelie I don't know. I do know he is being kept in an induced coma for a while.' Tom had noticed that Yvonne was not asking any questions about the prognosis for her brother's recovery. She didn't react when he told her about the induced coma.

Yvonne frowned. 'But surely you have all his details on file, and know that his wife divorced him, sensibly in my view, as soon as he was charged with murder so she won't be his next-of-kin. It's not as though he'd been dropped in a bath of acid, or his body found after weeks at sea? You don't need him to be awake and speaking, identification must have been easy with his prison record, and that's what led you to me?'

'Oh you know how these things work. Nothing is official until it's all been approved and signed in triplicate by several different people in offices in different counties.'

Yvonne knew he was evading the questions and felt her stomach clench as an appalling thought stuck her. 'You haven't come here to ask me to formally identify him, have you?' she asked.

'No, don't worry, I just want to know what he's been up to since he was released and wondered what contact you had with him. Did you not know he had remarried?'

'No! Who on earth agreed to marry him while he was in there?' Yvonne looked shocked.

Tom said 'Why didn't you say who he was when you saw him lying on the Common?'

Now it was Yvonne's turn to avoid the question. 'There was a lot going on that night wasn't there. You, Lindy and Alison were amazing trying to save his life. Thank you for that.'

Tom shrugged 'It's what I am trained to do. What about the murder victim. What can you tell me?'

Yvonne was quick to say 'Absolutely nothing, I promise. I didn't see them, I don't know who it was.'

Tom said 'Well if you didn't see them you can't say you don't know who it was.'

'Oh, you know what I mean! I didn't go over to that part of the Common. Do you know who it was?'

Tom nodded but didn't enlighten her about the identity of the deceased, and she didn't ask again.

They sat in silence for a while, each thinking about the events of that night. Eventually Yvonne said 'Do you have any idea who stabbed him?'

Tom replied 'I'm going to have to follow the official line here Yvonne, and say we have several lines of enquiry, but no arrests have been made.'

'You don't think I had anything to do with it do you? Because I can assure you I did not hire a hit man or anyone like that, as much as I hate him for what he did.'

'No, of course not, and obviously you had the best alibi of anyone remotely connected to Beau as you were riding with me when we heard him, er …' Tom faltered.

'It's OK, you can say it, when we heard him scream' Yvonne shuddered. 'That sound is haunting me. It was bad enough when we could hear those animals while we were in the woods, but to know it was a human making that noise is even more shocking. Knowing it was a human I used to be close to is something I am having a hard time processing.'

Tom shifted his chair closer to Yvonne's and put his arms around. She rested her forehead on his shoulder and let herself relax into the hug. No tears came this time, and she felt calmer. They sat like that for several minutes, until eventually Yvonne pulled away. 'Thank you' she said quietly. 'I don't know how I feel about the fact that Beau has been attacked, or that he was so close to where I live, where my business is. I do know it must mean he was trying to get back in touch with me, and all he has done is bring his troubles to my door.'

Chapter 11

Jack Perry Ritchie stepped back from the wall which formed the back of his stand in Angel Lane Antiques, looking every inch the movie star with his tall figure and good looks. He had his hands on his hips and a smile on his face as he surveyed the results of his hard work.

'Finished is it? Let's have a look' said Rob Kemp as he came into the room. 'Mmmh I'm not sure.'

'It's perfect' said Jack. 'That dark plum colour will set off my stock to look its best, you'll see.'

Rob did not look convinced but said 'If you say so' and returned to his seat behind the desk where he had been cleaning all the dirt and grime which had accumulated in the time the shop had been closed while the police completed their investigations. The last fortnight had seen a flurry of activity as Yvonne and her team of antiques dealers cleaned and painted the walls, ceiling and window frames before a new carpet was laid throughout. Tomorrow was the day the antiques shop would open its doors to the public for the first time in three months, and the eight dealers, including Yvonne, were busy putting the finishing touches to their individual stands. As part of her attempt to make a fresh start and clear out the negative memories, Yvonne had given each room the name of a local hamlet or village. Jack was in the room furthest from the front door and reception desk, named the Melbury Room, sharing the space with two other antiques dealers, and between them they had decided to mix their stock together so there was no clear division between them unlike in the other two rooms, the Bedchester Room and the Sedgehill Room, where each antiques dealer had their own space. The room at the back of the shop was of course Rob's domain and contained only his stock and was officially called Alcester but the name hadn't stuck and everyone always called it Rob's Garage or simply The Garage. Yvonne made sure that every dealer labelled each item with the price, a brief description and their initials so whoever took the money at the desk knew whose account to credit. Sometimes labels went missing, and sometimes unscrupulous customers attempted to change the prices, but because everyone took a turn at running the shop throughout the week small hiccups like these were usually easily spotted and smoothed out.

The wall Jack had just finished painting housed the door to the cellar, which in turn led to a system of tunnels which ran under the homes, businesses and roads of Shaftesbury. That door had been the focus of much of the police investigation, and Yvonne was keen to prevent it from becoming a destination for those with ghoulish inclinations, even though no one had been murdered behind it and no dead bodies had been hidden there. When Jack requested a change of colour from the clean and bright white paint of the rest of the shop, Yvonne had thought it was an excellent idea. Rob didn't think she'd approve of the finished result when she saw it but decided to let her find out for herself.

Jack checked his watch 'Raymond will be here in a minute. He's bringing a linen cupboard, and I said I'd give him a hand.'

'I'll help you' said Rob, and the pair of them walked through to the garage at the back of the shop.

Jack looked around the large room which had been built as a garage when the building was a family home and had been used for storing flowers when it had been turned into a florists' shop. These days the space was filled with automobilia in the form of classic cars and bikes, antique oil cans, car badges, vehicle manuals, and a selection of specialist paints. Rob's stock had not escaped the attentions of the forensic investigators, and everything had been checked and photographed before being packed away into boxes and stacked along one wall, except for the bones of the cars and motorbikes which were for sale as 'projects'. Tom Archibald was a keen enthusiast for Austin-Healey Frogeye Sprites and was proud of his own red Mark 1 kept safely in his mum's garage and only allowed out on warm and sunny days. Rob had at least two Frogeye Sprites in various states of repair in his part of the shop, and he and Tom spent quite a while chatting during the time the shop was closed to the public. When the police eventually moved out Rob had taken the opportunity to clean the floor and repaint the walls, before putting everything back in its place. To his satisfaction the garage looked almost exactly has it had before.

When opened the roller shutter revealed the courtyard where Yvonne parked her car, and beyond that were the electronic gates which led out to the Angel Lane public car park. There was space for up to six cars and vans in the courtyard, plenty of room for the couple of vehicles belonging to the dealers whose turn it was to run the shop for the day, plus Yvonne's car and a friend's or two. For the past three days the courtyard had been rammed with vehicles, and the gates had been permanently open so that more could park behind them as the dealers worked hard to fill the shop with their stock. There was nowhere to park at the front of the shop on Angel Lane itself, and the front door was a traditional single entrance into the building which was fine for carrying in jewellery and small items, but not ideal for something as large as a linen cupboard.

The familiar sight of Raymond's blue Vauxhall Movano van was visible through the open gates, and the back doors were open. Raymond was wheeling one of Yvonne's sack trucks towards the van when he caught sight of Jack and Rob.

'Aha just the people. Can you help me?' he called over, brushing back his shoulder-length grey hair as he did so. In his sixties, with a weathered face typical of someone who has worked outdoors most of his life and the stocky build of someone used to hefting pieces of furniture around, Raymond was five foot ten and all muscle, and one of the new members of the Angel Lane Antiques team.

Between the three of them they manoeuvred the large piece of furniture out of the back of the van, between the parked vehicles, through Rob's automobilia bits and pieces, and into the main shop where they pushed it through the other dealers' stands to the farthest room, the Melbury Room.

'Bloody hell that's a bit dark isn't it?' Raymond spotted the wall Jack had just finished painting.

'Great isn't it?' said Jack, beaming as he gazed on his handiwork. 'It's going to set off our cabinets perfectly. I'm just waiting for it to dry and then I'll push them into position. I can't wait; they are going to look amazing.'

Raymond caught Rob's eye and decided not to say what was on his mind. Diplomatically he asked 'Has Yvonne seen it yet?'

'No she hasn't. She's going to love it!' said Jack. 'Do you need help bringing anything else in?'

'Thank you, no I can manage the rest thanks Jack.'

'I'll go and put the kettle on' said Rob. 'I've made some apricot flapjacks.'

Raymond rubbed his hands together in anticipation 'They sound delicious, thanks Rob!'

While Raymond brought in a small old pine table and a set of six elm-seated chairs from his van, Jack began to drag the glass cabinets in front of the newly painted wall, taking care to leave a couple of inches between them and the wall. Once the four cabinets were in place he fitted the glass shelves and plugged in the spotlights so he could position them to maximise the visual effects. Rob brought a tray around to the Melbury Room with teapot, milk bottle, mugs and flapjacks, and he and Raymond sat at the table on the comfortable wooden chairs and watched while Jack began to unpack the jewellery, watches and silver which would fill the cabinets.

'It's going to be great to finally be open to the public again' said Rob. 'I'm looking forward to tomorrow. It's been a long time coming.'

'Three long months' said Jack. 'Fortunately my stock in the other two antiques shops I'm in has been selling well. I think my usual buyers have been spending more in them than normal, so I hope they will return here again.'

'I'm sure they will, after all it gives this place a bit of notoriety, and no one who was involved in all that criminal activity earlier in the year is here now.' Raymond said. 'Although now of course poor old Bernie Campling has died, who was also a dealer here, and there's all the revelations about the stock he had stolen as it now turns out. I'll admit it's a bit of a gamble joining you in here. Lots of people have been warning me off.'

'Have they? Like who?' asked Rob.

Raymond shrugged. 'Everyone, really. It's a running joke at all the antiques fairs, with people telling me to watch my back, watch what I eat, carry a cosh with me at all times.'

'I see you're not taking their advice' Jack nodded towards a piece of flapjack as it disappeared into Raymond's mouth.

Raymond laughed 'No I'm bloody not! Although I am old enough to remember when Christopher Boucher was murdered in his shop, and his cousin Beau Parker was found guilty and sent to prison for Life.'

Jack looked up from the silver-topped perfume bottle he was unwrapping 'Parker? As in Yvonne's surname?'

Raymond nodded. 'Beau was Yvonne's brother. Or is her brother I should say, and she was the one who walked in as Beau and some chap called Smith were attacking her cousin Christopher. Poor girl, that experience will have left a mark. She disappeared from the antiques scene for years, so I was surprised to learn she had this place.'

Rob said 'I think she wants to put all that behind her, and this shop was a fresh start for her.'

'You knew about all that?' Jack looked shocked. 'You never said anything!'

'Why would I? It's got nothing to do with us. It isn't as though it was Yvonne who killed her cousin is it? Why should she be tarred with the same brush as her brother?'

Raymond nodded 'You can't choose your family. Although I never would have guessed that Beau would turn out the way he did. I thought he and Yvonne made a great team, and I always had good dealings with them. They ran an honest and successful business, and I never heard of any threatening behaviour or rumours of violence.'

'Same here' agreed Rob. 'Beau and Yvonne made the Parker family businesses the gold standard for antiques centres and antiques fairs in their day. You knew where you were with them. They always paid out on time at the end of the month, their buildings were well-maintained and staffed with trustworthy people so you knew nothing was getting nicked from your stand.'

'You're right' said Raymond, as he helped himself to another piece of flapjack. 'The thing I liked about their markets was the marshals got everyone parked and ready to stall out quickly and efficiently so there wasn't any time wasted in the queue while our customers were running around buying from everyone lucky enough to get in position early. There wasn't any arguing about pitch space because anyone who thought they could impinge on someone else's stand was given one warning and then they were out if they tried it on again. It really cut down on the bad feeling which can build up when your neighbour is taking up part of your pitch or obscuring your stock with theirs.'

'Although there was that time when that ghastly auctioneer Sylvia Nelson went to one of the fairs and bought thousands of pounds worth of stock from a notorious family. Do you remember? I think it was the first and last time she went to an antiques fair on her own' Rob was giggling at the memory.

Raymond joined in 'Ha ha yes I remember! She was flirting her way through the deal, thinking she'd got special prices for everything and had really won the lottery when they loaded everything onto her van for her and then took her over to the onsite restaurant for a celebratory dinner.'

Rob continued the story 'But when she came back to her van they had robbed her of everything on it, including stock she had bought from other dealers. The rascals had packed up and gone, leaving nothing behind!'

Both Rob and Raymond were roaring with laughter at the memory, but Jack was watching them with a frown on his face.

'That doesn't sound very funny. I don't understand why it is funny.'

His unintentional impression of Penelope Keith's character Margot in the television series "The Good Life" only served to set Rob and Raymond into more spasms of laughter.

'Couldn't have happened to a nicer person' Raymond commented, his voice dripping in sarcasm. 'But it also had the result that Yvonne and Beau stepped up their security presence around that family whenever they turned up at a market, until they gave up coming to the Parker-run fairs. Once they realised they couldn't keep ripping off our customers they didn't bother stalling out and selling properly, which was good news for the rest of us because it meant we didn't need to be on permanent high alert in case any of our stuff was stolen, and nor were we all being tarred with the same brush.'

'There was no messing around at their markets' agreed Rob. 'The people who gave the trade a bad name stopped coming or were banned, and it made for a more pleasant experience for buyers and sellers alike. I miss those days.'

'Me too' said Raymond.

'I can't imagine doing all that driving and staying away from home for days at a time' said Jack.

'It was part of the job' Raymond shrugged. 'Although I think the whole landscape has changed now. The cost of fuel put paid to a lot of fairs because dealers could no longer afford to load up their vans at the start of the week, and travel from one county to another stalling out at several markets before returning home for a few days.'

Rob said 'I certainly scaled back the number of fairs I used to do and tried to stick to ones no more than a couple of hours from home rather than travelling from one end of the country to the other.'

'And across from one coast to the other!' laughed Raymond. 'I don't know how we did it.'

'Alcohol had a big part to play' Rob said. 'The number of deals we used to do at ten o'clock at night in the queue for the next day's fair over a bottle of whisky.'

'My tipple was vodka' said Raymond. 'Can't stand the stuff anymore. And then of course there were the antiques dealers who relied on coke to keep them functioning. Not many of them left now.'

'It's a different world now' said Rob. 'It's all working out down the gym and abstinence, isn't that right Jack?'

Jack flexed his biceps 'You don't get muscles like this by drinking and snorting shit.'

'Talking of abstinence, we used to have a good time in the back of our vans too' Raymond said with a grin. 'Do you remember that woman dealer, oh what was her name?'

Rob laughed 'I know who you mean! Sue! She was married to that scrap dealer. Tom? Tim?'

'Jim Cooper! Oh my god I'd forgotten about Sloppy Sue. Don't look like that' Raymond was laughing at the expression of Jack's face. 'She was a right goer. There weren't many men she hadn't been with.'

'She was never in the back of my van' Rob said primly.

'No, but you were always faithful to your wife. I never saw you play away with anyone else.'

'Unlike you' Rob teased Raymond. 'You were with a different woman every month! We gave up trying to remember their names because they never lasted.'

'Like I always told you all, they were only with me for work experience. Nothing happened. I never touched any of them.' There was a steely note in Raymond's voice and a chill fell on the room. Jack busied himself with unpacking the final item from the last of his boxes, a beautiful eighteenth century pearl and emerald pendant.

Rob leant back in his chair, and said 'Yes, you did always say that. Was it true?'

'Yes it was!' Raymond sounded exasperated. 'They wanted to learn the ropes and expected to go on and set up their own businesses. It was always useful to have another pair of hands to help with unpacking the van and staying on the stall when I wanted to go off buying at the fairs. At the time I enjoyed the nudging and winking and innuendo from you lot, but now it's not funny anymore.'

'Fair enough' Rob held his hands up as if defending himself from Raymond's frustration. 'I didn't believe you at the time, but if you're still sticking to that story then I do now. Not that it matters what I think.'

'But it does matter' Raymond leaned forward. 'Reputation is important, and I don't want people to think I was shagging teenagers when I was in my thirties and forties.'

'You were shagging teenagers when you were in your forties!' a woman with a mass of curly black hair and a big smile on her face walked into the room, carrying a cardboard box.

'No I bloody wasn't!'

'Don't worry darling, I'm only teasing. It was what we all thought at the time, and you can't blame us. What would you think if some bloke kept turning up with different young girls, sleeping in his van with them? You've got to admit it looked a bit suss!' Rachael Hall began to unpack a collection of oriental porcelain from the box and was creating a display in a glass cabinet on the opposite side of the room to Jack's statement wall while she chatted.

Raymond sighed and said through gritted teeth 'It wasn't just girls; don't you remember Darren? Lenny? Mike? They slept in the cab, and I slept in the back of the van.'

Rachael turned around to look at Raymond 'Do you know I had forgotten that Darren was one of your apprentices. He's made a good business for himself since then. Oh my god that wall is disgusting!'

Chapter 12

Yvonne walked barefoot around her shop, enjoying the feel of the new carpet beneath her bare feet and the smell of new paint and cleaning products intermingled with the evocative scent of the polished pine and oak furniture which took her back to happier times. It was five o'clock in the morning, and in another four hours she would be opening the doors for the first time in months to people who wanted to buy antiques, browse the stock, and those who just wanted to be nosy about the place which had too many connections to death. At least, she hoped people would walk in through the door. What if nobody came?

Originally she had been going to close the shop for a few days out of respect for the first known victim, but events had rapidly escalated and three months had passed. During that time a few members of her team had decided to withdraw their stock and leave, new dealers had joined, and she had taken advantage of the shop being closed for so long to have the rooms redecorated. The last time she had managed to do this was during the first Covid lockdown. She had also fulfilled a long-held dream of visiting Ireland, and had taken a fortnight's holiday with George and Zebedee, leaving Toby to be cared for by her friends at the farm.

Yvonne had been sure that she wanted to reopen Angel Lane Antiques, it hadn't crossed her mind not to, but as time went by and more revelations emerged about people she had thought she knew she began to wonder if her business could survive the notoriety. If she could survive the notoriety. Again. She contemplated closing the business and turning the whole building into a large home for herself, but she didn't need more room, and didn't think she would want to stay in Angel Lane if she wasn't working there. Selling the place to someone else to do whatever they wanted was an easy option because she knew it would be snapped up, and she and Zebedee could move further into the countryside, possibly buying some land and having Toby at home with two or three other equines. That was an appealing prospect and her plan B if Angel Lane Antiques failed. The difference between this time and last time was she had good local friends who were not involved in the antiques trade. Tabitha was a sheep farmer, and her wife Alison was a beautician with her business partner Maisie, and Lindy who was part of the family who ran a prestigious country house hotel, Kenyon Hall, and a fellow horse lover. The four women had provided all the encouragement and support she needed to keep going, reminding her she enjoyed managing her own business as they did with theirs. They were also reliable drinking buddies and at least one of them was always available for a meal at one of the local pubs or a takeaway, so even if she hadn't been staying with Tom she wouldn't have been left to brood.

In the end it had been the enthusiasm of the dealers which had given her the final push to reopen, in particular

Rob and Jack who had organised the other dealers into clearing and cleaning, painting and polishing. It had taken her a few days to get on board because Tabitha had spotted an ideal cottage and piece of land belonging to one of her farming friends who was thinking about selling, but once she committed to Angel Lane Antiques again she enjoyed getting stuck in with the rest of them. Now as she looked at the shining cabinets, the fresh stock, and even Jack's statement wall she smiled. She had a good group of people to work with, this was her business, and today was going to be a good day.

She ran up the spiral stairs from her kitchen to her bedroom and washed and dressed for the day ahead. Deciding on smooth straight hair and a red shirt over blue jeans, strong dark eye make-up and chunky gold jewellery, Yvonne was soon ready for anything. She called her dog and opened the door which led from her bedroom out onto the balcony and then to the wooden stairs down to the courtyard. She and Zebedee enjoyed a brisk walk down Shooters Lane, along Layton Lane to St James and over to Breach Common, before slowing down and enthusiastically climbing up to Castle Hill, pausing to look back and take in the fabulous views including across to King Alfred's Tower, and then striding back home along Bell Street.

By nine o'clock Zebedee was fast asleep on the sofa in the kitchen, and the shop was full of antiques dealers who had come to celebrate either their first day of business or returning to trading in Angel Lane Antiques. The air now smelled of coffee and pastries thanks to Jack bringing in a bag of filter coffee grounds, and his sister-in-law

Charlotte appearing with a present of a box of freshly baked goods from her bakery in neighbouring Coppice Street. Without any fanfare Yvonne unlocked the front door and turned the 'Closed' sign around to 'Open', and almost immediately half a dozen customers made their way through the door and began to browse, commenting favourably on the displays of stock. Jack's wall proved to be a marmite feature and divided the sexes, with the majority of women disliking it and the men loving it. By the time Keri from Shaftesbury's Alfred radio appeared to make some interviews for a piece on the reopening of Angel Lane Antiques a full-on debate about the colour of the wall was taking place between several customers and dealers, and there were no goodies from the bakery left.

Yvonne was relieved to see many of the original customers coming through the door and pleased to see several new faces too. Even a couple of dealers who had decided to relinquish their places in the shop appeared and expressed regret at not being a part of the enterprise anymore. Yvonne was happy to add their names to the waiting list, and promised to let them know if a space became available. It felt good to have the place busy with people who were not police or forensic experts, as had been the case for too long. The banter was flowing, as were the sales which was perhaps more important, although Yvonne felt that having such a positive atmosphere was essential for the future of both her shop and her home. It was just as well the full complement of antiques dealers were present as customers were buying heavy tables and chests of drawers which needed to be carried out through the back of the shop to the car park;

cabinets needed to be unlocked under supervision so that buyers could have a good look at the precious silver and gold antiques before deciding whether or not to buy, and cash and card payments needed to be processed. The noise level in the shop was high and lively, with occasional lulls as is normal when large groups of people are gathered together.

Some people seem to be able to move around without being noticed, while others always draw attention to themselves wherever they go. The front door opened and in walked an overly made-up woman, with jet black hair and matching eyebrows, and plumped up red lips, wearing a tiny tight black skirt revealing skinny white legs ending in eye-wateringly high heeled shoes which probably added four inches to her height and making her just over five foot tall. Her startling green eyes scanned the room until they spotted her quarry through the archway into the Melbury Room, at which point they became cat-like. Yvonne and Rob moved from behind the counter so they could watch, with faint grins, as the inevitable happened.

'Jack, darling' the woman stalked over to him, and reached up to pull his head down to hers, intent on planting a kiss somewhere on his face. Deftly, Jack managed to interrupt her assault by swinging around and picking up a tiny silver basket from inside the cabinet he had been about to lock.

'Sylvia! Just the person. I was thinking of putting this into your next sale.'

Sylvia Nelson appeared not to notice the obvious lie and examined the delicate item. 'Gorgeous. I know several people who will want to buy this. Bring it down tomorrow when I'm there' she instructed. She studied the contents of the cabinet and spotted a diamond ring on a gold band. Picking it up she fished out a loupe from her Aspinal of London cherry red Mayfair handbag and studied the ring. 'I'll have that' she announced and handed it to Jack without giving him any choice.

Sylvia scanned the rest of the cabinet, but nothing else met with her approval, and her face showed her distaste for much of the stock. Jack followed her to the counter where he handled the transaction as quickly as he could, Yvonne and Rob standing clear so they didn't need to be involved.

'Thank you Sylvia, and I'll see you at your auction house tomorrow' he said. 'Thanks for supporting Yvonne's first day back open here in Angel Lane Antiques.'

Sylvia glanced around at all the people and looked as though she was going to comment, but then sketched a wave and said 'Bye bye darling, see you tomorrow' and left as abruptly as she had arrived.

Jack looked over to where Yvonne and Rob were standing.

'Don't say a word' he growled, which was all they needed to erupt into giggles.

'She doesn't change does she' Yvonne said, wiping the tears from her eyes. 'I was impressed by your swerve when she was aiming for a kiss.'

'On the lips!' Rob dissolved into another fit of laughter. 'Oh my goodness she doesn't give up does she!'

'It's not that funny' muttered Jack, turning his back on them which only set them off again.

'You know she only buys anything from this shop belonging to you, and then only when you are in here?' Yvonne asked him.

Jack looked worried. 'No, I did not know that' he said, slowly.

'She's a vile woman' commented Rachael Hall.

Yvonne looked at her in surprise. Rachael was usually a smiley, sunny person, not given to making derogatory comments about anyone. 'What makes you say that?'

Rachael said 'You know about that poor elderly lady's medals, don't you?'

Both Yvonne and Rob shook their heads. Jack nodded, not meeting anyone's eyes. Rachael said 'You must have done. Early last year a lady put her late husband's medals in for the February sale with Sylvia. Sylvia divided them into two Lots, and the first Lot sold way over estimate for a huge amount, but the other Lot failed to reach its reserve and didn't sell. The widow was landed with a huge tax bill due to the big selling price, and as she is on a low fixed income she needed the other Lot to sell so she could pay the taxman. Sylvia has been hanging onto that second Lot ever since, refusing to return the medals to the widow because she claims to have an offer. The thing is, that offer is less than a fifth of the auction valuation, and in no way will touch the tax bill.'

'Nasty practice' commented Rob. 'She's the kind of auctioneer who gives the rest of them a bad name.'

'That sounds terrible!' said Yvonne. 'I had no idea.'

Jack looked at the floor and didn't comment.

The next person to come in was a notorious dog owner with her small terrier in tow.

'Don't worry, I'll follow her' Rob volunteered as he went to the small kitchen area at the back of the shop and retrieved a small bucket containing cleaning materials.

Yvonne's attention was diverted by a friendly gentleman who walked in and announced to anyone who was listening 'I've been left in the creche while she goes shopping!'

'You too' said another man, who had been studying a tray of old printing press letters. 'I am so pleased this place has reopened because it means I don't have to follow my wife around the lingerie shops and carry her bags.'

The first man laughed 'My wife is pleased because she doesn't have to tolerate me questioning everything she buys. Do you know she spent over an hour in one of those shops last week, and when she eventually found me in the Salt Cellar she said she had been having a lesson on how to put a bra on. I mean, she is sixty-two years old! I am sure she knows how to put her own bra on by now.'

'I know which shop you mean!' said the second one, and the two men, who had previously been unknown to each other, began to walk around the shop together exclaiming over the collection of copper jugs and pots and a particularly atmospheric seascape.

A couple of women were having a discussion over by a shelf of china ornaments. 'I think she would really love this' said one.

'I thought she told you not to buy her anything for her birthday? That is quite expensive.'

'Yes, she did. But she's my sister, and she's going to be cross with me anyway so I might as well buy something for her which is worth the argument.'

Rob returned with the bucket, as the woman and her dog left. 'She wasn't happy about me following her around, but at least her dog didn't cock his leg on anything this time.'

'Thank you Rob. It's a shame none of us caught him in the act before or I would be able to ban her, but perhaps if she knows we've cottoned on to whose dog it is she'll stop bringing him in here. Once one dog does it they will all do it.'

One of Rob's regular customers came in, so Rob disappeared to his room at the back of the shop, and Jack took his place alongside Yvonne behind the counter. They were kept busy dealing with customer enquiries, sales, and general chit-chat with familiar faces who had come in to see the new-look shop and wish them well.

Before she knew it the five o'clock closing time had been and gone, and there was still no sign of the dealers or customers wanting to go home. Finally, just before six o'clock the volume of customers slowed down and the dealers began to slip away, and then it was just Yvonne and Rob. Between them they wiped down surfaces where crumbs and spills had escaped earlier cleaning efforts and ran the vacuum cleaner over the carpet which had survived surprisingly well after the number of boots and shoes tramping over it, and together they totted up the cash and card sales. In less than half an hour the shop was ready for the next day.

'Phew! That was epic' Yvonne said as she sank into a fabulous red and navy-blue striped chair.

'Well done Yvonne' Rob said. 'You've worked hard to make today a success, and you did it.'

'Oh it was a team effort and you know it. Thank you. I am relieved today is over with; I was worried no one would come, or only people with a ghoulish interest would turn up, but most of the time it felt as though we had never been away.'

They both turned towards the sound of someone coming in through the back of the shop. Although the front door was locked and the 'Closed' sign visible, the gates which led out into the public car park were open, as was the roller shutter to Rob's garage.

'Hello! Is anyone here?' George Gumbleton appeared through the doorway. 'Ah there you are! How did it go today?'

'Really well' said Rob. 'Take this lady out for a well-deserved drink. I'm off home now, but I'll be here in the morning in time to help you open up, Yvonne. I think Jack is working with me tomorrow, and Rachael. Hopefully we'll be busy again. See you tomorrow. I'll shut the gates on my way out.'

'See you tomorrow Rob. Thank you for today.'

With a cheery wave Rob left the way George had come in.

George bent down and gave Yvonne a quick kiss on the lips 'You look exhausted.'

'Thanks!'

'I should have said you look beautiful. And exhausted' he teased. 'Is Rob right? Would you like to go for a drink or would you prefer to eat in? I could cook something here for you?'

'You are an angel!' Yvonne thought for a moment. 'I don't need to go down and see Toby, because Sally said she'd check and feed him for me today, but I would like to get out of here. Let's walk over to The Mitre for dinner. I feel the need for the chef's fish pie and a huge glass of Pignot Grigio.'

With Zebedee trotting along beside them, Yvonne and George walked arm-in-arm along the road to the pub, where Jonathan the landlord and a number of other local business owners asked with genuine goodwill how her day had been. It was just the relaxed and chatty atmosphere she needed after the stressful build-up and full-on busy day. Unlike many antiques dealers who only liked to deal with each other, Yvonne loved working with members of the public, answering questions and helping people to choose between one blue and white plate and another.

After an hour of quiet conversation, and with a belly full of seafood and potato, Yvonne was ready to go home. She and George parted company outside the pub with a warm embrace, and he crossed the road to his home and restaurant while Yvonne and her dog strolled home.

She and her dog ran up the external wooden stairs to Yvonne's bedroom, and within minutes Zebedee was asleep on the bed while Yvonne luxuriated in her Jacuzzi bath and contemplated the successful and fun-filled day.

'Here's to many more' she said to herself as she raised an imaginary glass in the air.

Chapter 13

The next day dawned bright and sunny. Yvonne awoke refreshed and ready for the day ahead, and she and Zebedee headed to the farm, for a quick ride around the fields with Toby. Tom had also made an early start, and together with his horse Ben and dog Stan they enjoyed an hour or so of walk, trot and canter in the peace and quiet of the October morning. No one mentioned Beau, in fact they didn't talk much at all, simply enjoying being out with their horses in the quiet of the day. They set out just as the sun was rising, and as they headed back to the farmhouse they could see three riders with a pair of chestnut Arabs and a palomino horse riding towards them. As they drew closer Sally called out 'Good morning!'

'You two must have set off early to be coming home already' said Charlotte.

'We did. It wasn't planned, but we were both here before sunrise. I have to be back to open the shop at nine o'clock so couldn't go too far' explained Yvonne.

'I've been riding early because I am on duty at ten down in Blandford all week, but this is the first morning we've had company' said Tom. 'Me, Stan and Ben have been out in time to watch the beautiful skies every morning this week as the sun comes up over Win Green. We've been lucky with the weather, because if it had been raining I wouldn't have been so keen.'

'Where are you all heading to?' Yvonne asked.

'I'm not working today, and neither is Sally so we're going out for a couple of hours' said Lindy. 'We're heading over to Ashmore Woods. It's been a while since I have ridden up there, and I really want to see the colours of the leaves before one of those Autumn storms brings them all down.'

'My lovely Dad said I could join them' said Charlotte. 'He's taking my shift in the bakery this morning. We don't usually let him work in there because he spends more time giving away freebies than he does selling, but if it means I can have some quality time with Sparkle then it's worth it now and again. It's not as though I pay him for working there' she laughed.

'Does your mum like working with him?' Sally asked curiously. 'My mum and dad wouldn't be able to work together, I'm sure.'

'I think her eyes get a lot of exercise, with all the rolling' said Charlotte.

'Your dad is so funny' said Yvonne. 'I'll make sure I pop in before I open the shop' she teased.

'Me too' said Tom. 'I can stop on my way to Blandford.'

'No!' Charlotte pretended to cry. 'I won't make any money today if everyone knows my Dad is in there!'

Laughing the two rides parted, Tom and Yvonne making sure their dogs were following the right sets of horses' legs. 'I was going in today anyway, because Charlotte very generously gave us a lot of pastries for our opening day yesterday, and I wanted to buy some today. I'll have to time it carefully because she is right, her dad does have a tendency to give away a lot of stock and she can't afford that two days in a row.'

'No one can beat their almond croissants' said Tom. 'I'll buy some for my colleagues on my way into work. That will help Charlotte.'

They had reached the farmyard, and as she always did Yvonne enjoyed the sound of the horses' bare hooves on the concrete, the clip-clopping echoing off the walls of the old farm buildings surrounding them. Some of the other livery owners had arrived and Stan and Zebedee joined a selection of Labradors, Jack Russells and spaniels, while Yvonne and Tom untacked their horses and walked them back to their field. All the horses lived out in herds of up to eight, depending on their management needs and how they got on with the other horses. One of the livery horses had moved to Devon during the summer, and Ben had taken her place, fitting easily into the same herd as Toby. The eight horses were still on restricted grass during the day with access to a number of large field shelters forming a square so that even those who didn't want to be inside could still have shade from the heat of the summer sun or shelter from driving wind and rain. At night they were turned out onto a four-acre field. In a few weeks, as winter set in, their four-acre field would be rested and they would have open access from their shelters to an eight-acre field which had been grazed by sheep from the time the horses came off it in February until June when the sheep had been turned away on the hillside overlooking the rest of the farm.

Horses fed and turned back out, Yvonne and Tom got into their cars with their respective dogs and went their separate ways. Yvonne was back home, showered and in Charlotte's bakery in less than forty minutes, and as she was ready she opened the shop a few minutes early. By the time Rachael, Rob and Jack turned up, also early for their day's work, there were already three customers in the shop. Any doubts Yvonne had about reopening were put to rest by the enthusiasm of both customers and antiques dealers.

'When are you going to put your stuff into Sylvia Nelson's auction?' Rob innocently asked Jack.

Seeing the teasing glint in his eye, Jack replied nonchalantly 'I think I'll give this month's auction a miss, and make sure I have a decent amount to put in next month's.'

'Chicken' was Rob's only comment.

The morning was filled with browsers, buyers and dealers replenishing their stands. Yvonne was particularly pleased that several of the buyers were trade, which confirmed to her that the dealers renting space in her shop were sourcing and selling items the antiques trade wanted. Shaftesbury is a popular town for visitors, and many tourists also wanted to buy something to take home with them. For those who had driven there and were staying locally in a hotel or bed & breakfast there was often the dilemma of where to fit that chest of drawers they couldn't live without in the car, and sometimes they would ask if they could pay for a big item of furniture and leave it with her until they returned in six weeks' time, deciding to make another visit to the hilltop town purely to collect their purchase. For others they knew they could only buy something small and light enough to fit into their suitcase for the flight home, or that they could carry onto the coach with them. Vintage toy cars, small brass candlesticks, delicate cloisonne vases, and a couple of well-carved wooden Buddhas were some of the purchases made that morning, while a large pine table and a small bookcase were measured and details noted so the dimensions could be checked back home. A chap with his gorgeous German shepherd dog came in, closely followed by a new father with his baby strapped to his chest. A couple of elderly ladies inspected the jewellery cabinets, and a young couple bought six pictures for their new home. A discussion about the latest potholes on the nearby main roads, and another about the proliferation of temporary traffic lights in the surrounding area. Complaints about the parking charges, and praise for the number of independent shops in the high street.

Suddenly the door was flung open, and a loud female voice demanded 'Jack? Is Jack in here?'

Yvonne looked over to the counter where she had last seen Jack, but he had disappeared. Only Rob was sitting there. Sylvia Nelson stalked into the shop, her petite stature no barrier to the chilling presence she exuded, green eyes scanning for signs of the tall young antiques dealer, her red-stained lips pursed.

'Can I help you Sylvia?' Yvonne asked pleasantly.

Sylvia Nelson waved a dismissive hand 'No, it's Jack I need. Is he here?'

Diplomatically Yvonne said 'I can't see him. Can I pass on a message for you?'

Sylvia's only reply was a loud tut, and she turned and left as abruptly as she had arrived.

'You can come out now' Rob said.

Yvonne laughed as Jack emerged from where he had been hiding on the floor behind the counter. 'She's not that bad!'

'It's alright for you' grumbled Jack. 'She doesn't try to snog you every time she sees you.'

'Don't you want to be a toy boy?' Rob asked innocently.

Jack looked uncomfortable. The silence lengthened, punctuated by the loud ticking of an Edwardian mantle clock, until eventually he said 'She's actually very pretty under all that make-up.'

'How do you know?' asked Rob. 'When have you seen her recently without it?'

More silence as Yvonne and Rob waited for an answer. Feeling the intensity of their stares, Jack blushed. The sound of the buzzer at Yvonne's electronic gates spurred him into action 'I'll go!' he said as he almost ran to the back of the shop to check the screen for who was requesting for the gates to be opened.

Rob and Yvonne raised their eyes at each other. 'There's a story there!' said Rob.

The lady with the leaky terrier came in through the front door, causing Rob to move quickly to collect the bucket of cleaning products and begin to follow her and the dog around the shop. Yvonne took up his position behind the counter, and Jack reappeared with Raymond carrying a medieval oak coffer between them, which they took through to the Melbury Room. They went back out to Raymond's van and when they returned they were both carrying paintings which Jack helped Raymond to fix to the walls of the room.

Stepping back Raymond studied one of the paintings. 'That is not a good picture, is it? I mean look at the way the artist has painted that woman's hands!'

Laughing, Jack said 'I hadn't noticed. They are out of proportion aren't they.'

'They are murderer's hands' commented Raymond.

Sylvia Nelson stalked through the front door again, and this time her quarry had nowhere to hide. 'Jack, darling!' she said, and walked up to him and succeeded in planting a kiss smack on his lips.

'Hello Sylvia' Jack said, extricating himself from her grip. 'Sorry, I'm just in the middle of helping Raymond empty his van.'

'I won't hold you up, promise' she said. 'I just wanted to give you this' and she handed him an envelope.

He took it gingerly, as though he was afraid it would explode.

'It's an invitation to my birthday party. You will come, won't you darling?' Sylvia said in her loud voice as she gripped his arm, her red nails digging into the skin of his forearm.

'Of course, yes, if I'm free' Jack tried to step away from her, but she followed.

'Oh I do hope you will come. It won't be the same without you. Say you'll come? Yes, I knew you would!' she said triumphantly as Jack nodded. Sylvia released his arm, and as she walked out of the shop with her nose in the air he rubbed the area just above his elbow.

'She's left her mark there' observed Raymond. Glancing down, Jack saw that Sylvia had been digging her nails into the tattoo of Chinese characters on his arm.

'How old is she going to be?' Yvonne asked. 'It must be ending in a nought if she's having a party?'

Everyone jumped when the door opened again, but this time a large quiet presence filled the doorway unlike the small ball of fire who had just walked out. Yvonne was temporarily stunned at the appearance of a man she had thought she would never see again, and briefly wondered if he had walked into her little antiques shop by accident.

'Hello Yvonne' the man gave a tentative smile as he approached the counter. 'How are you?'

'Terry? Hello Terry. I'm good thank you. How are you?' she managed to reply.

The man nodded 'Good, good thank you. Um, is there somewhere we can go to talk?' he looked around at the staff and customers who were staring at him, all of whom were still absorbing the recent interaction between Jack and Sylvia and not really seeing Yvonne and the newcomer, but Terry didn't know that.

For a brief moment Yvonne felt a shiver of panic at the thought of being alone with this man, but then common sense kicked in and she said 'Yes, of course, follow me' and with Zebedee at her heels having roused herself from the dog bed under the counter, beckoned for him to walk with her to her sitting room on the other side of the door at the back of the shop.

Once inside she asked 'Would you like a drink?' and without waiting for an answer refilled the kettle and switched it on.

'Oh, er, yes, thank you, a coffee would be nice' he said, appearing to be as nervous as she felt about their encounter.

'Sit, sit' she said, motioning to the chairs around her kitchen table. 'Have you come far?'

He took his time pulling out one of the elm seated chairs and sitting down, before answering 'I drove down from London this morning. I still live in the same place, above my shop.'

'I remember your home as being a lovely place to visit. I am not surprised you have stayed there. And your wife? And children? Are they well?'

While Terry relaxed into talking about his family, Yvonne made a cafetiere of coffee, pulled a couple of mugs from the cupboard, and fetched a bottle of milk from the fridge. As an afterthought she put the bowl of sugar on the table and a teaspoon, desperately hoping he didn't take sugar since it had probably all stuck together in the months since it had last been used.

She was in luck. They helped themselves to milk and coffee, Terry refused the offer of sugar, and then he said 'I hope you don't mind me coming down here like this?'

Yvonne was quick to reassure him 'No! I am really pleased to see you. And thank you so much for talking to me a few months ago about that jewellery belonging to the Speake family. I appreciate it. George and I found some of it in a field, where it had been abandoned by thieves. The family were grateful to have it returned.'

Terry smiled 'Yes, it was good to talk to you after all this time, and I was happy to help. I have dealt with the Speake family for years, and recognised it immediately. That's why I'm down here, actually, to see the family about some more of their jewellery which is legitimately for sale. I come to Dorset fairly regularly but didn't know this was where you lived until Lindy Speake told me about everything that had been going on' he nodded his head in the direction of the shop. 'She said you both keep your horses at the same yard, and often ride out together.'

The last time they had spoken was the first time in almost twenty years after a major falling out, and Yvonne was wondering if Terry's visit was purely as the next step in rekindling their friendship, or if he had an ulterior motive. He had always been a lovely chap, and his wife was welcoming and friendly. It was just his father who Yvonne had a problem with, and because of her testimony Terry's father had ended up being sent to prison for a few years which had resulted in Terry's refusal to have anything to do with her. Now here he was sitting in her kitchen, drinking coffee out of an 'I love horses' mug with a photo of Toby on one side, which Tabitha had given her one Christmas.

'I also heard about the recent attack on Beau' he said, quietly.

This was what Yvonne had been waiting for, ever since Terry walked through her shop's front door. She said nothing and waited for him to continue, after all he had made the first move. As if sensing her unease Zebedee came and laid her head on Yvonne's knee under the table.

'Yvonne, did you hear what I said?'

'Yes' was all she replied.

'I am sorry' he reached across the table and touched her arm. 'Is there any news? How is he?'

'Thank you' she shifted her arm so they were holding hands across the table. It was a comforting feeling, and she appreciated the gesture. They had been good friends once upon a time, their relationship platonic, and it made Yvonne realise it was a long time since she had a male friend like Terry in her life. 'As far as I know he's doing as well as can be expected. Isn't that the phrase? How did you hear? I didn't think it was common knowledge?'

Slowly Terry withdrew his hand and shifted in his chair as if trying to get comfortable, but Yvonne knew he was stalling. Eventually he said 'I have a confession to make. I am sorry I let you believe it was solely your testimony that sent my dad to prison. I am sorry I let you believe I blamed you for it.'

Yvonne allowed herself to be side-tracked and was on the verge of stating that it was his dad's actions on the night her cousin Christopher was murdered that had caused his prison sentence, but she stopped herself. It was uncomfortable to have to talk about those horrific events, and as she looked at his soft round face, short thinning grey hair and worried-looking grey eyes she wondered what was coming next. He had aged considerably in the intervening years, but then she supposed so had she. He had always been slightly overweight, looking like an overgrown schoolboy even on his wedding day when he was in his early thirties, but now he looked more like someone's cuddly grandad in his late sixties, albeit a worried cuddly grandad who has the sad news to tell you that your pet rabbit has died.

'Well it was because of my testimony, wasn't it?' she stated simply. 'I saw what your dad did, and what Beau did, and that was what I told the court.'

Terry nodded 'yes, yes, you did, and I let you believe you were the only witness.'

Yvonne looked at him, trying to understand what he was saying. She WAS the only witness, other than his father and her brother Beau. Puzzled, she asked 'What do you mean?'

'I was there too' he said in a quiet voice. 'I saw what happened. If you hadn't been prepared to stand up in court, I would have had to.'

Yvonne hadn't realised she had been holding her breath until she sat back in her chair and forced the air out of her lungs. She was having trouble comprehending what Terry was telling her. He was there too? Why hadn't he said anything at the time? Why hadn't he helped her when she tried to defend Christopher? If Terry was there he must have seen his father threaten her, see her grab the nearest thing to hand and hit his father with the Victorian croquet mallet which was standing up with the rest of the lawn set just inside the door of Christopher's shop. She could still remember the awful crunch as she broke his father's arm, the one which held the knife. Immediately she saw her brother Beau turn towards her and she had swung the mallet so it connected with his knee. Another crunching sound; another broken bone. She wasn't taking any chances after she had witnessed Beau smash Christopher to the ground.

Abruptly she stood up, sending her chair flying over onto its back, and rushed over to the sink where she threw up. When she was sure there wasn't anything else to vomit she ran the tap, rinsed her mouth, and turned back to look at Terry. He was sitting with his elbows on her table and his head in his hands. From the way his shoulders were shaking she guessed he was crying. She felt no sympathy for him. She tore off some kitchen roll and put it on the table in front of him. While he blew his nose and dried his eyes she cleaned out the cafetiere and put the sugar bowl back in the cupboard, resolving as she did so to empty and clean that out too at some point.

Eventually he said 'I am so sorry.'

Yvonne made no comment. She didn't know what to say. Several minutes passed with neither of them talking or making eye contact with the other. Eventually Yvonne asked 'Where were you?'

Terry shifted in his chair. When he spoke his voice was shaky. 'I wasn't in time to get inside before Dad turned up. I was outside the window. I knew what my dad was planning to do, and I went to warn Christopher to lock the doors to his shop, and not let my dad in.'

Yvonne studied him for a while. The whole incident had been so ghastly it had left its mark on her memory. She realised as she was sitting here in her kitchen with another witness that she had never heard what the argument had been about, why Terry's father and her brother had been in Christopher's shop, and how it had escalated to the violence which ended her cousin's life. 'Come on then, tell me everything from the beginning.'

As Terry began to talk Yvonne could see the tension in his face and body rise as she began to relax. To finally understand what it had all been about was a relief she didn't know she needed.

In an almost toneless voice, Terry began 'Firstly I want to say how sorry I am for taking so long to talk to you about it all. I saw what you were going through, and I was afraid. My wife has been telling me for years I should contact you, but the longer time went on the harder it got.'

Yvonne replied 'I was alone. My marriage broke up over it. At least you had your wife.' She heard the bitterness in her voice, and so did he.

'You are right, you are right, of course you are. I do know what a coward I was, and in the years since then. I could have picked up the phone at any time but I didn't. You were well-supported by the trade, I could see that. Maybe if they had turned on you I would have found the courage to come forward.'

'If you saw it all then what was stopping you?' now Yvonne was curious.

The initial shock was wearing off, and reason was creeping in. It had been a terrifying time, that level of violence was not something she had ever witnessed in real life, only on the television, and even though the police had reassured her she was safe and did not need to go into witness protection or change her identity or anything drastic like that, she had been unable to continue living as she had before. She would never have thought Beau was capable of such aggression and would not have believed it if she hadn't seen the results for herself. Terry's father was another story, and Yvonne had not been surprised to see him draw a flick knife when things got heated.

Terry shook his head 'I was scared of what my dad would do to me, and what he would do to my family. He's always been a violent shit and used to beat us up all the time when we were kids. I managed to keep him at arm's length from my own children, but I knew he would find a way to get to them, and my wife, if he found out what I had done if I spoke up.'

'Why are you speaking to me about it now?'

'Because he's no danger to anyone now. He had a stroke last year and has been in a nursing home ever since.'

Yvonne absorbed this information. She didn't know how she felt about any of it. Then she thought of something, and asked 'Was anyone else involved, or a witness to what was happening?'

Terry nodded. 'Yes. Bernie Campling was there at the beginning of the argument.'

'What did he have to do with it?'

Terry sighed. 'My dad and Beau had given a few items to your cousin Christopher, who had given them to Bernie to sell. Bernie was saying he hadn't had some of them, and my dad didn't believe that your cousin had indeed given them to Bernie, because he and Bernie had been mates for years whereas he rarely had anything to do with Christopher. You must be careful Yvonne. My dad got his stuff from some dangerous people, and that's why everything got so heated.'

'What about Beau?' Yvonne asked. 'I can't believe he was dealing with anyone who wasn't reasonable. What triggered him to be so aggressive?'

'You know what my dad was like. I firmly believe Beau was trying to hurt your cousin so my dad wouldn't. I know, I know, it sounds mad' Terry said, seeing the look on Yvonne's face. 'But your brother wasn't a violent man, but I think he saw Dad pull that flick knife of his and got a punch in first. I believe his thinking was that with your cousin down there was no reason for Dad to inflict anymore pain.'

Yvonne looked sceptical. It was a theory she wanted to believe and was more in keeping with her brother's nature than the apparently random act of violence she had walked in on. 'If that's true it was a risky thing to do.'

Terry nodded, and they both thought about the fact that the risk had all been with Yvonne's cousin, who had lost his life as a result.

'Why did Beau never enter that as a defence?' Yvonne asked, reluctant to accept that her beliefs about her brother for the past twenty years were wrong.

Terry shrugged 'I don't know, but did you not think the Judge's sentence was unduly lenient?'

'Beau was serving a Life Sentence!' exclaimed Yvonne.

Terry looked at her, trying to gauge if she was being genuine. 'No, he didn't' he said slowly.

'Yes, he did.'

'No, he didn't. He pleaded guilty to involuntary manslaughter, which immediately means he had a third of the time spent in prison taken off the life sentence. He had more time off for good behaviour, part of his sentence was commuted to a suspended sentence, and he was out after two years. Surely you knew that?'

Yvonne sat back in her chair, her face a picture of shock. Her vision blurred and she suddenly felt very cold and then very hot. She heard 'Oh my god' and the scraping of a chair on the floor, and then Terry was beside her, putting a glass of water in front of her and crouching down next to her.

'Yvonne? Are you alright?'

Shakily Yvonne put her hand out to the glass. Terry guided her gently, and she took a sip of water. Her vision cleared and she felt stronger. 'Thanks' she muttered. 'No, I didn't know that. I thought he was still in prison until I saw him on the ground with a hole in his side.'

Terry was confused, but seeing the colour return to Yvonne's cheeks he went back to his chair. 'I knew you had distanced yourself from the antiques trade, but I didn't realise you had cut yourself off from it completely. Beau has been working in an auction house since the day he left prison. Only small time, and in the back rooms, not customer-facing. He was the one who has been encouraging me to come to see you and explain my involvement, but as I said it wasn't until my dad became too ill to be a threat that I felt I could.'

Yvonne was still trying make sense of what Terry was telling her. 'So you have seen Beau?'

'Oh yes! We meet up probably every two or three months for a meal out and a chat. His second wife is lovely' seeing Yvonne's expression, Terry said 'Oh! I don't suppose you know about her, either?'

Shaking her head, Yvonne said 'I have only recently been told about her.'

There was a long silence. Yvonne did not know what to think or say, it was all such a shock.

Eventually Terry said 'I'd better be going' as he stood up. He walked around to where Yvonne was sitting on the other side of the table and put his hand on her shoulder. 'I am sorry.'

After a moment's hesitation Yvonne put her hand to his. 'Thank you for telling me all of that. I need some time to take this in. I am sure you understand.'

Terry stepped away and said 'Of course I understand. I am really pleased to see how well you are doing in business, how great you are looking too. I appreciate you even listening to me, and I don't expect your forgiveness, but please, phone me or text or whatever. I would like to stay in contact. Please.'

Yvonne didn't reply, but stayed where she was until he had closed the door behind him. A soft knock followed his exit, and George stuck his head around the door 'Can I come in?'

Yvonne didn't really want to see anyone, but forced a smile because George was probably the only person she could tolerate at this time. His dark eyes were gentle and smiling and she needed a bit of comfort after speaking with Terry. 'Hi George, yes of course, come on in. How are you?'

'Fine thank you. I had a spare half an hour and thought I'd wander down to my favourite antiques shop. Rob said you were in here, are you alright? You look a bit pale.'

'I'm fine, thanks. I could do with a walk. Fancy coming with me?'

George, Yvonne and Zebedee left through the back of the shop and out of the electronic gates into the car park beyond. George took her hand, and together they strolled up Coppice Street, waving to Charlotte through the window of her bakery, walking through the park at the back of the youth club and on up to Barton Hill, down to Bell Street and back to Angel Lane Antiques. Yvonne enjoyed walking along with George, someone who cared for her, was attracted to her, and was a lot of fun to be with, and very good-looking. She reflected that perhaps if she and her husband had this type of relationship their marriage might have lasted. Theirs had been all lust in the bedroom and rivalry in business, with no quiet and relaxed times in between. When Yvonne needed a shoulder to cry on and someone to talk through the events she had witnessed in her cousin's shop, her husband was not equipped to be the person she needed. It wasn't his fault, or hers, but now she knew better, and certainly sexual attraction was an essential part of her relationship with George, but they also had the emotional range to spend time enjoying other activities too. George was an intelligent man, and Yvonne enjoyed their discussions because he listened to her, and she learned from him. Her husband had been knowledgeable about his hobby of rock climbing but had little interest in anything else which made for limited conversation over the dinner table. Yvonne didn't tell George anything of what Terry had revealed during his visit. She wasn't sure she had the words and needed some time alone to make sense of it all. Instead, they chatted about the buildings they passed, the lovely sunny weather, the robin who appeared to be following them, the traffic on the A350.

Outside the electronic gates at the back of her shop Yvonne kissed George goodbye and they agreed to meet up later that evening. She walked back into her shop feeling a little lighter and happier than when she left, but with more questions about the past than she had when she woke up that morning.

Chapter 14

The next day Tabitha bounced into the shop. 'Yvonne, just the person. Keep October twenty-first free, because that is when we are having your birthday party!'

'What's this?' Jack asked. 'A party?'

'It's not a party party' Yvonne was quick to explain. 'Just a few friends gathering to celebrate my birthday.'

'Sounds like a party to me' observed Jack.

'And me' piped up Rob. 'Where's my invite?'

'It's not that sort of party' Yvonne explained defensively.

'Yes it is!' said Tabitha. 'We're having it at the courtyard at TAA, and we're having a Barn Dance and Line Dancing. You are both invited, as is everyone else who works here.' She produced a poster from her rucksack and handed it to Rob.

'Thanks, I'll put it up in our kitchen' he winked at Yvonne. 'Looks like you're having a party party!'

'Let's see?' Yvonne asked. Rob held the poster up so she could read it. Laughing she said 'I like the look of that, I think I'll come.'

Grinning, Tabitha said 'You'll need to brush off your cowgirl boots and dig out your hat. Yee-haw!'

'Is that what you're into?' Rob asked Yvonne.

Yvonne shrugged 'Not so far, but I'll give it a go. I like the tassels and boots but I'm not keen on the music. Isn't it all Kenny Rogers and Dolly Parton?'

'Dolly Parton's alright' said Rob, and started singing "Working nine 'til five"

"What a way to make a living" sang Tabitha.

'Is it a big birthday Yvonne?' Jack asked.

Yvonne laughed 'No! I think everyone just wants an excuse to celebrate something. I am going to be forty-nine but think I may plan something special for my fiftieth.'

Jack looked at her speculatively 'In that case you're looking good for your age. Wouldn't have said you were much older than me.'

Yvonne gave him a look. Jack was well-known for using his good-looks and charm to entice women into his bed, and his track record was infamous. Unlike his younger brother Charlie, who had fallen in love and married in his early twenties, now thirty years old Jack always claimed to be uninterested in 'being tied-down to one woman' as he put it, and his behaviour appeared to back that up. He never had the same girlfriend for more than a few months, although was rarely without female company. There were not many women in the area, single or in relationships, who Jack hadn't had some sort of dalliance with, but so far he had never been foolish enough to try it on with her. She hoped he wasn't going to start now, because that could only make it awkward to have him in her shop. He really wasn't her type, and he was so young. And she was far too old for him, it could only be embarrassing to hook up with him.

Seeing her face Jack hurriedly said 'What? I mean it! She looks like someone in their late thirties, don't you think?' he looked at Rob for support, worried that he had gone too far.

Holding his hand up in defence Rob laughed 'I am not getting involved, you're on your own mate.'

Jack was saved from further embarrassment by the next people through the door. Nigel and Rufus Campling walked in, and both smiled when they saw Yvonne.

'Hello you two. How are you both?' Yvonne asked.

The older brother, Nigel replied with a wry smile 'Oh, you know, trying to live down being the sons of one of the biggest thieves in the antiques trade.'

Rufus nudged his brother 'It's not that bad. Fortunately for us the police have been brilliant, and almost everything has been returned to its rightful owner.'

'Already? That was quick work. These things normally take forever' said Yvonne. 'I wonder if my brother has had his stock back.'

Rufus said, shaking his head 'Oh was he another one who thought he'd lost items in the burglary? I didn't know you two were in contact anymore. Sorry, we haven't been involved in any of it thank goodness. The police have given us permission to put the house on the market if we want to, and we were wondering if you would come and see if there is anything you want to buy from there and of course Dad's shed? You'll be the first person we are offering his things too, and we'll be guided by you about what we do with the rest, if that's alright?'

'Thank you, I am honoured to have been asked. Let me know when's convenient and we'll go through everything. What are your plans for the house?'

Rufus said 'Thanks Yvonne. Once you've finished we'll be in touch with estate agents because we are not going to keep the house.'

'We probably wouldn't have done anyway' explained Nigel, 'but after this we can't stand the disgrace. Neither of us wants to live there now.'

'I still can't believe my dad did it' said Rufus.

'Nor me' said his brother. 'Particularly on such a grand scale.'

'If it is any comfort I still can't get my head around your dad doing something like that either' Yvonne said. 'He was always genuine in the dealings we had together. I never had any reason to doubt his integrity before, unlike numerous other dealers I could name.'

'Thank you Yvonne, that means a lot' said Nigel. Noticing the poster Rob was still holding he asked 'What's all this?'

'Oh it's my birthday coming up.'

Rufus said 'Of course, I had forgotten with everything that has been going on recently. It must be your forty-ninth isn't it? Fifty next year? Beau's must be this year. You're exactly between me and Nigel, although I have to say you look ten years younger than either of us.'

'Thank you Rufus, that is very kind of you to say and not true! Yes it is my fiftieth next year. I wasn't going to do much for my birthday this year, but my friends wanted to celebrate and so here we are. Of course, you and your wives are invited, if you'd like to come. Let Tabitha know if you can make it because she's doing all the hard work; I am just turning up, isn't that right?' she winked at Tabitha, who nodded, smiling with relief that Yvonne appeared to be happy about their plans. 'Come on, let's go and sort out a date for looking at your dad's remaining stock.'

As the brothers followed Yvonne through to her kitchen, Jack turned open-mouthed to Rob and Tabitha 'Did you see that? He said exactly the same thing as me and got an invite to her party!'

Tabitha laughed 'Um, he didn't say exactly the same thing though, did he?'

Once Yvonne and the brothers agreed a date she let them out through the back of the shop to the car park. When she returned she found Tabitha had gone, and Rob and Jack had been joined by Rachael Hall and Raymond Wise and the four of them were huddled in deep discussion.

'Hi Yvonne, was that Bernie Campling's sons you were just talking to?' Rachael asked, her mass of grey curls held back from her face by a moss green coloured scarf.

'Yes, Nigel and Rufus are selling their family home and they asked me for some advice about the remaining items in there.'

'Including Bernie's shed?' Rachael's face lit up. Yvonne nodded, and Rachael said 'You lucky thing. I would love to see what is inside there.'

Jack said 'I wonder how much that house will sell for?'

'More than I can afford!' said Raymond.

Jack looked thoughtful. 'How many bedrooms does it have?'

'Are you thinking of setting up a little love nest with Sylvia?' Raymond teased.

'What's this? Are you and Sylvia an item again?' said Rachael.

'Again!' Raymond looked astonished.

'Oh yes, didn't you know? Jack and Sylvia had a fling last year, didn't you Jack?'

Everyone looked at Jack, waiting for an answer. He shifted uncomfortably on his feet. 'We dated each other for a while. It wasn't serious. Anyway, she's married.'

'Is she? I did not know that. Who is the lucky man?' Raymond said wryly.

'She's alright' Jack defended her. 'She's married to a man who works in finance, nothing to do with the antiques trade.'

'Are they still married then?' asked Rachael. 'I heard she left him last year.'

'Sorry, I have to take this' said Jack, holding his phone to his ear and walking off.

'I didn't hear it ring' Rachael commented.

Rob, Raymond and Rachael left Yvonne at the counter while they went to their respective areas of the shop to restock and tidy up. Idly Yvonne logged on to the computer and began to browse clothing with a Western theme. She added a few things to her shopping cart, looked at the total, added a few more things. 'You're only forty-nine once' she muttered, and pressed Pay.

George walked in through the door of the shop looking every inch a tall and muscular cowboy in blue jeans, black long-sleeved shirt and black baseball cap. Yvonne noted he was wearing red trainers. Oh well, she thought, you can't have everything.

'What's wrong?' he said, looking at his feet.

Blushing at having been caught out, Yvonne hurriedly said 'Nothing! I'm guessing you know about the party Tabitha and the girls are planning for me as it's at your place.'

He grinned 'You like the idea?'

'I do! I didn't know I did until Tabitha told me earlier, but now I'm all for it.'

'Good' he said. 'I am glad. You deserve to have fun after all you have had to deal with recently. Talking of fun, would you like to go out for dinner tonight? My treat?'

'Thank you but I feel I have been eating all day long. I need to take Zebedee out for a walk, so I'm going to pop down to the yard and ride Toby around the fields in the dark, and Zebedee can come too. Do you want to come and walk around the fields with us?'

'Good idea, I would love to. Give me ten minutes to go and change' he said looking down at his jeans and shirt. 'I could do with donning my running shoes and putting in a few miles.'

'Great. It will take me more than ten minutes to sort all my riding gear out, but I'll message you as I'm leaving and pick you up outside TAA.'

After George had left Yvonne stayed sitting where she was for a few minutes, enjoying the feeling of the building which had turned back into a safe and positive space after an unsettling few weeks. Eventually she hauled herself up and went to find her dog, who had been supervising the occasional use of the kitchen by Rob.

There was a large bunch of flowers in a big glass vase on the middle of her kitchen table, with a note which read 'Congratulations on a successful reopening of Angel Lane Antiques! Love Tabitha and Alison' and a bottle of chilled orange wine, Yvonne's current favourite from Shaftesbury Wines, with a note saying 'Drink Me! Love Lindy'.

'You are a rubbish guard dog, thank goodness' Yvonne teased Zebedee, who wagged her tail enthusiastically.

The pair of them ran up the spiral stairs to Yvonne's bedroom, where she completed a quick change from shopkeeper to horse rider, and minutes later they were driving up the High Street, where George was waiting for them outside The Abbess Aethelgifu, his tall athletic figure making Yvonne's heart jump.

The five-minute drive to the yard was filled with Yvonne sharing the story of the return of the lady with her leaky terrier, and George telling her about the time he banned the woman from bringing her dog into his restaurant, when they pulled into the yard. They were greeted by Tom's dog Stan, and seeing Tom bringing Ben in from the field George said 'Why don't you see if Tom wants to ride with you instead?'

'Don't you mind?'

'Not at all. I'll make up a route and run home from here, and we could meet later for supper if you feel like eating then?'

'That would be lovely' Yvonne gave him a kiss on the cheek, and watched as he jogged down the beech tree-lined drive to the lane beyond.

'Where's he off to?' Tom asked as he tied Ben's lead rope to one of the rings outside barn.

'He's going for a run and will finish back at his apartment. Rather him than me, because knowing him he won't take a direct route up the road. How's your return to running going?'

'Not bad. I keep having to drop back to nice and easy five kilometre runs but am determined to get back to running at least ten kilometres three times a week.'

Yvonne shook her head 'I can't imagine describing running five kilometres as nice and easy. I was going to take Toby and Zebedee for a ride around the fields if you'd like to join us?'

'Love to, thanks' said Tom as he energetically brushed Ben's thick dark brown tail.

It took Yvonne less than five minutes to bring Toby in from his field and tack up, because she didn't bother with brushing more than the area around his head where the bridle would fit and roughly where the saddle and girth would go. They set off on foot to let the horses warm-up under saddle, and mounted at a convenient bank in the field at the back of the farm house.

'Is there any news on the person who attacked my brother?' Yvonne asked in what she hoped was a casual tone. It was on her mind, but she didn't want it to occupy too much brain space. She had learned to compartmentalise her brother's choices and behaviour a long time ago so that they did not impact on her peace of mind. But his stabbing, and the place where it happened, could not be pushed to one side. While they were out here, in the open, with the horses seemed like a good time to ask.

Tom wasn't fooled by her act but answered in an equally casual manner 'I think there is some progress, but I couldn't tell you what it was. The other victim has been identified but I can't tell you who it was.'

Yvonne was about to ask Tom to qualify his answer as to whether he knew but wasn't allowed to tell her or didn't know and therefore couldn't provide her with an update, but she decided instead to let it go. If Tom wanted her to know he would tell her, or if Commander Tattersall needed more information from her she knew where Yvonne lived.

'I can tell you a body was found in the pond down in Semley' said Tom.

'No! Really? A body? Whose?'

'She has been identified, and the family informed so I can tell you who she is. It's Bernie Campling's sister.'

'What? Oh that's awful, the poor family. Poor Nigel and Rufus. They were close to their aunt. Both of them had been working for her since they left school. They must be devastated, particularly as this is so close to death of their father. Would it be alright if I give them a ring?'

Tom said 'Of course, they would probably appreciate it. I haven't been working with the family, but you know them. I saw how you were with them when we discovered Bernie's stash of antiques, and people in their situation often need someone to talk to who knows the family like you do.'

An awful thought struck her. 'She didn't commit suicide did she? It's not the first place I'd think of for drowning myself. It's only a little lily pond.'

'No, she was definitely murdered. The poison that was used to kill Bernie was found in her system. The pond is probably bigger than you think. All that foliage around it obscures the size, and you could easily drown in it.'

Yvonne nodded 'I suppose you're right. I have never really thought about it before. They do say you can drown in a puddle. But that is horrible, to think her body was dumped in that lovely village pond. I will never be able to look at it again in the same way. I wonder why Semley has become the focus of all this violence?'

Tom said 'I can't explain that, but I can tell you something else you may find interesting, When the forensic team were down there after your brother's attack they drained and searched the pond looking for the weapon. They didn't find that, but they did find a number of items on our list as being given to Bernie by other dealers for him to sell.'

Yvonne looked astonished. 'Bernie hid them in the pond? The one by the pub? Are we talking about the same one?'

'That's the one. The pieces had obviously been in there a while because they were sunk into the mud. Our experts reckon at least twenty years, all perfectly preserved in the mud.'

'But that pond dries out sometimes in the summer. Surely everything dumped in there would be exposed?' Yvonne was trying to picture the pond, but all she could think of was an area of water roughly the size of a large garden pond.

Tom shrugged 'Apparently not. Everything was deep in the silt, and probably not visible even if the water level dropped.'

'Still, it's a bit of a risk. Why on earth did he dump the antiques there, when he had his purpose-built room?'

Tom said 'We don't know that it was Bernie who put them in there, but it does seem possible considering he had the rest of the supposedly stolen antiques. Obviously he can't have been involved in his sister's death because whoever murdered her and dumped her body in there must have done it in the past few days because the pond has only just begun to refill since it was drained.'

Yvonne's mind was reeling with this new information. She asked 'Do you think it is a coincidence that his sister's body ended up in there too?'

Tom shrugged. 'I don't know, and if I did I probably couldn't tell you. However if putting her body in the same pond a load of stolen antiques were found in was meant to serve as a warning, then who was that aimed at?'

Yvonne didn't have an answer for that. 'I don't want to think that any more people I work with are involved, and would like to think it wasn't Bernie who hid those items in the pond because I believe he had more respect for antiques than that.'

It was a beautiful warm October autumnal evening. The sun was low behind them and would disappear long before it reached Duncliffe woods. The horses settled into an easy stride side-by-side even though there was a significant height difference, and their riders were lost in their own thoughts about recent events. Eventually, both feeling they had exhausted the subject of the murders of Bernie and his sister and the recovered antiques without more information, Yvonne and Tom changed the subject with relief, and chatted about this and that while the dogs ran ahead only stopping to sniff intently for a few seconds before dashing off again. Yvonne could feel her shoulders relaxing and dropping as her body moved with her horse's.

'This is just what I need' she said as she rolled her shoulders, enjoying the crunching sound they made. 'I hadn't realised how worried I was about reopening the shop. There was a possibility no one would want to come in, and there would be a strange vibe about the place, but so many friendly faces have come through the door, and sales have been really positive, it feels great to be back in business again. It's just all these other dreadful events which are stopping me from feeling one hundred percent positive about the future.'

'It's all going well then?' asked Tom. It was the first time they had talked about the reopening of Angel Lane Antiques since they started their ride.

'It is, thank goodness. No thrill seekers or ghost hunters, and plenty of buyers and enthusiastic antiques dealers. We even have most of our familiar locals coming into see us and telling us how happy they are we are open again.'

'Good. I'm glad. After all your hard work it's what you deserve. Let's hope this marks an end to all the shit you've had to deal with this year.'

'Thank you Tom!' Yvonne was a little taken aback by the emotion in Tom's voice. They carried on in silence for a while, until they came to an open gate into another field. 'Shall we go in here and have a trot and canter?' she asked.

The horses trotted along one side of the field in a comfortable steady gait, and as they turned the corner to go slightly uphill they both broke into an easy canter. Yvonne and Tom were both riding in a half-seat, slightly leaning forward with their backsides out of the saddles and enjoying the rhythm as their horses covered the ground. Glancing back Yvonne could see both dogs following behind, with Zebedee slightly ahead of Stan. The six of them continued along the third edge of the field which was relatively flat, and the horses slowed to a trot and then a walk before turning down the final side and walking on a loose rein back to the gate, and then returning to the yard.

'Aren't we lucky to be able to ride off road at this time of year' said Yvonne. 'No need for lights or watching out for other road users as it gets dark.'

Tom nodded. 'These dark evenings always catch me out when I'm walking Stan. The thing I love about having a horse is that you can see beautiful sights like that which you rarely see while walking or running.'

Yvonne looked over to where Tom was pointing and saw three deer grazing close to a hedge-line, an owl swooping along the field edge, and something which may have been a bat flew over her head. Blue flashing lights making their way up the beech drive to the yard caught her eye just as Tom said 'Uh oh, that doesn't look good.'

Chapter 15

The horses raised their heads and their steps became more staccato the closer they got to the police car which appeared to have been abandoned in the middle of the yard. Yvonne and Tom jumped off their horses and lifted the reins over their heads to lead them to where their headcollars were hanging by the lead ropes from the brick wall. As they walked around the car, the blue coloured lights bouncing off the floor and walls of the yard with a strange disco effect, the horses snorted and stepped sideways. Three unmarked black vans were lined up blocking the drive, blue lights flashing behind the grills. There didn't appear to be anyone around, and so they untacked the horses, gave them a quick brush where their tack had been and picked out their feet, before leading them out to the fields, followed by the dogs. As they walked back, rope halters slung over their shoulders, two more police cars with lights flashing sped up the driveway.

'What's going on?' Yvonne asked Tom, who didn't answer but instead pulled his phone out of his pocket.

'Where the bloody hell have you been!' Several police officers wearing protective helmets with visors covering their faces were striding towards them, and the one in front continued to shout. 'Don't you ever turn your phone on?'

'Who's she talking to?' Yvonne asked Tom, who again didn't respond to her although now that his phone was back in range of the farm's Wi-Fi Yvonne could hear the constant pinging indicating there were several missed calls and voice messages. The area was notorious for limited if any phone signal, which was one of the reasons it was so peaceful to ride out with the horses. Through the visor Yvonne recognised the voice, Police Commander Jemima Tattersall.

'Yvonne, you need to come with us' The Police Commander modified her tone. 'We need to take you to a safe house immediately.'

Yvonne stood still and stared at her, taking in the rest of her police uniform including the solid looking body protector, and was that a gun? Yvonne's heart was thumping, and she was terrified. It was like being faced by a team of black-clad Storm Troopers, and she had never seen anything like it in real life. She half-expected to see running riots and police vehicles on fire, but in the silence all she could hear were the crows arguing in the trees and an owl, typical for an evening in the countryside. When she spoke she was surprised to find her voice was strong. 'What? No! No way. No. I'm not going anywhere with you.'

Tom, who had been rapidly catching up with the messages on his phone came and stood by her and put his hand on her arm. 'Yvonne …'

Yvonne snatched her arm away and whirled round to face him. 'Don't touch me! I have only just moved back into my own home. I am not leaving it again.'

Tom tried to explain 'Something's happened.'

'You know how hard it has been to reopen my business! I can't close it down again!'

'You won't have to. Yvonne listen to me please!' Tom held his hands up as if surrendering. 'Whoever tried to kill your brother is making credible threats against you. Not to your business, just you. I'm sure Rob and Jack and the rest of them can keep the place open in your absence while we put all our resources into catching these people. This is serious, and not worth losing your life over.'

Police Commander Tattersall took a small step forward. 'Yvonne, we would like to keep you safely out of the way while we pursue this person. If you won't leave your home then we need to make your home and business premises secure, which will take a lot of manpower and I am sorry but your shop cannot be open during the time it takes us to bring these people into custody, because if it is open to the public then you will be a sitting target. I do appreciate how disruptive the last few weeks have been to your life, and I have absolutely no wish to add to or prolong the distress you have been experiencing. As Tom said if you're happy with the arrangement your colleagues can keep the business running as normal, but please, we do need to take you out of harm's way.'

Reluctantly Yvonne asked 'How long for?' She could see that other livery owners were being kept up at the yard and was aware they needed to feed their horses. Embarrassment washed over her at yet again being the from the police concerning events surrounding her before she had.

In less than a minute Tom was yelling at her to keep her head down as they passed under the terrifying rotor blades and in through the open door, and she was strapped into the helicopter cab alongside Tom, behind the pilot. The incredible noise of the blades beating the air was competing with the high pitch whine of the engine, and it was with relief she found the headphones Tom handed to her cancelled the sound.

It was all happening so quickly she didn't have time to prepare herself for the lurch in her stomach as the pilot took them up and away and was momentarily distracted by the tingling in her feet. She felt Tom place his hand over hers and heard him speaking through the headphones, but she couldn't spare the brain space to listen to what he was saying. She was fully occupied with keeping as still as possible and staring at the back of the pilot's head, her body rigid with fear, one hand firmly placed on the seat next to her, the other gripping Tom's hand despite the fact she was angry with him and would rather not have been anywhere near him let alone having physical contact. Tom continued to talk to her, until eventually his calm voice seeped into her consciousness, and she heard him say 'We are heading to Kenyon Hall. You'll be safe there. You probably haven't been back since you were helping Tabitha and Alison plan their wedding there? Not long now.'

Slowly Yvonne began to feel less anxious although she was aware that her shoulders were almost up to her ears and she was clenching her jaw. Yvonne forced her eyes to move away from the pilot's short ginger hair at the back of his neck where it disappeared inside the collar of his jacket, and she risked looking past his head through the windscreen at the landscape ahead. As she tried to work out where they were the pilot's voice came through the headphones 'There, can you see King Alfred's Tower up ahead?'

They flew past the tower, and then the noise of the rotor blades changed as they banked right. Yvonne relaxed enough to turn her eyes and then her head and look out of the window to her left, although all she could see was streetlights and vehicle lights in the darkness.

A few minutes later the pilot said 'Here we are' and Yvonne could see the welcome lights of Kenyon Hall. Tom was correct, and she hadn't been back since Tabitha and Alison's wedding plans had been aborted, but for several months it had been somewhere she had visited regularly. It was an impressive building from the ground in daylight, but at night from above it looked huge. She could see the lights on either side of the long winding drive, and the outdoor swimming pool looked warm and inviting as the water twinkled in the pool lights. There were pathways through the gardens picked out in bright lanterns, and the Orangery was stunning as she looked down on the warm lighting surrounding it and big lanterns shining up through the glass ceiling.

Yvonne had been expecting to feel the downwards transition, but she barely noticed how close they were to the ground until the pilot smoothly landed the helicopter on the landing area to the side of the hall. He shut the engines down and looked over his shoulder and said 'You can relax now, it's all over.'

Yvonne managed to nod her head and even forced a smile when she said 'Thank you'.

While the rotor blades were slowing down to a stop, Tom gestured to her to take off the headphones, and he undid his harness. Still in a daze Yvonne copied him and undid her own harness, and then followed Tom through the open door where the pilot was waiting to help her out of the cab and onto the safety of the grass. She was grateful for his support because her legs buckled as she stepped down, and he kept her moving away from the helicopter, and upright, until the strength returned to her body.

'Sorry' she mumbled. 'That was absolutely terrifying.'

He grinned 'You did very well. Next time you'll enjoy it' and with a wink he walked back to the helicopter.

'Next time?' Yvonne said through gritted teeth to Tom. 'There is not going to be a next time.'

Tom said nothing and led her away from the helicopter and towards the building.

Following in his wake Yvonne said 'That was no accident was it? You being at the yard when I got there and just happened to be ready to ride out. You knew this was going to happen. And how come George was back at the yard to take care of the dogs? When I last saw him he was heading home! And when did you ask Rob and Jack to take over the shop, and Tabitha and Alison to sort out clothes from my home for me? What the bloody hell is going on, and why am I the last one to know?'

Chapter 16

Tom ushered her through the door into a brightly lit corridor, its stark off-white walls and ceiling and brick-tiled floor giving the impression of a cold and utilitarian part of the luxurious building.

'Welcome!' Lindy Speake appeared at the end of the corridor. 'Oooh I do love flying in a helicopter. You are lucky.'

'Am I?' Yvonne asked coldly. 'That was awful. I hate heights almost as much as I hate being left in the dark. This all seems a bit over-the-top, and as you are clearly yet another of my friends who knows what is happening I want to know too.'

'Let me show you to your room' said Lindy, ignoring her friend's attempt to extract an explanation and trying to take Yvonne's arm to lead her up the narrow wooden stairs which were a far cry from the grand carpeted sweeping staircase at the entrance of the hotel.

Yvonne snatched her arm away 'No. I am not going anywhere until one of you tells me what is going on! You are clearly in on it, Lindy. Tell me. Now.'

'No, not here' Tom said quietly. 'Let's go with Lindy, and we can talk about this in private. It really is not something we can discuss here. Trust me.'

Yvonne bit back a sharp retort, closed her eyes and let out a long breath. 'OK, let's go' she gestured to Lindy. As they began to climb the stairs she heard the helicopter taking off behind them. She followed Lindy as they reached a polished wooden landing, the change in décor indicating they were moving into a more habitable area of the house and continued up the stairs to the next floor and another landing, this time covered in a good quality dark red carpet.

'This way!' Lindy said brightly, and led them along another corridor, which was decorated with old-fashioned gold and red wallpaper and lit by gilt wall lamps. She stopped next to a huge wooden door, opened it, and ushered them inside.

Yvonne walked through the door and came to an abrupt halt as she took in yet another change of décor. Tom just managed to avoid walking into her by executing a smart step to the side.

Lindy closed the door behind Tom and continued 'This is your home now for as long as you need it.'

Yvonne ventured forwards a few steps taking in the three huge plush yellow sofas arranged around an open fireplace where a fire was burning in the grate even though the outside temperature was not chilly. There were double doors to the right slightly ajar through which she could see an elegant dark wood four poster bed, and to her left a fully equipped modern kitchen with sliding glass doors opening out onto a wooden deck softly lit with uplighters and furnished with a long wooden table and some comfortable-looking steamer chairs.

'Sit down and I'll explain what is happening' Tom was already seated on one of the sofas, and Lindy sat down on one of the others. Yvonne wavered for a few seconds, but reluctantly walked over to the third and perched on the edge of the cushions, determined not to show any sign of agreeing to whatever was being proposed despite feeling she didn't have any choice.

'The Ronco brothers attacked your brother and killed the other man, they killed Bernie Campling by poisoning him, and murdered his sister in the same way and dumped her body in the pond at Semley. Your life is in danger because they will use you and Beau's wife and children to get to him. Up until now they haven't been interested in you, but he survived their attempt to murder him, and as far as they are concerned he is unfinished business and they intend to finish it.' Tom waited, watching Yvonne's reaction.

She gasped and put her hands up to cover her mouth. 'No' she breathed, and then in a stronger voice, vigorously shaking her head 'No! Beau wouldn't be mixed up with them.' She looked from Tom to Lindy and back again, seeing the concern in their eyes.

'I am sorry Yvonne.' Again Tom waited, before continuing 'Now you can see why we had to act quickly, and remove you to a safe place. Lindy has kindly agreed to hide you here for the next few days while we complete our operation. The staff are used to having celebrities and rich people staying here incognito while they recover from scandals or plastic surgery, and they think you are a member of a German aristocratic family recovering from some sort of unspecified operation. Lindy is the only person in the whole place who knows the truth, and that is the way it needs to stay.'

Lindy spoke up 'You can order anything from our kitchens or have a food delivery brought to the hotel and cook for yourself. This suite is one of our private family residences, so you won't be disturbed by the hotel's guests.'

Yvonne leant forward, her head in her hands. It had occurred to her as they were walking up the stairs that this was some elaborate joke, but the number of people who would have been needed to play the parts of the police at the livery yard in addition to the expense of the helicopter meant she discounted that idea almost immediately. The Ronco brothers were ruthless killers, notorious in the London-based antiques world but rarely heard of outside of the capital city. Of course she knew of them because some of the Parker antiques business had touched on their turf, but she had never had anything to do with them and she couldn't understand how anyone in her family had come into their orbit. Her eyes narrowed as she looked up at Lindy.

'How are you connected to the Ronco brothers?' Yvonne asked abruptly.

Lindy was taken aback by Yvonne's expression, which was cold and threatening, and wondered how best to answer. In the end she decided honesty was the way forwards.

'I used to be married to one of them. To Antonio.'

Now it was Yvonne's turn to be lost for words. After a moment of shocked silence she said 'You did? You were married to a Ronco brother? How on earth did that happen?'

Lindy shrugged. 'I was young, he was charming, handsome, knew all about me and my family's wealth, made me fall in love with him.' Seeing a sceptical look on Yvonne's face she said 'I know it's no excuse, but he did. I was nineteen, he was twenty-three, I had never heard of the Ronco brothers, no one had at that point. Luca is a year younger than Antonio and they hadn't got into their stride as violent thugs.' She shivered and stopped talking.

Tom waited a moment, and then said 'Do you mind if I continue explaining to Yvonne?'

Lindy shook her head 'No I don't, please go ahead.'

Tom said 'Lindy was one of the lucky ones and escaped the marriage after less than two years. I'm sure you know that Antonio has a string of accusations and convictions for violence against women against him. There is also a list of missing people we can only suspect have disappeared thanks to the Ronco brothers. Lindy and her family have been incredibly generous over the years in providing a safe place for those victims and their families who have needed somewhere to live in the months preceding and during those trials.'

Yvonne looked at Lindy who had stood up and was staring out of the windows with her back to them. Slowly she said 'I think I owe you an apology, Lindy. I am sorry for the way I have been behaving since I arrived. It is very kind, and as Tom said generous of you to provide me with shelter. I am just a bit taken aback by it all, and I admit out of my depth.'

Lindy turned around 'Don't mention it Yvonne. My family will do this for anyone. It was only when the security detail turned up an hour before you did that their name was even mentioned.'

'My what?'

Lindy looked at Tom, who explained 'You don't need to worry about any of that. We have a number of people in all areas of the hotel and its grounds to ensure your safety. We know how these men operate, and we are close to arresting them and closing down their business, but we're not there yet and until then we do not want you to become yet another casualty of their violence.'

'Am I under house arrest?'

'You do need to stay in here, yes' he said, not directly answering her question. 'Are you ready to message Tabitha or Alison now?'

Yvonne sighed and flopped back into the sofa, looking more like herself than the menacing person a few minutes earlier. 'Alright. Will they be the ones bringing my stuff here?'

Tom shook his head 'No, they don't know where you are and that is how it needs to be. Lindy is also going to be staying here until this is over, to keep you company.'

Yvonne looked at Lindy 'Don't you mind?'

'No of course I don't. You haven't asked for any of this, and if I can help you to pass the time away then I will. I can't do much, but this is something I can do to help put those bastards out of business.

'Wow' said Yvonne. 'That is incredibly generous of you.'

'Not really' said Lindy, coming over to sit next to Yvonne on the sofa. 'I am not restricted at Kenyon Hall in the same way you are, and I often spend days at a time here. Sorry, I didn't mean to make you feel worse.'

'Who is going to look after our horses?'

'Lindy can still go back to the yard, in fact it will be better if she does carry on her routine as usual. I am going to ask Sally and Charlotte to take care of Toby and Ben, and I'll do what I can, of course' Tom replied. 'We couldn't hide the fact you were taken off in a police helicopter or that Commander Tattersall turned up with a protection squad, so they have probably heard by now. I am sure Charlotte and Sally will keep an eye on our horses like they usually do.'

'What story are you telling everyone? There were a lot of people witness to me being taken off by more police than we see in a year in Shaftesbury.'

The return of Yvonne's belligerent tone riled Tom 'Look, we are doing this for your own safety, do you understand? You might not care if the Ronco brothers catch up with you, but we do. And by "we" I mean the policemen and women who are giving up their rest days to do everything they can to catch your brother's attackers and to keep you alive.'

Suitably chastened Yvonne was silent. Eventually she sat up and looked at Tom. 'I do understand. I am sorry. This is all a bit of a shock, and unsettling. To be honest I am absolutely terrified, and that is making me behave like a right bitch. Sorry.'

'Good. Thank you' he said. He paused, because he knew that what he was about to say next would undo the small progress he had made. 'We have told everyone at the yard we have taken you into custody in connection with your brother's attack so, um, sorry about that.'

'You what!' Yvonne exploded. 'You mean everyone is going to think I tried to murder him? Oh great. That's not going to affect my business is it.'

Tom tried to explain and attempt to regain the lost ground 'We don't want to tip the Ronco brothers off that we know what they have done, and neither do we want them looking for you.'

'It makes sense' Lindy ventured. Tom flashed her a grateful look. He was more used to hunting down criminals and arresting violent thugs than explaining life-threatening situations to a friend. If he had been talking to anyone else he would have been a lot less tolerant with Yvonne's ungrateful behaviour, but after the weeks they had spent sharing the same house and enjoying quality horse time he had grown to like and respect Yvonne and knew her current reaction was out-of-character. He could empathise with her fear but was feeling a little frustrated that he was on the receiving end of her fury.

'Come on,' Lindy said 'let me show you around and then you will know what to ask Tabitha and Alison to pack for you. Hopefully you won't be here for more than a day or two.'

Without giving her much of a chance to object, Lindy stood up and motioned for Yvonne to join her. As they walked around the apartment, Yvonne's sense of injustice at the way she had been publicly removed from the farm was replaced with trepidation as she took in the fantastic living space Lindy was lending her. This really was a beautiful suite, luxurious and practical, with a better equipped kitchen than her own which she had designed and installed only eight years' earlier, and a gorgeous decking which was giving her ideas about how to upgrade her own outside her flat. For the police to have contacted Kenyon Hall and organised for this to be her safe house when surely she could have stayed at Tabitha's farm or George's apartment above The Abbess Aethelgifu must mean they took the threat of the Ronco brothers seriously and didn't want them to threaten either her or her friends. She also wondered if installing her in such a well-appointed place might mean this wasn't for the day or two Lindy was suggesting.

Tom appeared on the decking, and said 'I've got Tabitha on Facetime, so keep the phone facing this way' he indicated the brick wall behind him. 'Don't tell her where you are, but you can talk her through what you would like her to pack for you? She's in your flat now.'

Yvonne took his phone, trying to keep the picture in the same place he had it. She didn't want to put her friend in danger too. She smiled at the welcome sight of Tabitha's smiling face but could see DS Smalley in the background. 'Hi Tabs, thank you for doing this' she said, attempting to sound upbeat.

'No problem! I've always wanted to go through your knicker drawer' Tabitha winked.

'And me!' Alison pushed her way into view.

That was all it took for Yvonne to start laughing, much to Tom and Lindy's relief. It didn't take long for Yvonne to talk the women through what she needed for a minimum of two days stay in a well-appointed apartment.

'Do you want to talk to them?' she asked Tom when she was ready to hang up.

'Yes, thanks' he said and took the phone from her, again keeping the screen angled so they only had a view of the wall. They talked through the arrangements for handing over Yvonne's bag to the police.

Once Tom had hung up Yvonne asked 'What have you told them is happening?'

'We told them you have been taken into custody in relation to the attack on your brother. As you can see it hasn't occurred to them you are in danger, nor that you are suspected of anything. I know you are upset about the implications for your reputation, but we are trying to keep this as low-key as possible.'

Yvonne sighed. She was tired and wanted to be left alone. Seeing her yawn, Lindy said 'If you need anything, whether it is some company or to ask how to work the television, just press 1234 on this internal telephone and I'll be here for you.'

Smiling weakly, Yvonne said 'Thank you Lindy. Sorry I was bad-tempered earlier.'

Lindy gave her a hug 'You had every reason. It's a big upheaval, but I hope these surroundings make things a little easier.'

Yvonne hugged her back 'They do, thank you. It is very generous of you.'

Tom said 'Do you want to be left alone for a while, or would you prefer one of us to stay here with you?'

Yvonne let go of Lindy, and hugged Tom 'Thank you Tom, I do appreciate what you are all trying to do for me. I think I'd rather be on my own for a bit.'

They both looked out of the window at the sound of another helicopter coming into land. Tom shifted uneasily. 'Um, you won't be on your own for long. Your brother Beau is being flown in. He'll be in the suite next door.'

Chapter 17

Yvonne marched out onto the decking and peered over the clear barrier. She watched as her brother was helped out of the helicopter by a couple of burly men in black, and as he walked, limping but unaided, out of sight below her. Folding her arms across her chest she stood with her back to the garden, glaring at the sliding glass doors of the apartment next door, waiting for a glimpse of the brother she had not seen for twenty years and who had put her in this awful situation. The two decking areas were separated by low black railings, and as soon as Yvonne could see figures behind the glass she stepped over the railings and strode up to the window.

Beau's first sight of his sister after so long was of a furious-looking woman glaring in at him. His two minders had already seen her, and Tom had warned them in advance she would be next door. One of the minders unlocked and slid the huge window open, and both men looked ready to tackle her if she posed a threat. Tom was also ready to catch hold of her, more to save her from harm than to prevent her from dishing it out.

Brother and sister stared at each other. The onlookers held their breath. Behind her Yvonne could hear the helicopter taking off and wondered if it had been the same pilot who had flown her to the venue.

Beau was overcome with emotion. Here was the sister he had never thought he would see again. Once they had been so close, but for twenty years there had been no communication between them. Yvonne had been the first person he had wanted to talk to when he was being held in the police station but he had not been allowed to communicate with her. While he was being treated for the damage she had inflicted to his knee he wanted to message her to tell her about his rehab because Yvonne was always the first person he spoke to about things like that. He knew she would have been traumatised by the scene she had walked into in their cousin's shop and had wanted to comfort her and explain things to her, and being prevented from doing so hurt him almost as much as his knee did. When his wife made it clear their marriage was over, when he was released from prison, when he met someone new and fell in love and married her it was Yvonne he wanted to tell, share his feelings with, ask her advice, be there at their wedding. Even though he had been able to contact some of their other siblings, they had never been on the same wavelength as he and Yvonne had been, and they had not had the same close relationship. As much as he felt grief for the ending of his and Yvonne's relationship, he knew she must have been feeling the same, and that only added to the pain. Seeing her now, even with that furious look on her face, all those feelings flooded their way up through his body and he could feel tears run down his cheeks. Yes she was twenty years older, and her long auburn hair had been cut short and dyed brown with a hint of red, but he recognised that furious expression on her face as being the same as the time their older brother had pinched her bicycle and left it at the nearby playpark overnight to be rained on.

Yvonne saw a smaller, thinner, weaker-looking man than she remembered her brother to be. His head had been shaved and the hair was growing back, but there was an angry red line where a wound had been stapled together clearly visible through the stubble across one side. He was holding himself a little crookedly, which she guessed must have been due to the gaping wound in his side which had hopefully been stitched and was healing. All the feelings of hatred which had consumed her memories of Beau slipped away. She tried to hang onto them, to remember why she had cut herself off from so much of her past, to justify the image she had built of her brother in her mind. But then she saw the tears on his face and rushed towards him. Tom and the security guards moved quickly to block her way, but Beau said 'It's OK, I'm alright' and they stepped away.

Brother and sister hugged each other tightly for a long time, until eventually Beau said 'I'm sorry, but I am in a lot of pain there' and shifted his left side way from her arm.

Yvonne stepped back and put her hands over her face 'Oh Beau, of course you are, I am so sorry! How are you? How bad was the injury?'

Tom signalled to the other two men to step outside with him, and they left Yvonne and Beau to talk, keeping a close eye on them through the windows just in case.

Beau was able to reassure Yvonne that no major organs had been damaged in the knife attack, although he had suffered significant blood loss. The more worrying injury had been the blow to the head which had resulted in swelling and the necessity for a couple of operations, in addition to the operation to repair the stab wound to his side. He showed her the medication he had been discharged from the hospital with, and listed his upcoming appointments, of which there were many. The noise of a helicopter approaching caused them both to stand up from the sofa they had been sitting on and move to the window. Sliding the door open, they stepped out to see who was arriving this time.

'It's Lucy and the girls!' Beau exclaimed. 'My wife and our daughters' he explained to Yvonne, as a woman and two teenagers emerged from the helicopter, assisted by the pilot Yvonne recognised from her flight. 'They had to go into hiding after I was attacked, and we haven't seen each other since that morning. You are going to love them' he said, his face a picture of joy. Yvonne couldn't help but smile too.

'I'll give you all some time alone' Yvonne said, not wishing to intrude on this family reunion.

'No, you must meet them' Beau tried to insist, but Yvonne shook her head and stepped back over the railings to her side of the decking.

'I will, I can't wait to get to know them, but you and I still have a lot to talk about first. It's getting late, and it looks as though we are going to be here for a day or two, so be with your family tonight, and we'll meet up in the morning' Yvonne said gently.

'Of course, you're right. God I have missed you Yvonne' not ready to let her go just yet, Beau leaned over the railings to hug her again, wincing as he did so.

'Go on' Yvonne pushed him away even though she wanted to stay with him and get the answers to all the questions that had been burning up inside her for two decades. 'Your wife and daughters need you, and I am sure you need them. Rest up, and we'll see each other tomorrow.'

Smiling Beau said 'I didn't think you and I would ever be in this position again. I can wait until the morning, but if there is anything you need just come in. You know where I am' he grinned.

Yvonne returned to her apartment with a huge smile on her face. It felt good to be back in contact with her brother.

Somehow while she was outside her belongings had materialised, and unsure how long she was going to be staying at Kenyon Hall, Yvonne decided to put her clothes away in the wardrobe and chest of drawers and put all her wash things and cosmetics in the spacious shower room. Hopefully she could pack everything up again tomorrow, but she didn't want to jinx anything by living out of her suitcase and ending up being away from home for long. She had a quick shower and put on her pyjamas, before heading through to the kitchen area and familiarising herself with its contents. Lindy had provided a few essentials, and Yvonne made herself a cup of tea and some toast. Her mind was whirring, and at the same time she felt a heavy peace wash over her. She curled up on the sofa and drank her tea and ate her toast, missing her dog at the end when there was no one to feed the last piece of crust to. She wondered how Zebedee was, and if she was confused with all the to-ing and fro-ing between Tom's house and her own home and now George's flat. The room was quiet, too quiet, and so for some background noise and distraction Yvonne worked out how to operate the remote control for the huge wall-mounted television and found an episode of The Detectorists. She was soon immersed in gentle humour and intrigue, enjoying the frustration of Andy and Lance as arch-rivals nicknamed 'Simon and Garfunkel' foil another potential search site.

Blearily Yvonne opened her eyes and was momentarily disorientated. There was daylight streaming through the windows and an old episode of Bergerac playing on the television. She sat up on the sofa on which she had fallen asleep, and wondered what the time was. Looking around the room she realised there were no clocks, she had taken her watch off before showering and she couldn't remember where she had left her phone. She stretched, and as the memories of the night before gently seeped back into her mind she felt an enormous sense of calm, despite the disruption to her life and the danger the police believed she was in. She walked barefoot over to the kitchen area and spent a bit of time working out how to make herself a cappuccino in the coffee machine. The morning outside looked cold and frosty, brightly lit and warming up rapidly by a persistent Autumn sun. Yvonne stood behind the glass and sipped her coffee as she gazed out at the tops of the trees beyond the decking, which was all she could see from her vantage point. She was looking forward to seeing her brother again, and to meeting his new family, although she reflected they weren't new if he had teenage daughters. Finishing her drink, she headed back to the bedroom and found her phone where she had left it, plugged in and now fully charged on the bedside table. She was shocked to see the time was after ten o'clock in the morning, and calculated she must have been asleep on the sofa for over twelve hours. She couldn't remember the last time she had slept for so long, and certainly she didn't think she had ever slept so well in a strange place. Quickly she dressed in jeans and a red and blue stripey jumper, slipped her feet into the pair of white moccasins Tabitha and Alison had packed for her, and walked back to the kitchen area. Sliding open the large glass window she stepped out into the sunshine onto the decking, popped over the railings and before she could knock on the corresponding glass door it was slid open by one of Beau's minders who stepped back to allow her through.

'Yvonne!' her brother eased himself up from the large table in the part of the room between the kitchen and living area and greeted her with a big kiss on the cheek and a tight hug. 'Come and meet my wife, Lucy.'

Beau's wife stood up and shyly walked towards them. Yvonne thought she was probably in her late forties, with greying brown hair styled attractively in a shoulder-length bob which curled up at the ends, brown eyes and with soft pink skin. She was a couple of inches shorter than Yvonne, who stepped forward and hugged her new sister-in-law. 'Lucy, I am so pleased to meet you.'

centre of police attention, but before Police Commander Tattersall could answer everyone turned to look up at the noise of the police helicopter flying over the hill behind them.

Tom, who had been transformed into another black clad, weapon-carrying figure while Yvonne was distracted put a hand on her back and said 'Come on Yvonne, we need to go in the helicopter. George will take the dogs back to my house in your car, and Tabitha or Alison will pack some overnight things for you. Message them once you're on board with what you need.'

Before she could process this Yvonne realised that while her attention was on the helicopter, which had now disappeared and must have landed behind the farmhouse in the field she and Tom had been riding in minutes before, the police officers had surrounded her and were shepherding her at a brisk pace towards the landing site. She had little option but to go along with them, and as they walked she saw George reappear, and gather up Stan and Zebedee who happily jumped into her car with him. She glared at him, but he was either deliberately avoiding eye contact or was occupied with securing the two dogs inside her car. The horse owners always left their car keys on a hook inside the kitchen in case the farmer needed to move their cars for some reason, and George sometimes drove her car home from a night out so he knew what he was doing. She wanted to know how he had been recruited to collect the dogs. Although they had never discussed it, she found out that George used to be in the special forces, and several times in the few weeks they had known each other he had been privy to information

Lucy hugged her back, and then turned to introduce her daughters, who both came forward and loosely hugged Yvonne before returning to the table, their eyes watchful of this new relative. Yvonne wondered how much they knew about their father's past, and what they understood about their present situation.

'They are a bit annoyed because they have had their phones confiscated' Lucy confided. 'We can't risk them giving away our location or anything about what's going on. I don't think either of them have spent this much time without their phones since they were given them for their eleventh birthday.'

It was only then that Yvonne realised the girls were twins, identical-looking faces and build but differing hairstyles. Although both with their father's auburn hair.

'We have been trying to introduce them to the fun of playing board games' said Beau, 'but we're failing so far. We have tried Monopoly, obviously, Scrabble and The Traitors board game.'

Yvonne had never watched the television programme with Claudia Winkleman, and wasn't sure what that game would entail, but remembered many family arguments with the other two and thought the girls were probably right to object to playing. She hoped for everyone's sakes they weren't going to be cooped up in the apartment for much longer. While she had clearly enjoyed a good night's sleep despite the unusual bed, she didn't think a couple of teenagers would find the experience as calming as she had done. Beau and Lucy were engaging in a muttered conversation, during which they seemed to reach an agreement. While Lucy went over to speak to the bodyguards, who were surprisingly unobtrusive despite their size, Beau took Yvonne's arm and led her to one of the sofas. A double yell of 'Yes!' came from the table, and his wife and daughters left the apartment with one of the bodyguards, leaving the other standing by the window at the far end of the kitchen.

'Lucy is taking the girls down to the swimming pool. I'm going to stay here and talk to you, but they can so long as a member of the security team is with them' Beau explained. 'I think we can go out and about if we have one or more of these guys with us?'

Yvonne said 'Yes, I can go anywhere within the hotel and grounds, and I haven't been assigned a minder so either I am expendable, or the threat is not so great to me?'

Beau said 'It's probably more because I am the target, but you and my family are not so likely to be identified by anyone who works for the Ronco brothers.'

'So come on then Beau, how on earth did you get mixed up with those two thugs?' Fear was making Yvonne sound more aggressive than she felt.

Giving her a forgotten but familiar look, the one where he knew he had done something wrong but was going to make everything alright again, Beau began to explain. 'I think I had better start at the beginning. Our cousin, Christopher, had a gambling problem. He was an addict. Did you know?'

Yvonne shook her head. 'No, I didn't know that.'

'He was. He would bet on anything. The rise and fall of the gold price, what something would make in auction, how many items he could sell from his shop in a day, whether or not one of our antiques fairs was going to be rained on, Christopher would bet on anything. The day he died was the day I found out he had used our takings on the gate for the last three Sunday markets to bet that our Twickenham shop would lose money that month, and to make sure he won he had …'

'… been bribing our staff not to come into work!' Yvonne finished for him. 'Oh my god, the bastard! No wonder we had that sudden plague of staff sickness there! Well I hope he paid them well because they were all out of a job soon after that when I sold everything and the new owners didn't take them on. How could he mess around with people's livelihoods like that?'

Beau looked down at his hands. 'I have had a lot of time to reflect on his actions, and mine, and the sad thing is that he was behaving as addicts do. He was in debt to the Ronco brothers for an obscene amount of money, and he was frightened. In order to pay off his debts he told them he could get us to sign over our shop to them.'

Yvonne looked shocked. 'How on earth did he think he was going to persuade us to do that?'

Beau swallowed, before saying 'Chris came to see me in an absolute state that morning. It was the first I had heard about his situation, and like you I had no idea about his addiction. But it turns out he started on fruit machines, then betting on horse racing, and in the previous eighteen months or so he had got further and further into debt with the Ronco brothers, and kept making more bets to get him out of the enormous hole he was in. He came to see me because those men had given him an ultimatum. He told me that either you and I willingly signed the shop over to them, or they were going to take it in their own violent way. But that isn't why he died, I promise you Yvonne. I am not a violent man and that thought never crossed my mind.'

Beau looked so pale and frightened Yvonne leaned forward and hugged him as tightly as she dared, taking care to avoid the area on his side she was sure was giving him a lot of pain. Quietly he said 'It is important that you believe me, Yvonne.'

'Of course I do,' Yvonne said, and the calm which had been enveloping her for the past twelve hours was replaced with an overwhelming grief for the years without her brother in her life, and she began to sob. By now Beau was crying too, and brother and sister stayed locked in their distressed embrace for several minutes, oblivious to the presence of Beau's bodyguard in the corner of the room. who was doing his best not to let tears form in his eyes too.

Eventually they drew apart, and Beau fished a handful of tissues out of his pocket, passing some of them to Yvonne and using the rest himself. He said 'I can't tell you what a relief it is to finally be able to talk to you about all of this, Yvonne.'

'Why haven't you?' she asked in a small voice.

'Because once I confessed to murdering Chris you made it very clear you wanted nothing to do with me. I don't blame you; I would probably have done the same thing in your shoes.'

'Tell me what happened' she said, quietly, ready to finally face the conversation she had not wanted to have for such a long time.

Beau sighed as he tried to find the words. Eventually he began 'I'll be honest, your determination not to have any contact with me made it easier. I didn't want to put your life in danger. Christopher owed the Ronco brothers an enormous amount of money, and they wanted it and they didn't care how they got it. That is why Terry's dad was there.'

Yvonne looked questioningly at her brother. He explained 'He was one of their enforcers. Did you know that?'

She nodded and said 'No wonder Terry was always so frightened of him.'

Beau said 'He had good reason to be afraid of him. His dad was evil. He was the one who dealt that final blow. He killed Christopher, not me, but I didn't save him. We knew Terry's dad was going to be paying him a visit, so Christopher and I came up with a plan where I would pretend to beat him up, and then Terry's dad wouldn't need to do anything. Unfortunately he stepped in and smashed Terry's head after I thought I had knocked him out cold. I have never seen anything so horrific before or since.'

Brother and sister were quiet for a few moments, each lost in their own memories of that tragic evening.

Eventually Beau said 'You know he's now in a care home?'

Yvonne nodded. 'I do. Terry came to see me the other day and told me.'

Beau judged it was safe to continue, guessing that Terry had finally told Yvonne the whole story. 'So he also told you he was there? On that evening?'

Yvonne nodded. 'You knew?'

Beau shook his head 'I didn't know at the time, but yes, he contacted me while I was in prison and asked if he could visit me. We have kept in contact ever since, meeting up every now and then either just the two of us or with our families.'

Yvonne understood that by removing herself from the familiar world of friends and family she had also removed herself from the truth. While she was intent on shutting down her past and making a fresh future without them, everyone else had been continuing with their lives and she had missed out on a lot of love and friendship during that time. She was beginning to wonder if she had made a mistake in cutting herself off from everyone and everything she had known, particularly as her life appeared to have come almost full circle.

Resolving to make up for lost time Yvonne stood and asked the remaining minder 'Are we allowed to go for a walk?'

He nodded 'Yes, of course. I'll follow you down.'

The trio left Beau's apartment, which Yvonne now noticed was as beautifully furnished and decorated as hers, but in more practical colours and furniture, presumably with a family in mind rather than a single woman or a couple. As they walked down the corridor to the stairs Yvonne could hear the minder talking on his radio. By the time they had walked down the flights of stairs and reached the cold, white corridor leading to the outside a couple of Kenyon Hall's security personnel had joined them, at a discrete distance, and the five of them walked around the grounds in a sprawling group. Yvonne and Beau talked non-stop, walking with their arms linked and catching up on almost twenty years of adventures and experiences. Yvonne was not surprised to learn which of their siblings had maintained contact with Beau, and it felt good to have that in common with her brother. All six of them were beneficiaries of the trust, along with their parents, set up when Yvonne sold the family business of antiques centres, shops and markets, and none of them needed to work, but in true Parker-family style everyone had been busy in their chosen businesses. Beau had joined their older brother Gabriel working in an antiques auction house, and although both intended to work in the background lotting up the items and making collections and deliveries, eventually the auction owner decided to retire and wanted them to take over. They kept the name of the auction house, and the staff, employed three more auctioneers as the business grew, and carried on as before even though they were now the owners. Gabriel had never wanted to be in the spotlight, and Beau had no intention of going back there.

'Why did no one tell me when you were released from prison?' Yvonne asked curiously. 'I would have thought Amelie would have done. We're in contact.'

'She did ask me if she could, and I think she tried to bring up the subject with you but you shut her down.'

'But if I had known what was going on I would have listened!' Yvonne was not having that. 'I believed you had murdered Christopher, even though I couldn't believe it, but you told me yourself you had done it so why would I think any different?'

Beau shook his head. 'I know, but at the time I thought I had, or at the very least contributed to his death, and I do still believe I was responsible for his death even if I didn't make the final blow. I didn't know until all the evidence had been gathered for my trial that it wasn't me who had killed him, because even though I saw Terry's dad hit him I thought I had knocked him unconscious and it was me who had caused his death. By the time the truth had been found out I felt it was too late. Your husband was being an arsehole, and Amelie and I didn't want to add to your stress. You were doing a great job at managing the family business on your own while finding the best deal for the family with the buyers for all the various parts of it, as well as coping with the divorce. From what Amelie told me you didn't have the headspace to bring my problems into the mix too, after all the Ronco brothers were still hovering in the background at the time. I am sorry if we were wrong, but we were trying not to add to your burden. Would it have made a difference if you had known at the time?'

That brought Yvonne up short. Why on earth would her brother and sister think the information she was now being given would not have helped her. There was so much she could have done for Beau; their estrangement had been devastating for her, and she was sure it would have been worse for him because of all that he was accused of and having to cope with at the time. They had come to a bench by a duck pond and sat down in the sunshine watching the birds swimming, grooming, and diving for food.

'When did you last see Amelie?' Beau asked gently.

Yvonne had to think back. She and her sister would send each other Whatsapp messages, videos and photos now and then, but they hadn't seen each other for many years. She wasn't in touch with any of their other siblings, not because they had fallen out but because they didn't have any reason to contact each other.

'I'm not sure. I visited her over in Norway before Christopher's death. I don't think I have seen her since then.'

Could it really be nearly twenty years since she had any physical contact with her family? Surely not. They had once been so close, meeting up for birthdays, Christmas, Easter, Mothering Sunday, and any other family celebration. She and Beau had rarely gone more than an hour during waking hours without being in contact one way or another. Twenty years since she had last seen a member of her family, other than her sister Catherine on the television. She supposed it must have been that long.

'So what has changed? Why did you end up lying on the ground in a village near where I live with a knife wound in your side and a significant head injury, and a dead body nearby? Were you coming to see me?'

Beau was silent while he thought about how to reply. Yvonne waited, watching as two ducks swam across the pond in perfect unison. Eventually he said 'I wasn't, no. At least not on purpose.'

Yvonne looked at him sharply. 'So what were you doing in Semley? Why did someone try to kill you? And who was the unfortunate person who was killed?'

Beau let out a sigh and leaned forward, his head in his hands. Yvonne looked at his short greying auburn hair, and while she was still trying to take in everything he had told her in the past few minutes she found herself wondering if that was what her hair would look like if she didn't dye it dark brown. It wouldn't be so bad to let it go naturally grey, she decided.

Beau raised his head and looked at her. 'It's a long story, but it all started when Christopher got mixed up with the Ronco brothers, and it didn't end with his death. You know, if I had better legal representation I wouldn't have spent time in prison for murder? It's why I was given such a short sentence, and ended up being released almost immediately.'

'Oh? I heard you had been released on a suspended sentence?'

Beau gave a rueful smile 'I was given a suspended sentence for my part in Christopher's death but had already served that by the time I was released. I'll always have to live with my actions that night, it doesn't matter where I am.'

'It sounds as though the Ronco brothers would have got him sooner rather than later' said Yvonne.

'Possibly. His gambling addiction was so out of control I don't suppose he could have ever got to a stage where he wasn't in huge amounts of debt to them. They are a pair of evil bastards.'

'They haven't really been on my radar' said Yvonne. 'One of the many benefits of living and trading in a rural North Dorset town like Shaftesbury is we don't have enough business to be of interest to people like them. So what happened to his debt when he died?'

Beau shrugged 'For a long time I was worried they were going to try to collect from us, or from his wife, but it appears they simply wrote it off. Possibly because the police were all over it, and also by that time it was entirely interest accrued on interest accrued on interest so they weren't out of pocket by any means. I have never heard from them directly, and I hope you haven't either.'

Yvonne shook her head. 'No, they have never been anywhere near me thank goodness. When Terry came to see me was the first time I had heard of them for a long time.'

'That's a good thing' her brother said.

Yvonne asked 'Once you left prison how did you decide to work with Gabriel? I always thought you hated the idea of working for someone else.'

'Of course I did, while you and I were a team. We had plenty to do with our fairs, markets and antiques centres and I would not have worked all those hours for someone else. But when I was released from prison I had no desire to go back to those insane working hours, let alone the miles we used to clock up on the motorways driving from one place to another.'

'I know what you mean' agreed Yvonne. 'I don't know how we did it.'

Beau said 'I was probably as surprised as you are, but Gabriel came to me saying he had spoken to the owners of the auction house where he had worked since he left school and they were happy for me to join him. Although I am not sure that "happy" is quite the right word; probably "tolerant" of me, but because Gabriel was a good employee for them, and of course they knew my track record with our business, they agreed. It's been great working with Gabriel for all these years, and I probably would never have had this experience if it hadn't been for that terrible night in Chris' shop. I used to really enjoy turning up for work at half-past eight in the morning and leaving at four o'clock in the afternoon, with occasional road trips rather than every day. Of course now we own it my work life is a little different, but I am not going to make the same mistakes I did before and I make sure my family life nearly always comes first. Working with Gabriel is great, although it is not the same as working with you, Yvonne. You and I had the same way of working and thinking, whereas Gabriel and I are very different characters.'

Yvonne said 'That's no bad thing though, is it? I have changed my way of working too and can't imagine going back to those mad and stressful hours we used to do.'

Beau nodded 'We were young and keen, though. Something had to give eventually, although someone's death is an awful way for it to happen. I am older and wiser now, and my family see a lot more of me too. To coin a phrase, I have a good work-life balance. I enjoy running the auction house with Gabriel, and working with antiques dealers and yes, members of the public, and I do still travel but not anywhere near as much as we used to. Did you never remarry?'

'No! I can't imagine marrying again; I have been on my own too long to start sharing my home with anyone else. But there is someone I am enjoying spending time with. I'll introduce you once we're out of here.'

'I look forward to meeting him' said Beau. 'I assume it is a him?'

'Yes' Yvonne laughed. 'I haven't changed that much! He isn't involved in the antiques trade, his name is George, and he does travel quite a bit but that's a good thing because it means we get to miss each other when he's away. I have a horse and a dog now, both of whom keep me busy in Shaftesbury, so I don't tend to go anywhere else. I don't need to travel for pleasure, or business anymore.'

Beau said 'Which brings me to why I was in Shaftesbury. Do you remember a dealer called Bernie Campling who was a regular at our antiques markets, or maybe you came across him since you moved to the town? He used to live here until his recent death. In fact he died on the Green opposite the pub in Semley.'

Yvonne nodded 'Yes, of course I remember Bernie. He was also one of the dealers in my antiques shop.'

'Interesting. Well, Bernie and his sister were in a way responsible for what happened in Christopher's antiques shop. Bernie had begun to steal, for want of a better word, antiques from his fellow dealers, although I think it was his sister who was actually behind it all. To this day I cannot believe the Bernie Campling you and I knew and worked with, father of our childhood friends Nigel and Rufus, would behave in such a deceitful way. But his sister certainly did. Did you ever meet her?'

Yvonne shook her head. 'Not really, only at his funeral and then at the wake. I think it was all a bit overwhelming for her, and she left early on from the wake in Shaftesbury. I still can't believe the revelations of that day. It was a shock to many of the people there, and I think they would all be relieved to hear it wasn't all Bernie'

'I bet she felt overwhelmed' said Beau drily. 'I heard about that. Didn't Nigel and Rufus find where Bernie and his sister were storing all those stolen antiques, and bring some of them to the wake?'

This time Yvonne nodded, realisation dawning. 'So Bernie's sister walked into the courtyard, saw some of the items they had stolen, and walked back out? She must have been horrified when she saw them!'

'Not as horrified as she will have been when the Ronco brothers got wind of where their missing antiques were' said Beau. 'Anyway, I had a delivery to do from our auction house to an address in Semley. I did know you lived nearby and deliberated whether or not to contact you. I must admit I hadn't made a decision about that. I had one of our lads with me, well, when I say 'lad' Gregory was in his sixties and had been working for the auction house since he left school. He was a quiet, hard-working member of the team.'

Yvonne looked away from the pair of ducks, and said sharply 'Was?'

'Yes, was.' Beau sighed heavily. 'Honestly Yvonne, those men are like a cancer in our trade.'

'Who, the Ronco brothers?'

'Yes. Neither Gabriel nor I had any idea, but it turns out that our porter was another of their henchmen, like Terry's dad. Whereas with Terry's dad we all knew he was a vicious thug, Gregory as I said was just one of those people who get on with the job without any fuss or argument. He was the obvious choice to come with me to deliver the mirror and pictures the client had bought in our recent sale, and I didn't give it a second thought. We unloaded and carried everything into the client's house just up the hill from the pub, climbed back into the van to go home, and decided to stop at the pub for a bite to eat. I didn't want to leave the van in the pub's carpark because it is covered in our signwriting, but the client said I could leave it in their drive outside their house.'

'I'm sure it would have been perfectly safe outside the pub' Yvonne commented. 'This isn't London, you know.'

Beau shrugged 'That's what the client said, but I'm not used to this country living like you, and as it turned out it was much, much worse than simply having my empty van broken into.'

Beau took a shuddering breath, and Yvonne put her arm around him 'You don't need to tell me, if you don't want to. It must have been terrifying. There is no need to relive it.'

'No, no I need to tell you' Beau pulled away, and continued 'We walked down the hill, and Gregory was on his phone a lot, until he lost signal, but that wasn't unusual. I can see why you have chosen to live round there, that pub was really great. Everyone was friendly, and we were lucky to get a little table, and enjoyed a very good steak and kidney pie by the way. We didn't hang around, although I could have spent all evening in there, but headed back to the van as soon as we had finished eating. We had just walked past the school and the village shop when Bernie's sister appeared. Of course, I didn't have a clue who she was at the time, but she and Gregory clearly knew each other. Gregory told me he'd catch up with me, so I carried on walking and left them to it. I must admit I wasn't really paying attention because I was thinking about the drive back home, and what the A303 and M3 would be like at that time of the evening. I thought we'd probably be home by half-past nine, which wasn't bad.' He looked at Yvonne, who nodded for him to continue. He was still looking a bit shaky, but Yvonne thought he was looking a little stronger, so she didn't interrupt. 'The next thing all hell broke loose. Two men, who I now realise were the Ronco brothers, Antonio and Luca, emerged from somewhere ahead of me and headed towards Gregory and Bernie's sister. I didn't recognise them immediately because they were out of context. You don't expect to see two London gangsters walking down a quiet country lane in Dorset.'

Yvonne resisted the urge to correct him about the county. It really wasn't the time for a geography lesson about the Dorset and Wiltshire borders.

'The next minute everyone was running hell-for-leather down the road as though they were in a silent movie. No one was making a sound other than the noise of their boots on the road. I could not believe what I was seeing!'

'Oh my god, what did you do?' Yvonne asked, dreading to hear what he was going to say next but wanting to know.

'I ran after them. I didn't have a plan of what I was going to do when I caught up with them, but then right in front of me Luca grabbed hold of Bernie's sister and held a knife to her throat before forcing her to climb into the boot of a car. I didn't even see what was happening to my porter, Gregory, but I guess Antonio must have killed him because when I had my first interview with the police after I had regained consciousness they told me he had been found, dead.'

'Surely there must have been other witnesses? There are always people outside that pub either sitting on the benches or parking their cars and vans?'

'There were, but apparently no one else saw or heard a thing' Beau shrugged. 'I haven't been back there, but there were a lot of vans and cars parked opposite the pub, and a few people sitting on the table and chairs outside the door, as well as others on the Green. No one would have thought twice about the sound of a car boot slamming shut, and everything happened so quickly I don't suppose Gregory had time to shout for help. Bernie's sister certainly didn't resist once Luca showed her the knife. Anyway, I don't think either Luca or Antonio had noticed me, even though they walked past me a few seconds earlier, but they certainly noticed me by the time I reached the Common. I tried shouting for help, but I couldn't find my voice. Have you ever had that?' Yvonne shook her head. 'It's awful, like being in one of those stress nightmares where you are running through treacle. The last thing I remember is Luca running at me and feeling this incredible pain in my side. The police have since told me there is a boot print on my head, so one of those two bastards stamped on my head too.'

'Oh Beau, you are lucky to be alive' breathed Yvonne, putting her arm around him again. This time he didn't pull away.

'I am, and I intend to stay that way. But that is why you are here, and why my lovely Lucy and girls are here. I can identify Luca as the kidnapper of Bernie's sister, and as my attacker too, and I can place Antonio at the scene, even though I didn't see him kill Gregory. The Ronco brothers know you are my sister, they know you gave evidence at my trial and were a witness to Christopher's death, and they know where you live. There is no way I want you to be used as leverage by them to get at me, and we know they don't have any qualms about killing members of someone's family to get their message across. Look what happened to Bernie.'

Brother and sister sat side-by-side on the bench with their arms around each other for the first time in many years, at peace with each other, united by the terrors they had witnessed, both feeling a sense of calm neither had felt for a very long time, watching the ducks busily getting on with their lives on the water and the bank.

Their three security guards kept watch, alert to any movement in the surrounding area, watching for the slightest sign of attack.

Chapter 18

Beau and Yvonne parted in the corridor outside their temporary front doors, and Yvonne walked through into her apartment and threw herself onto one of the sofas. Beau's daughters had sent him a message to say they had loved swimming and wanted to spend the afternoon watching a trilogy of films in the apartment, and although Yvonne was invited to join them and wanted to meet everyone properly, she declined. She had a lot to process and knew she wouldn't be good company. She desperately wanted to talk to George about it all, and although she would have preferred to have him here on the sofa next to her, she did the next best thing and called him on video chat. When he answered she burst out laughing, because instead of George's face appearing Zebedee was looking quizzically at the screen.

George's handsome smiling face appeared 'Hello!'

'Oh George that was so funny! Is she alright?'

'She's absolutely fine. Stan is here too, hang on' George angled the phone so that Yvonne could see both Stan and Zebedee sitting next to each other.

'Where are you?' Yvonne asked.

'We're in my flat. I offered to take Stan for Tom, because he is working on some special mission which I assume has something to do with your situation and I thought Zebedee might appreciate the company. The pair of them are being as good as gold. The three of us went for a run this morning over in Wardour Woods, and they have been sleeping ever since. We'll probably take a stroll later on and end up at The Ship Inn.'

'That's really kind of you George, thank you. Are you able to get any work done?'

'Don't worry about that, I'm spending all day on the computer, so these two are giving me a good reason for leaving my desk and getting some fresh air and exercise. How are you? I know you can't tell me much about where you are or anything.'

Yvonne gave him a look. 'Tom told me you are in on all this, George. You probably know more than I do at this stage.'

George had the grace to look a little abashed. Yvonne saved him from trying to explain 'Don't worry, I know you can't tell me anything' she smiled at him.

Earnestly he said 'I will do, as soon as this is all over. How are you coping?'

'Beau and I have had a really good chat, and things are a lot clearer now. It feels good to be back on speaking terms with my brother, and I understand a lot more than I did this time yesterday. Oh sorry!' Yvonne stifled a yawn. 'I have suddenly come over all tired, which is ridiculous because I must have slept for about twelve hours last night.'

'That's a good sign, your bed must be comfortable' said George.

Yvonne laughed 'I didn't make it as far as the bed; I fell asleep on this sofa!'

She yawned again, and George said 'It looks as though you're about to do it again. I'm really pleased you phoned me. I have been worried about you.'

Yvonne glowed inside. It felt good to have someone out there who was concerned for her welfare. She reassured him 'Please don't, I am being very well looked after here, and now that I know Zebedee is not missing me one little bit I can relax.'

George smiled 'I wouldn't go so far as to say she isn't missing you, but she is certainly happy here with me and Stan. I miss you' he said.

Yvonne was a little taken aback by the emotion in his voice, and suddenly felt a rush of love for him. She would be very glad when all this horror was over, and she could return to her quiet life as an antiques dealer and horse rider. 'I miss you too, that's why I called. I want to tell you everything that is happening, but it doesn't feel right doing it this way. Hopefully all of this will be over very soon, and we can get back to normal whatever that is.'

George laughed 'It has been one thing after another since we met hasn't it!'

They said their goodbyes and hung up. Yvonne made herself comfortable on the sofa expecting to fall asleep even though it was the middle of the afternoon and she was fully dressed, but her head was full of everything Beau had revealed that morning. She wished she had paid more attention to Bernie's sister at his funeral, but she really had not been a noticeable woman, in fact Yvonne was struggling to recall her face. She wondered how

Nigel and Rufus were coping with the discovery of their aunt's body so soon after their father's funeral.

Taken by a sudden urge she sat up and messaged her sister, Amelie. There is only an hour's time difference between Britain and Norway, and within minutes Amelie was on the phone.

'That was good timing, Yvonne. I was having a quick tea break when your message came through. How are you?'

Yvonne sank back into the cushions and enjoyed a long phone conversation with her favourite sister. Amelie was hugely relieved to discover that her younger sister and brother had finally healed their rift, and that Yvonne was now up-to-speed with all that had been going on in Beau's life. She confessed it had been very difficult to be in the middle of the two of them and apologised for her part in the emotional distance between herself and Yvonne. Although Yvonne had been feeling upset that Amelie had kept so much from her which could have brought her and Beau back together many years earlier, she knew that the responsibility for the division lay solely with herself and was grateful that her sister felt as happy as she did to be back in proper contact again. They ended the call promising to speak again soon and meaning it.

Next, feeling on a roll, Yvonne phoned her eldest brother Gabriel. As soon as he answered the phone she knew she had made a mistake, and this wasn't going to be the feel-good reunion she had enjoyed with Beau and Amelie. It wasn't that Gabriel was an unpleasant person, or that he didn't like her, it was just that he was not someone she would choose as a friend if they weren't related. After a few minutes of stilted conversation, they both felt they had caught up on each other's lives as much as they needed to, and politely hung up without the promises of being in touch again soon that had ended her conversation with Amelie.

Wondering if it was a good idea, especially after that last conversation, Yvonne contemplated her younger sister, Nicole, but as she wasn't sure where in the world she was living these days and therefore what time zone she was in, it wasn't long before Yvonne had talked herself out of it. Briefly she thought about contacting her youngest sister Catherine, but as they had never been particularly close she felt no guilt about deciding not to. Three in one day was enough to be going on with.

Her phone pinged with a message from Lindy 'Hi Yvonne, just checking in. How are you? I'm around if you want some company.'

Now that sounds like a great idea, thought Yvonne. She messaged back 'My place or yours?'

Lindy replied with a laughing emoji and said 'Come over to mine! Turn left and keep walking and come on up!'

Yvonne did as she was told and found herself at the end of the corridor where there was a lift. She pressed the button, the lift doors opened, and she stepped in. Looking at the choice of buttons she pressed the only up option. A short ride upwards and the doors opened onto a beautifully appointed penthouse suite.

'Wow Lindy! This is gorgeous!' Yvonne looked in wonder at the apartment located in a glass turret. It wasn't a big area, and there didn't appear to be an outside space like the one she was staying in, but when the grounds of Kenyon Hall were yours she supposed you probably didn't need anything else.

Lindy beamed 'Thank you, although this isn't mine. You know I sold my cottage in Shaftesbury last month and have been temporarily living with my parents over in Somerset, at Kenyon House. I admit I jumped at the chance to move out from there even after only a few days and am staying here for as long as you and Beau have to be here, and I am not going to complain. Look at those views!' The two women gazed out over the trees, orangery, walled garden, outdoor swimming pool, and fields. 'I bet you are missing your dog and horse aren't you?'

Yvonne said 'I suppose I am, but I haven't really had time to think about it. George was really sweet and put Zebedee on to our Facetime call earlier. We don't spend much time apart, but she looked happy. He has taken on Tom's dog Stan too.'

'He's a keeper' Lindy winked.

'Maybe' Yvonne was non-committal. 'It is good of you to give up your freedom too. Let's hope it isn't for too long.'

'That's OK, it's not the same as you and your brother and his family. I work here anyway. The only difference for me is I am not going back to sleep and eat at Mum and Dad's, which isn't a bad thing, and I can still go and see Astrid. It's tempting to stay on here after you and your brother go back home to be honest.'

Yvonne asked 'Are you looking for somewhere new to buy?'

'I am looking for somewhere, and I definitely want to stay in Shaftesbury. I love living there, and it's close to Astrid. I only sold my cottage because my marriage broke-up, which was sad but not a bad thing in the end.'

Yvonne wasn't sure if Lindy was referring to her home or her marriage but didn't like to ask. They had only recently become friends, having known each other for many years to speak to at the livery yard and occasionally riding out in the same group. She said 'Yes I love living in Shaftesbury too. Recently I did consider selling up and moving away, but I like being able to go for walks on quiet country lanes and footpaths with Zebedee for half an hour or two hours from my door and going to have a cuppa in one of our cafes or a glass of wine in a pub nearby. There is nearly always someone I know to talk to.'

'Exactly that!' said Lindy. 'Divorce is a lonely experience, made easier by the people I saw regularly while it was going on, many of whom I don't know their name, but they always say hello when we meet on Park Walk or on the High Street.'

'Is your ex-husband staying in Shaftesbury?' Yvonne had never met Lindy's husband, and didn't know the circumstances of the break-up, but knew how difficult it would have been if she and her husband had stayed in the same town.

'No, thank goodness.' The bitterness in Lindy's voice was strong. 'He and the woman he was cheating on me with have gone away. I will never see either of them again. Come on, let's have a drink. White wine?'

Lindy and Yvonne sat on a curved sofa in one window of the glass turret, the sofa curving in the opposite direction to the glass, and watched the sun go down over the trees as they compared notes on their respective ex-husbands. Yvonne had never talked about her marriage breakdown in detail with anyone else, because until she moved to Shaftesbury she hadn't had any female friends who were not also work colleagues, and Beau would have been the only one of her siblings she would have talked to but of course she wouldn't have anything to do with him by then. Her husband hadn't cheated on her or been violent or anything like that, but he hadn't been there for her, and she knew she hadn't been there for him. They simply drifted apart through lack of effort with the stress of Beau's conviction and having to sell the Parker family business, but their divorce was still acrimonious.

Yvonne said 'I have never seen my ex-husband since he left either, and I don't want to now. We were vile to each other at the end.'

Lindy said 'I suppose that means you still had feelings for each other, which must be a good thing, surely? By the time our decree nisi came through I didn't have any feelings for my ex, other than not wanting to see him with his girlfriend every time I left the house.'

'How long had you been married?'

Lindy said 'Nine years. He was my third husband. I'm not planning on having a fourth.'

'Three? Blimey!' the wine was dulling Yvonne's filter and she said it more loudly than was polite. Lindy laughed at the look of horror on Yvonne's face and topped up her glass for her.

'It's not as bad as it sounds!' Lindy tried to defend her marital decisions. 'The first one was when I was nineteen and over by the time I was twenty-one. The second one I was twenty-five and he was a couple of years younger, and that lasted about ten years before we went our separate ways, and this one I was forty and he was ten years older when we met. I really thought we'd grow old together.'

Yvonne didn't know what to say, or indeed if she needed to say anything. She sipped her wine and said nothing.

'What's going on?' Lindy sat up, looking out of the window.

Yvonne followed her gaze. 'That doesn't look good.'

Half a dozen black clad figures were running through a formal garden carrying guns. As the two women watched a man ran out of the trees behind them and quickly turned and ran back the way he had come. Over to the right they could see someone else ducking in and out of the trees.

'Oh my god, look over there!' Lindy pointed to their far right. Yvonne looked to where she was indicating, and from their high vantage point they could see over the wall of the secret garden. A couple were strolling along one of the white gravel paths inside, oblivious to the drama going on just metres from them.

Both women checked their phones, but no one had sent them a warning or alert. Lindy started to pace in front of the windows, trying to keep tabs on all the people on the ground outside.

'I have to admit' Yvonne said as she placed her wine glass carefully on the glass table in front of them 'that until this moment I have not been taking the threat too seriously.'

Lindy looked at her 'What? We're talking about the Ronco brothers. Those men have already been responsible for the murder of two people and the attempted murder of your own brother in the last week. You don't think the police would have gone to these lengths to keep you and your brother and his family safe in my own hotel if there wasn't a serious threat to your life?'

Yvonne said 'Things like this just don't happen to people like me.'

Lindy gave a harsh laugh 'Yvonne they obviously do. Look at what is happening now, out there!'

They hadn't seen anyone for a few minutes or heard anything although Yvonne guessed the soundproofing on the turret was effective considering its location. The couple were still strolling along the paths, pointing to plants and flowers, unaware of the potentially deadly activity going on outside of their little piece of paradise.

Lindy spun round as the sound of the lift being operated could be heard. 'Shit' she said under her breath and began to move towards the doors.

For the first time since she had arrived at Kenyon Hall Yvonne wished one or more of the minders and security guards were with them. She had found their nearby presence claustrophobic, but now she missed their comforting protection. She didn't know how Lindy knew whoever was coming up in the lift was a danger, but she wasn't hanging around to find out. Lindy picked up speed and ran past the lift and up a staircase Yvonne had not noticed before. They were to one side of the lift, going up and over the kitchen area, and following the theme of the room were all glass, including the bannisters, the safety panels and the stair treads. Yvonne was disorientated by the experience of appearing to walk over the top of the hob, sink and work surfaces, and tried to focus on Lindy's legs as she ran up the steps ahead of her. By the time they reached the top Yvonne thought she was going to be sick, but there was no time to stop because the lift doors were pinging open. Lindy was running along the glass mezzanine floor towards a door which Yvonne assumed led back to the main building. Terrified by the sounds of people coming fast up the stairs she had just climbed, Yvonne raced after Lindy, who was already through the door which had swung shut behind her.

Yvonne could hear shouting from whoever was chasing her, and managed to pull open the door and rush through before they caught her.

She was in a corridor which in blinding contrast to the glass turret they had left was dark with no natural light. Surrounded by infinite blackness Yvonne could hear the running sounds of Lindy fading into the distance, but unable to see where she was going after a few seconds she froze to the spot. The door opened behind her, flooding the way forwards with light, and Yvonne didn't need to think twice. She ran as fast as she could following her friend. The people behind her were running too, and she could hear someone shouting her name. She thought it was Lindy and coming to the end of the corridor she hurled herself down the stairs at the end, using the wooden bannisters to jump two and three steps at a time.

She was terrified, and her lungs were burning. She was regretting the wine. At the bottom of the stairs she couldn't hold it in any longer, and collapsed onto all fours, throwing up everything she had eaten and drunk that day onto the polished wooden floorboards. Even with the noise of the people behind her now jumping over the top of her and running past, she couldn't stop being sick. She tried to count how many pairs of legs ran by, but a fresh bout of vomiting combined with the difficulty of catching her breath meant she had no idea other than there were far more people than just a couple of brothers.

'Here' a male voice said, as Tom squatted beside her and handed her a wad of tissues which she used to wipe her mouth. He helped her to sit on the bottom step. 'It's all over now. Breathe out, now breathe in, and out, there you go.'

The sounds of shouting made them both freeze and look in the direction of the noise. 'Can you stand up?' Tom asked as he put his arm around her waist and helped her to her feet. 'Now don't throw up on my boots, or my boss will put me on a charge for having dirty uniform' he teased.

Despite her fear Yvonne gave him the ghost of a smile. 'Keep breathing out, and in, out and in' he said as he steered her to a door under the stairs. 'We'll be out of harm's way in here.'

Tom helped her into the room, and over to a sofa against a wall just inside the door. Yvonne slumped into the depths, but unable to stop her legs from shaking she shifted onto her right hip and tucked her legs under her on the deep red plush to hide them and leant against the arm of the sofa. She looked around at the ornate décor of a grand dining room, unconvinced by Tom's words. The room was huge, with at least three other doors opening into it, and a bank of windows along two walls. She could see the stone balustrades of a terrace outside. Plenty of access for the Ronco brothers and their killing team to reach her.

'Oh my god, where is Beau and his family?' she asked, feeling a fresh wave of nausea and trying to stop it from overwhelming her. That was the last time she was ever going to drink wine. She really couldn't throw up in these expensive surroundings. 'We have to go and save them!'

One of the doors opened, and Yvonne thought she was going to die from terror long before a knife or bullet hit her. It took her a few moments to recognise Police Commander Jemima Tattersall, closely followed by Detective Sergeant Bridget Smalley. They went into a huddle with Tom, murmuring so Yvonne could not hear, although she was trying to interpret the numerous hand gestures. More police came through the door, more whispering and unintelligible radio noise was added to the mix. Eventually the other police left the way they had come, and Tom walked over to Yvonne with Commander Tattersall and DS Smalley.

The Commander sat next to her, while DS Smalley and Tom stayed standing in front of her. 'We have a medical team coming into see you shortly. They will check you over, and if they feel it is necessary they will take you to hospital.'

Yvonne had no idea how dreadful she looked, with her washed out skin, huge dark circles under her eyes, and vomit running down her front. Her body was shaking, not just her legs. In a weak voice she admitted 'It's only alcohol. What just happened? Is Lindy alright? My brother?'

Tom answered 'Beau and his family are absolutely fine. We have a team with them now, and they will be able to go home, as will you. They know nothing about what has just happened, as is the case for the guests here at Kenyon Hall. It's all over Yvonne, it's all over.'

Again Yvonne jumped as a door opened, and three people in green jumpsuits appeared, one of them carrying a large bag. 'Here are the medics' the Commander said. 'We'll leave you in their capable hands. I will come and find you later, and we'll talk.'

Frustrated, Yvonne gave in to the endless questions of the medical team and tried to convince them she was absolutely fine, she had drunk too much before running halfway around the hotel, and should be allowed to go and see her brother and Lindy. Apparently this wasn't going to be possible as Beau and his family were already being taken home, and in a daze Yvonne allowed herself to be helped up from the sofa, and taken to her suite to pack her things, ready to leave for Angel Lane.

Chapter 19

George was waiting for her when Tom escorted her back to her temporary apartment. Yvonne had given up asking questions and was feeling exhausted by the events of the past few hours. Had it only been yesterday she had been riding through the fields with Tom, enjoying the last of the Autumn sun?

'I might have known you'd be here already' Yvonne snapped when she saw George standing by the open door to the decking. 'One day I would like to be the first to know something, not the last.'

She went to the bedroom and the sight of her packed bag sitting on the bed made her even more furious. Aware of how ungrateful she was being she tore off her vomit-stained top and pulled a clean one out of the bag, not caring that Tom would see her half-naked. She flung the top she had been wearing into the bin and searched in the bag for her toothbrush and toothpaste. Marching into the bathroom she was pulled up short by the sight of herself in the mirrors. There were a lot of mirrors, and she couldn't escape the image of an old woman staring wildly back at her. Horrified, she went over to the sink and splashed cold water over her face, before cleaning her teeth and running her hands through her hair. She tried smiling into the mirror, standing up straighter, taking a deep breath and letting it out slowly. Eventually she decided she looked more like herself and walked with less temper and more humility back into the bedroom to repack her bag, and carry it through to where George and Tom were waiting for her.

'Sorry' she said, 'Thank you. Both of you.'

Relieved that they were not going to be yelled at again, George stepped forward to take her bag and Tom opened the door. 'George is going to take you home, and if it's alright someone will come later to talk to you.'

'Will it be you?' Yvonne asked.

'Possibly, if you would like me to. Commander Tattersall and DS Smalley need to talk to you too, and if they are able they will come tonight, but if not they will speak with you tomorrow.'

'I want to know what just happened' said Yvonne. 'Are we really all safe?'

'Yes, you are all safe.'

Yvonne's voice hardened. 'What. Just. Happened?'

'We are still sorting it all out. I don't want to give you half an answer at this stage, so please, bear with us. We still have a lot to do.' said Tom. 'Beau and his family are already in a car heading home, and I am sure he will be in touch as soon as they are back. You don't need to worry about them, I promise you.'

Begrudgingly Yvonne said 'Alright, thank you. Shall we go?'

George nodded, and led the way down the corridor, and down the flights of stairs to his car parked outside. Yvonne was still shaking when she got into the Aston

Martin and had a little difficulty pushing the seatbelt buckle into the clip. George took it and pushed it in for her, and then leant across to hug her. Wrapped in his arms she felt safe for the first time in hours, and clung onto his warm solid body. With her head buried in the curve where his neck met his shoulder she took a few shaky breaths before whispering 'I thought I was running for my life.'

George felt helpless and hugged her slightly trembling body tighter. 'I know' he murmured. 'I know. It's all over now. We're going home where Zebedee will be ecstatic to see you. We can drive down to see Toby, and you can have some quality horse time with him to get your feet back on the ground. Even though you have been through a terrifying ordeal, everything back home is the same as before you left, you'll see. In less than an hour everything will be calm and familiar and normal. Tomorrow the antiques shop will open to the woman with the weeing terrier, Sylvia will fly in looking for Jack who will be trying to hide from her in vain, and Rob will have made something delicious for us all to eat. I am so sorry you have been put in danger, but it really is all over now.'

Yvonne nodded and released her grip. Pulling slowly away from him she looked into his eyes and smiled weakly. 'Thank you' she whispered.

'Come on, let's go home. I left Zebedee and Stan in my flat. No doubt they have made my bed their own. Let's go and get them.'

Yvonne sank back into the seat, reluctant to let go of his hand so he could drive the car but even though it was an automatic he did need his left hand some of the time, and appreciated the fact she was being driven rather than flown home. That was another experience she didn't want to repeat.

In the end they drove straight to see Toby. They stopped on the road outside so as not to disturb the owners in the farmhouse next to the yard, and by the light of the full moon they leant on the wooden fence, careful to avoid the electric tape which ran along the inside and watched as Toby and his herd grazed together. All eight horses were in the same part of the field, and edged their way towards Yvonne and George without lifting their heads and continued to eat the grass as they took one step after another in their direction. After a couple of minutes Toby gave a low snort and picked up his pace, arriving at the fence and nudged Yvonne's outstretched hand.

'Sorry Toby, I don't have anything for you' she said.

'I do' said George, as he pulled some horse treats out of his pocket. 'Since I met you my pockets are filled with pony nuts, dog treats and poo bags, and I don't even own a horse or a dog!'

It was almost midnight by the time they drove back to Yvonne's home, and after a short discussion Yvonne ran up the external wooden stairs to her flat while George left his car in her courtyard and walked to collect the dogs from his home less than five minutes away. It wasn't long before the clatter of dog claws on the spiral stairs down to her kitchen announced their arrival, and George wasn't far behind.

Yvonne was opening cupboards and the fridge. 'I am absolutely starving and can't find anything to eat! I think I threw everything up all over the floor at Lindy's hotel.'

Smiling, George produced a bag containing milk, bread, cheese and eggs. 'Would you like marmite and toast or an omelette?'

'You are a star' said Yvonne. 'Toast and marmite please.'

While Yvonne sat on the sofa cuddling Zebedee, and Stan inspected the dog toy box before choosing a long toy snake which he proceeded to throw up in the air and run around the kitchen chasing until he realised toast was being made, at which point he sat by George's feet watching in the hope of crumbs.

Yvonne could feel her body relax and her mind clear as she and George spent half an hour eating their toast, drinking their tea, and watching the dogs, while chatting about this and that to do with George's work.

Eventually Yvonne said 'I don't suppose anyone is coming to talk to me tonight, so we might as well go to bed. Are you staying?'

'If you'd like me to.'

All four of them climbed the spiral stairs, and while Yvonne and George took it in turns to use the bathroom, Stan and Zebedee settled down together in Zebedee's large grey fluffy donut-shaped bed on the floor.

Yvonne thought she would fall asleep quickly, but once George climbed into her bed next to her she found she had other ideas. Touching, kissing, caressing each other's bodies, murmuring endearments, lost in their own world under the covers, neither heard the message alert on Yvonne's phone.

Sunlight streaming through the window across her eyes awoke Yvonne. George was fast asleep next to her, and when she looked over she saw two dogs watching her from their bed. Carefully she slid out of bed so as not to disturb him, picked her phone up from the bedside table, and beckoned to the dogs to follow her down the stairs. She could have sworn they tiptoed after her, their usually noisy claws making tiny tap tap tapping sounds. She filled the kettle and switched it on as she passed, unlocked the back door to let the dogs out to the courtyard, filled a couple of dog bowls with food and made herself a coffee. She pulled on a pair of wellies by the door, slipped her phone into the pocket of a long riding coat which she wrapped around her naked body, and carried the mug outside. The dogs let themselves back in and had finished their breakfast before she made it to the bottom step of the wooden external staircase. The three of them climbed the steps, and Yvonne padded along her decking to the area she called her Treehouse, where she settled down on the large teak swing seat, nestled in the wine-coloured cushions, and watched the Autumn sun rise, zipped into the long coat and holding her coffee mug in both hands. The dogs busied themselves with exploring the greenhouse, decking and planters while Yvonne sipped her coffee, gazing over the rooftops of her little part of Shaftesbury in the sunshine.

Finishing her mug she placed it on the wide arm of the swing seat and delved into her pocket for her phone. There was a message from Tom. 'Hope you're OK?'

Yvonne replied 'All good, thank you. Stan is here with me.'

Seconds later he was ringing her. 'Hi Tom' she said quietly, aware that George was asleep just feet away inside her bedroom.

'How are you this morning?' he asked.

'Relieved yesterday is over.' There was a lot more Yvonne could say about the past thirty-six hours, but she didn't want to lose the mellow feeling of sitting on her swing seat in the sunshine.

'I'm sure you are. The Commander wants to come and see you this morning.'

'Good, because I want to see her. I have a lot of questions.'

'I don't know what time she is planning to see you, but you'll be at home all morning?'

'I am going to go to the livery yard to see Toby and prove to everyone I haven't been arrested for trying to murder my own brother' Yvonne said a little more coldly than she intended. 'Hopefully she's not going to turn up at the yard again.'

Tom gave a laugh down the line. He could imagine Yvonne's face. 'I'm sure she won't. Do you mind if I join you? I could pick Stan up from there if you like?'

Yvonne would have preferred not to see Tom for a while, because she was still annoyed about the way she felt he had tricked her into riding out with him before the entire Dorset and Wiltshire police force turned up in front of her fellow livery-owners and dragged her away, but she knew she needed some perspective and he was only acting to save her from harm. Taking a deep breath she said 'Of course. It will be good to see you away from all that shit we were in yesterday.'

They said their goodbyes, and Yvonne stood up, collected her empty mug and walked down the wooden steps, followed by the dogs to her kitchen. She made George a cup of coffee, and when she climbed the spiral stairs to her bedroom she didn't creep around, feeling sure George would want to wake up and get ready for his day too.

As she suspected he was awake. 'Thank you!' he said when he saw the coffee. 'How are you feeling this morning?'

'Much better than last night' she smiled at him, loving the way his dark hair was ruffled from sleep. 'I'm going to have a quick shower and then I'm heading out to see Toby. I'll take the dogs, and Tom can have Stan back.'

Watching her naked body disappear into the bathroom George debated joining her in the shower, but when she closed the door behind her he decided he probably wouldn't be welcome and settled into the pillows to enjoy his coffee instead.

They were ready to leave at the same time, and kissed goodbye in the courtyard, before driving their separate cars in different directions, each with a smile on their lips and the horrors of the day before dulled by their night together.

Chapter 20

When Yvonne arrived at the yard Tom was already there. He had brought his horse Ben up from the field and was brushing him in preparation for riding out.

'Hello boy!' he said as he and Stan greeted each other with equal enthusiasm. Yvonne gave up being cross with him, because how could you stay angry with someone who loved his dog that much, and whose dog clearly loved him? 'How are you feeling this morning? Did you manage to get any sleep?'

Yvonne couldn't prevent the corners of her mouth turning up into a smile at the memory of George a few hours earlier but she didn't explain, and simply said 'Yes, it was good to back in my own bed. You're up and about early. You can't have been in bed for long either?'

'I haven't been to bed yet. I'm going to take these two out for half-an-hour or so, grab a shower and some breakfast, and head back to the station. The Commander is planning to come to see you at about eleven o'clock, if that suits you?'

'Yes, the sooner the better' Yvonne replied. 'I need some answers.'

'Of course you do.' Suddenly Tom stepped forward and gave her a hug. 'You are one of the bravest people I know. It's good to see you looking so well this morning. I was worried about you yesterday.'

'I was worried about me yesterday' she replied, but before she could say any more or ask any questions Tom turned and put on his riding hat.

'I'd better get a move on or I'll be late, and I don't want to delay the Commander, for your sake as much as hers.' With a wave he led Ben out towards the fields, Stan realising where they were going and rushed to be in front. Zebedee looked back at Yvonne, who shook her head and indicated the car.

'Come on Zeb, we'll leave them to it today.'

It was still early in the morning when she returned home, and after making herself another coffee she wandered through to the shop to check the book for the takings for the day before, and then walked through the rooms, revelling in seeing her business looking so good. Raymond's stock was proving to be popular with the customers, and she could see he had a couple of large empty spaces on his stand. No doubt he would be replenishing his stock during the day. Although she did not like the colour, she had to admit that Jack's painted wall did highlight the objects in the cabinets in front of it, but she hoped he would agree with almost everyone else and repaint it a lighter colour before too long. Rachael Hall's stand was looking beautifully presented, and Yvonne inspected some of the vintage decorative lamps she had displayed on an old cast iron table. She sat down on a chaise-longue which had been re-covered in a pink flowery material and sent a message to Lindy. The police had assured her Lindy was alright, but Yvonne thought it odd that she hadn't already been in touch and was worried the Ronco brothers had caught up with her and although the police undoubtedly rescued her and caught them, perhaps they had injured her and she was in hospital.

While she was waiting for Lindy to respond, an unknown number flashed up on her phone. She hesitated before deciding to answer it. Normally she never answered unknown numbers, but she wondered if Lindy had needed to use a different telephone to answer her message. As usual she waited for the person at the other end to speak first, so she could hang up if it was a cold caller without engaging with them.

'Hello? Yvonne?' a man's voice asked.

'Beau?'

'Yes, how are you this morning?'

Yvonne was so happy to hear her brother's familiar voice on the phone she forgot to reply and smiled as the warm feeling of being back in contact with her brother washed over her. His worried voice snapped her out of her reverie.

'Yvonne? Are you there?'

'Yes, yes sorry!' she said. 'I'm so happy we are talking again. That was all a bit dramatic yesterday, but I'm fine, how are you and your family?'

They chatted as though they had never been estranged in that relaxed way siblings who see each other regularly talk to each other, almost a secret code no one else has access to, knowing what the other one is talking about without the necessity of complete sentences. They didn't discuss what had happened the day before, instead they arranged a date to meet-up. Beau was keen to bring his family down to Shaftesbury, and Yvonne was eager to meet them properly in more relaxed circumstances than their first encounter. They ended the call like old times with 'Speak later!'

Yvonne stayed where she was for several minutes, enjoying the liberating feeling of being back in touch with her brother. It had been a tough few years while they had been estranged, and although she knew she was in a good place now, and that their work/life balance had been out of kilter when they were together, she revelled in the loving emotions which washed over her in waves, feeling knots in her shoulders she hadn't been aware of dissipate, and the soppy smile permanently spread across her face.

Rousing herself she decided to open the shop a little earlier than advertised and spent the next few minutes switching on lights and the computer, and unlocking the doors. First in was a lovely couple who never bought anything but always enjoyed browsing. Next was a husband in a desperate search for a birthday present for his wife. To Yvonne's astonishment his gaze alighted on the box of random old keys, and minutes later he walked out with a grin on his face and thirty rusty keys which he planned to thread onto a red ribbon and present to his wife who apparently loved old keys. Yvonne wasn't sure if that was going to be the present the wife wished for her thirtieth birthday, but he assured her that combined with a bottle of champagne from Shaftesbury Wines, and a day trip to Longleat Safari Park, she would be very happy with his gifts.

Jack Perry Ritchie appeared, looking handsome in a blue shirt which complemented his black curly hair and blue eyes. 'Yvonne! You're back! What on earth has been going on?' he asked, worry creasing his forehead.

'Yvonne! How are you? We missed you yesterday. I hope everything is alright?' Rob Kemp came to join them at the counter and gave her a brief hug. As a general rule Yvonne didn't hug her fellow antiques dealers, but Rob was an exception and had never paid any attention to her stand-offish body language. She hugged him back, appreciating the gesture and his concern.

She smiled and reassured them. 'Everything is fine. In fact it is better than fine. Everything is very good. I will tell you all about it, I promise, but there are still a few loose ends which need to be tied up. Thank you for holding the fort yesterday. How was it?'

Rob and Jack launched into a complicated story about the lady with the leaky terrier which involved another shop owner running into Angel Lane Antiques and strongly remonstrating with the woman about allowing her dog to cock his leg all over a display of cushions which had been piled up on the floor in front of a table where matching throws were neatly folded. The angry shop owner had been joined in his diatribe by another business owner who happened to be looking for more cutlery for her café. She joined in with the dressing down of the dog owner because the terrier had pee'd on a chair leg the same day and the owner had been seen rushing out onto the High Street without informing the staff let alone apologising or offering to clean it up.

'She tried to deny it was her dog, but they weren't having it' laughed Rob. 'Jack and I just stood and watched as they made it very clear to her that she was never to walk into their business premises again either with or without her dog.'

Jack nodded 'They were an impressive team. They both stressed how they welcome dogs onto their premises but because of her behaviour they had both considered banning them.'

Rob asked 'Is there something wrong with the dog?'

'No!' Yvonne was quick to explain. 'He has still got his balls and is marking his territory at every opportunity. She knows what is going on. I wonder if she will stop taking him into our shops and cafes now someone has managed to hold her to account.'

'I think she probably will stop' said Jack. 'She did look highly embarrassed, and quite an audience built up to watch the dressing down.'

Rob didn't look so sure, but a well-dressed elderly gentleman wanted to talk to him about an Automobile Association car badge so he reluctantly left the counter to engage in the conversation. Jack and Yvonne busied themselves with rearranging stock and chatting with customers, until Tom and Commander Jemima Tattersall arrived and Yvonne ushered them through into her kitchen. She saw Jack's questioning look but didn't feel the need to explain.

The three of them sat around Yvonne's kitchen table. She wasn't sure whether to offer them a tea or a coffee, but the Commander started talking before she had made up her mind. 'How are you feeling this morning?' she asked.

The question took Yvonne so by surprise it was a moment before she could answer. 'I'm fine, thank you. Honestly I am. Although I would like to know how Lindy is please?'

Tom and the Commander exchanged a look. Yvonne watched their faces, and her heart sunk. 'What? What's happened to her? Is she dead?'

The lovely feelings which had been enveloping her since her brother's phone call disappeared as she broke out into a cold sweat. Tom stood up from the table and went to fill the kettle and switch it on. The Commander held Yvonne's gaze and said 'Lindy Speake is alive and well and has been charged with numerous offences.'

Yvonne's mouth dropped open. 'What?' was all she could manage.

'Please accept my apologies for everything that happened to you and your family at Kenyon Hall. I should also apologise for the way we plucked you to safety from your horse's stable yard too. We had a credible threat to your life and needed to be proactive. In hindsight we were trying to protect you from the right people but for the wrong reason. Let me explain. Lindy Speake was controlling the Ronco brothers, but we did not know that. Our fault, I am sorry. We had no idea until they turned up yesterday at Kenyon Hall.'

Yvonne said in a shaky voice 'That was who was coming up in the lift?'

Tom placed a mug of tea in front of her, and she held it tightly, not caring how much it burned her hands.

The Commander explained 'No, that was us. Lindy ran because she realised we were finally wise to her. We picked up the Ronco brothers shortly after you arrived at Kenyon Hall, and they were only too pleased to serve up Lindy. Of course we didn't believe them at first, but they also implicated one of her uncles, and when we questioned him he too named Lindy as part of the gang.'

Yvonne let go of the mug and buried her head in her hands. 'I can't believe this. Not Lindy.' She tried to think back over the past few months for an indication that Lindy had been involved in anything other than being a friend she enjoyed horse riding with but couldn't think of a single moment when she feared Lindy, or felt she was putting her life in danger. 'No, I don't believe it. You're wrong. All these men are putting the blame on someone who cannot defend herself, after all how can you prove you are not something?'

'Very easily' said Tom, who finally broke his silence. 'I understand you are having difficulty in accepting this because I am too. This is Lindy we are talking about, our friend at the stables and an all-round lovely person. But don't forget that she was married to Antonio Ronco, and you don't get involved with someone like that without knowing something of what they do and you certainly don't escape unscathed as she appears to have done. It was also relatives of Lindy who were the ones behind all the trouble you were having in your shop a matter of weeks ago. It appears she moved into the space created when we cracked the murders and thefts earlier in the year, but she must have already been deeply involved to be in a position to do so.'

'Tom is right' said the Commander. 'For operational reasons I can't give you more information, but having seen how Tom has been struggling with accepting Lindy's role in all of this, and listening to his account of her character as he knew her, I wanted to come and tell you personally.'

Yvonne nodded her understanding. 'Thank you' she said in a quiet voice.

The Commander stood up 'I need to go now, but Tom can stay with you?'

Yvonne shook her head. 'No, no, I'll be OK, thank you. Both of you go and continue to work this case. Although Tom probably needs to sleep at some point today.'

'If you're sure you don't want me to stay?' Tom asked.

'I am. Thank you.'

After they left Yvonne continued to sit at the kitchen table, trying to make sense of everything she had just been told, and failing.

A gentle knock on the kitchen door leading in from the carpark preceded George, who said 'Tom phoned me and said you may need some company. He didn't explain why. Are you alright?'

'Not really' said Yvonne and burst into tears.

Chapter 21

Feeling wrung out and exhausted Yvonne left George in her kitchen to make a few phone calls, and went upstairs for a bath. She lay in the soothing bubble-filled hot water and let her mind wander. She noticed a mark on the ceiling above her and realised it was a spider. Her heart rate rose a little at the thought the spider was going to drop and land on her, but then it scurried across to one corner where she saw it had created a web. She continued to lie in her bath looking up in wonder at the hard work which had gone into making the deadly pattern.

After a while she sunk down under the water so she was completely submerged, listening to the unfamiliar noises wash around her, successfully silencing the feelings of betrayal until she re-emerged when they all came rushing back. It had been a confusing forty-eight hours, when the brother she believed had been a person she couldn't understand turned out not to be, and the friend she believed had been wronged by her own family had actually been one of those in the wrong. As she continued to lie there, now with her face above water, she thought about those who she believed she could trust. At that moment there was only really Zebedee and Toby she could be sure of, which was a depressing thought.

A gentle knock on the door, and George's voice calling 'Yvonne? Are you alright?'

'I'm fine!' she called out. 'I'll be out soon.'

She hoped George was someone she could add to the list along with her dog and her horse. The bathwater was now too cool and she heaved herself out of the bath to dry herself and get dressed. She decided on jeans and a grey woollen jumper and was soon back in her shop with familiar customers, visitors to the town, and a few of her antiques dealers ribbing each other about sales and purchases, sharing gossip, and congratulating each other's clever buys.

The afternoon passed surprisingly quickly, and before she realised what the time was Jack was turning the sign to CLOSED and locking the front door.

'Are you looking forward to your party next week?' he asked.

'Next week?' Yvonne was confused. Her friends were planning a birthday party for her, and her birthday wasn't until next month.

Jack looked at her a little oddly but made no comment as he totted up the sales for the day and wrote them in the book. Glancing over Yvonne caught sight of the date. 'Oh, next week! It's my birthday next week! So much has happened I have lost track of the date.'

He put his hand on her shoulder and said kindly 'It's your age' before moving smartly away.

'Cheeky sod' she laughed, his handsome face smiling back at her.

'Shall I write in the diary that you are taking the day off on your birthday?' he asked.

Yvonne paused. She had always worked on her birthday, and it wasn't as though this one was a so-called big birthday. It hadn't occurred to her to take the day off, but now Jack had asked the question she was finding the thought of a day doing something different appealing.

'I haven't decided yet. Who's working that day?'

Jack checked the list in the diary. 'Raymond and Rachael'

Yvonne thought for a moment, and then said 'Yes please Jack. Those two will be fine on their own. I'll treat myself to a day off.'

Together they finished switching lights and the computer off, plugging in the card machines to charge ready for the next day, and doing a final walk around to check windows and doors were closed.

Yvonne messaged George to see if he was free for dinner. They had made a loose arrangement earlier, but she hadn't been concentrating and now she did want to see him. As though he had been waiting for her to contact him he answered immediately in the affirmative, and they agreed to go for a walk with Zebedee before eating at his flat. Yvonne and Zebedee walked up to the front of TAA, where George joined them and together the three of them strolled down Gold Hill and then walked a series of lanes and footpaths, enjoying the cooling Autumn evening as they passed the hard work several locals had been putting into their allotments, they stopped for a drink at Ye Old Two Brewer's pub, and then climbed back up Gold Hill. George's flat was now a place Yvonne could relax in, and Zebedee certainly felt at home as she went and sat by the fridge where he now kept dog food especially for her, and for Stan on his increasingly regular stays with George.

Dog fed, dinner cooked and eaten, the first of Jennifer Aniston's 'Murder Mystery' films watched, and everyone was ready for bed. While George took Zebedee out for a last wee, Yvonne washed and tidied up the kitchen, and then went up the stairs to his bathroom. By the time George came up to bed, without Zebedee who he had persuaded to stay downstairs with a chew, she was undressed and under the covers. When she heard the shower running she pulled back the duvet and went and joined him.

The next day Yvonne began to feel her life was returning to normal, with an early morning hack with Toby and Zebedee, a full day in the shop, and then meeting Tabitha, Alison and Maisie for a drink in the evening. They wanted to know all about her adventures at Kenyon Hall and what was happening with the police investigation, and so the evening ended up in one of the local Indian restaurants, Aroma, because Yvonne had so much to tell them.

'Have you spoken to your brother since you last saw him at Kenyon Hall?' Maisie asked.

'Yes, we have spoken several times already and it's only been a couple of days. It is so good to be back in touch, I can't tell you!' said Yvonne.

'Are you going to meet up soon?' Tabitha asked.

'Yes, he and his wife are coming down for the day early next week. His daughters will be at school, so they can't join us this time. He wants to meet you, and Tom, to thank you for saving his life Alison.'

'It was mainly Tom, but yes I would love to see him and then perhaps that awful image of his bloodied body will fade from my mind.'

'Oh Alison' said Maisie as she put her hand on Alison's arm. 'It must have been so distressing.'

'It wasn't at the time' said Alison. 'We were all so busy working on him that how he looked and what had happened to him didn't really feature in my mind. But since then I keep having nightmares and flashbacks. It's disturbing, and I am sure seeing him up and about and looking healthy and alive will help. Would you like him to come to your party?' she suggested.

'Yes please, that's a good idea. I don't think I can remember us having birthday parties as adults, so this will be a first' Yvonne laughed. 'He and his wife are so very grateful to you. It was an amazing thing that you did, thank you.'

As they passed around Peshwari naan, mushroom rice, chicken Ceylon and tandoori salmon, the conversation turned to Lindy.

Tabitha was the first to bring up her name. 'I don't suppose he'll be wanting to thank Lindy, as the third person supposedly trying to save his life. What was she doing there?'

Yvonne guessed it was a discussion she and Alison had had several times before by the way Alison simply shook her head and didn't reply.

Tabitha continued 'I didn't know her very well, but I'll admit I liked her, and she was a good customer of yours wasn't she?' she said, looking at Alison and Maisie.

Maisie said 'I am having a hard time believing she was part of a crime gang, let alone a ringleader. She was so nice!'

Alison shook her head. 'I am sure the police have made a mistake, you know? She has a lovely manner about her, is always asking after the children, telling us stories about guests at Kenyon Hall, she absolutely loved her horse and really enjoyed riding out with you and the rest of the livery owners, Yvonne.'

Yvonne shrugged her shoulders. 'I agree with you, I am having difficulty accepting it too. But she has been charged and is being kept without bail, so they must have some pretty strong evidence against her. Tom says the police are sure they know what happened at those awful events on Semley Common, starting with the poisoning of Bernie Campling while they sat around the picnic table on the green opposite the pub all those months earlier, and then killing the auction's porter Gregory and attempting to kill my brother, and finally poisoning Bernie's sister and dumping her body in the pond where those antiques had been hidden for so long. I don't think she ever held the knife or the poison, but she was deeply involved in the circumstances around it all. I'd like to think she really was trying to save Beau's life.'

Tabitha nodded 'Me too. She just doesn't strike me as the sort of person who could or would kill somebody.'

Alison asked 'Have you been told about any suspicion or proof the police have that Lindy has killed anyone?'

Yvonne shook her head. 'They don't have any evidence or suspicion that she has, or at least that is what both Tom and Commander Tattersall said. One day I would like to talk with Lindy and ask her how she got involved, that is if she is willing to tell me. By the way, did you know they found the knife buried under the Plague Stone on the way up the hill out of Semley?'

'What plague stone?' asked Maisie.

Yvonne explained 'There's a plague stone on the right, you'll notice it next time you go that way. It has a green sign explaining what it is all about. Tom says the police believe one of the Ronco brothers, probably Antonio because he was the more violent of the two, managed to pass it to Lindy as they drove up the hill to get away from the scene. Of course because she was apparently helping to save Beau's life she was covered in his blood too, and her coat pockets weren't checked for weapons because she was one of the people trying to keep him alive. It shouldn't have happened, but it did, and she could have made it up to the plague stone before the forensic investigation team turned up, hidden the knife, and come back without anyone noticing she was missing for a few minutes in all the bright flashing lights and darkness everywhere else.'

'Of course yes, she is very fit isn't she' said Maisie. 'She could probably run up that hill in no time, and if she was out of breath and sweaty when she got back everyone would think it was because she had exerted herself helping your brother.'

'Except she didn't actually get involved with the first aid we were giving him. It was me and Tom who were working on him, while Lindy was encouraging us. She was really great, it would be odd behaviour if she wanted him dead.' said Alison.

'True' said Yvonne. 'Although I keep thinking about her reaction when that lift started to travel up to her apartment, I mean she was running hell for leather without a moment's thought for me. I believed it was the Ronco brothers, but she must have guessed it was the police coming for her. She wouldn't have been afraid of the Ronco brothers. That is the only explanation I have for why she behaved in the way that she did.'

'I suppose you're right' said Maisie. 'I can't imagine how frightened you must have been when you thought those thugs were chasing you.'

Yvonne felt a cold knot in her stomach as she relived the terror of those few minutes. Tabitha put her arm around her and hugged her. 'You're safe now' she whispered.

Yvonne leaned into the hug and rested her head on Tabitha's shoulder, while the other two watched with concern. Yvonne closed her eyes and concentrating on her breathing, and her surroundings, and the friends who were with her.

Feeling better she sat up and said 'I'm OK now, honestly. That whole episode was surreal, but look what happened, it brought my brother back to me, and although it would have been less dramatic if we had actually just spoken, or even written to each other before now, we're back in contact and that for me is the main thing.'

Smiling, Alison raised her glass of Kingfisher lager 'Cheers to families!'

'Cheers' everyone said as they raised their pint glasses.

Chapter 22

Beau and his wife Lucy came to Shaftesbury for the day as promised, and Yvonne took great pleasure in showing them around the town she called home. As luck would have it the weather was dry, and warm for an October day. Shaftesbury Abbey gardens and Gold Hill museum were still open, and the trio spent a lovely few hours wandering between the two, enjoying the views of the surrounding countryside from Park Walk as they walked, adventuring along to Castle Hill and even more views all the way to King Alfred's Tower, and then sitting down for lunch at King Alfred's Kitchen where they enjoyed the view along the High Street. Lucy and Yvonne found they had many things in common, including a love of horses, and Yvonne was pleased that her brother had found someone who loved him. Yvonne and his first wife had never seen eye-to-eye about anything, although they were happy to spend time in each other's company for family get-togethers they just didn't click. Yvonne wondered if her brother's first wife was a little jealous of their relationship, and she hoped that by getting back in contact with Beau she wasn't going to be the cause of any conflict within their marriage.

'We are looking forward to your birthday party' said Beau. 'Where is it taking place?'

'Come on, I'll show you' said Yvonne, and they walked up the High Street along to Bell Street where she pointed to the large wooden black gates which hid the courtyard from view.

Lucy said 'This is an easy walk from our hotel. We have booked into The Grosvenor Arms for a couple of nights. We're going to come down for your party and then stay another day. The girls are staying with my parents for the weekend, so we decided to treat ourselves to a child-free getaway.'

Yvonne smiled 'That sounds like a lovely idea. I am sure you will find plenty to do, and I'm happy to be your tour guide if you like.'

They parted at Angel Lane Antiques, but only after Beau had been around the shop looking at every item, and they had all had some of Rob's delicious chocolate and banana cake with a mug of tea.

For the next few days Yvonne relaxed into her normal routine of riding Toby and working in the shop, usually accompanied by Zebedee, and meeting up with George at various times throughout the day and of course at night. Tabitha, Alison and Maisie insisted there was nothing she could do for her birthday party, and she felt a little silly that she was even having one but decided it was a good thing for everyone else so she might as well enjoy it. On the morning of her birthday she, Tom, Charlotte and Sally went for a two-hour hack across the fields up to Ashmore Woods, and in the afternoon she discovered that she had five birthday cakes in the shop from various customers and antiques dealers. Every person who walked through the front door was offered a slice of cake, and most accepted.

George arrived at half-past six wearing a black Stetson, black t-shirt, blue jeans and brown cowboy boots. The party wasn't due to start until seven o'clock, and Yvonne declared it was fashionable to be late for your own party and pulled him upstairs where he was soon naked, as was she. In the end they arrived at the courtyard only a few minutes after seven o'clock, to be greeted by Tabitha wearing very short shorts and a denim bustier, Alison in a long flowery maxi dress, and Maisie in blue jeans with rhinestone decoration. All three were wearing cowboy boots and hats, and the courtyard was filled with the sound of country music. Yvonne had been trying to get into the mood of country music for a few weeks, and was pleased she recognised Morgan Wallen, the Brothers Osborne and Kip Moore.

At eight o'clock the doors were opened into the large room off the courtyard, and the company who ran a series of Country Fit classes in the area, Wild Active, were ready to teach the partygoers some steps. Lorah Wild led the dancing, and it wasn't long before everyone was stomping and clapping, not necessarily at the right times. Yvonne was impressed that Alison and Maisie knew all the moves and resolved to join them at their regular Friday evening class with Lorah.

Beau came over to give her a hug. 'Happy Birthday little sister' he teased. 'This is great fun! I didn't know you were into all this' he gestured at the room full of jeans, flowery skirts and cowboy hats.

Yvonne laughed 'I wasn't until this evening, but I definitely am now. I love it!'

'What are you going to do for your fiftieth birthday!' he asked.

'I don't know! This is amazing, so I think I have peaked at my first adult birthday party. My friends are amazing, aren't they? They have done all this for me.'

Beau hugged her again 'You've done well sis, you've done very well. If anything good can come out of all the shit we went through, then your life here and my life with Lucy and the girls show that we survived, and better than that we are enjoying ourselves.'

It was a brief sombre moment during the evening as brother and sister took stock of how their lives had turned out, and how they probably would have been if they had stayed working at the rate they were before everything came to a tragic halt. They didn't have long for reflection, because another song started up and they were pulled back into the lines to begin scuffing and stamping and grape vining along with their friends and family.

Lesley and her catering team enticed everyone away from the stone floor and back out into the courtyard with the smell of cooking, and soon the sofas and chairs were filled as everyone tucked into fried chicken and steak, and bowls of brisket and chilli, washed down with plenty of lager, cider and wine. The Autumn air was beginning to chill, but everyone was so hot from dancing and eating, and the braziers were lit and giving off a lot of heat, Lesley decided not to close the roof.

By eleven o'clock the party came to a natural end, and the guests began to make their goodbyes.

'Are you walking back home?' Yvonne asked Tabitha and Alison.

'Yes, we'll walk back, once we have helped Lesley to clear up' said Alison.

'In that case I'm going home to fetch Zebedee and I'll walk with you.'

'What's that?' George appeared next to her.

'I was just saying I'm going to go home to get Zebedee, and then I'll walk these two home. It's too early to go to bed, and I am buzzing from this evening. These boots are so comfortable! I can easily walk to their farmhouse and home again in them.'

'Mine are killing me' confessed Alison, flexing the white sharp toed high-heeled boots.

'They don't look comfortable' said Yvonne, pleased she had chosen square-toed low-heeled boots.

'Fortunately I thought this would happen and brought some trainers to change into' said Alison.

'Mine are alright' said Tabitha, smugly.

'Mine are better than I thought they would be' said George, 'but if you don't mind me tagging along too I'll change into my trainers too. Don't worry about clearing up; Lesley and her team will do it. Honestly they're much happier doing it on their own because everyone knows what needs to be done.'

'Did you hear that?' Tabitha said to Alison. 'We'll be in the way' she laughed.

Ten minutes later when Yvonne returned with Zebedee the courtyard was clear of guests, plates and bottles, and only the braziers remained glowing in the dark. As she walked in looking for her friends, Lesley appeared with a watering can and doused the remaining fires. Yvonne said 'Thank you Lesley, that was amazing. The food was fantastic!'

'Thank you! It is the first time we have catered for a Texan Country event, so I am pleased you liked the menu. It certainly looked as though you were all having fun.'

Tabitha and Alison joined them, Alison now wearing her trainers and carrying her boots in a bag. George walked over to them and said 'You can leave your boots here and pick them up in the morning if you like. No point carrying them all the way home.'

'Thanks George and thank you for letting us have Yvonne's party here, and the food was fantastic!' Alison have him a big hug, and then hugged Lesley too.

'Yes, thank you George!' said Tabitha. 'It is very generous of you to provide all the party food for everyone.'

'He did what?' asked Yvonne.

'Oh yes, George paid for everything tonight. Didn't you know?' not waiting for Yvonne to answer, Tabitha said 'Come on, let's get walking if you're coming with us. I am afraid if I stand here much longer I'll discover just how much my legs ache from all that dancing. Maisie has headed home to Victoria Street, and she's probably already showered and in bed.'

The four friends and one dog walked down the hill to Tabitha and Alison's farmhouse, said their goodbyes at the gate, and then Yvonne, George and Zebedee turned back and walked the way they had come. There were no streetlights or a moon, and they walked carefully along the road, enjoying the quiet of the night until a rustle and an owl hooting above them made them both jump.

'I'm going to put my torch on, if you don't mind' said George.

'Go ahead' said Yvonne. 'That made me jump out of my skin!'

George had worn a light-weight harness and he turned its torch on and directed the beam to the ground. 'This should alert the nocturnal creatures to our presence before we're next to them I hope.'

Zebedee was happily trotting alongside Yvonne on a lead, and together the trio walked at a decent pace through the lanes and a couple of dark footpaths, until they reached Gold Hill, where George turned off his lights and they were walking in darkness again. Their eyes adapted quickly, and Yvonne marvelled at how different familiar places looked in the dark. They strolled along the High Street, glancing into shop windows as they passed, enjoying having the town to themselves, and with unspoken consent headed back to Yvonne's home. No more screeches and screams interrupted their progress, and they chatted in low voices, sharing their joy of the evening, and how much enjoyment the guests had been having too. It felt to Yvonne as though the tragedy and drama of the past were a long way behind her, and she relished the calm of the moment, and was excited for the future. It may not have been her fiftieth birthday, but today felt as though she had passed a milestone, and the future was bright.

No one else was around, and as they climbed the wooden stairs to Yvonne's bedroom all they could hear was the tap tap tap of Zebedee's claws on the treads. At the top George pulled Yvonne close and murmured 'Happy Birthday Yvonne. I love you.'

After a moment's hesitation she replied 'I love you too.'

THE END

I hope you enjoyed reading 'Death on the Village Green', the second in the Yvonne Parker Mystery series. If you haven't already, you may like to read the first book 'Field Murder'.

I love writing. For several months I spend a lot of time in an alternative world, dipping in and out of real life. Then the time comes to share my alternative world with the real world, but over the years this has become more a case of welcoming a group of people to join me. Martin the Editor is the first person who sees inside, and his insights into the structure and composition of the story are invaluable, and I love reading his notes and enjoy learning from him. It's a humbling time, which leads into several people kindly giving up their time to help. Fiona, Lydia, Hazel, Nova, Annette and Jeannette settled down in Yvonne Parker's Shaftesbury and Semley, and shared their thoughts, concerns, joys and feelings about what they read, sometimes agreeing with each other, sometimes reading a different meaning or experience. After this it's just me reading aloud to the dogs, horses, cat, chickens, and Bob, none of whom stay awake for long and are not great for positive feedback. Once I am as happy as I can be, I format the story into a paperback version and an e-book version, and thank you to Karen for letting me use a photograph of her gorgeous horse Brandy Girl for the cover, and press the button to order. The point of no return. All mistakes are then going to be available for you to see. That isn't the end of it though, because I read the story aloud to someone who is listening AND stays awake, and also gives me feedback in between tea and cake as Ed of Sylvafield Studio helped me to turn this into an audio book.

I am very grateful to everyone involved, and thank you all for stepping into this alternative world.

Printed in Dunstable, United Kingdom